BRO

Jón Atli Jónasson

Translated by Quentin Bates

Published by Corylus Books Ltd

Jón Atli Jónasson

One of Iceland's foremost playwrights, Jón Atli Jónasson has made a significant contribution both on stage and screen. He started out in experimental and political theatre working with independant theatre groups. His plays have since gone on to be performed in major cities including London, Paris, Berlin, Stockholm, Copenhagen and Athens.

He has also written a number of film scripts, most notably The Deep, produced by 101 Studios Iceland and based on his own play, which was shortlisted for Best Foreign Feature at the 85th Academy Awards in 2015. In addition to his theatrical and film achievements, he has been nominated for the Nordic Film Prize three times and was named the Nordic Radio Dramatist in 2011.

His literary work includes four novels, a short story compilation, and a novella. His crime novels all take place in modern-day Iceland and focus on themes such as corruption within the police force, changing dynamics in Iceland's society, the evolving underworld and shifting power structures in politics and business. Jón Atli lives in Reykjavik.

Quentin Bates

Translator Quentin Bates has roots in Iceland that run very deep. In addition to his own fiction, he has translated many of Iceland's coolest authors into English.

Broken is first published in English the United Kingdom in 2025 by Corylus Books Ltd, and was originally published in Icelandic as *Brotin* in 2022 by Forlagið – JPV útgáfa.

This book has been translated with a financial support from:

 **ICELANDIC LITERATURE CENTER**

Corylus Books Ltd

corylusbooks.com

ISBN: 978-1-917586-00-9

1

There was a giddy home-free vibe there in the squad car. The night shift was coming to an end and it had been a quiet one. They had pizza around midnight. Dóra paid. Elliði promised he'd pay next time. They listened to the radio and cruised around. Around two a drunk tried to get into the wrong house. Then a heart attack up in Breiðholt. Not much else. Until the call came.

Neighbours reported screams from a big house in one of the city's new districts. Dóra didn't recall them making a joint decision to respond to the incident. Elliði just swung the car around and right away they were pepped and ready. Foot to the floor up Ártúnsbrekka under lights and bells. Nobody was about.

It was after they had googled the address and gone wrong on a couple of roundabouts that they ended up in the cul-de-sac where the house stood.

It was a big white box, flanked by smaller white boxes. The drive was paved. This wasn't a house that belonged in this Icelandic scrub. It looked like a villa out of a French thriller. It would have been better placed among palm trees or overlooking the Mediterranean.

Two cars on the drive. A black Range Rover and a Porsche sports car that her memory told her was pink. Pretty much the colour of human skin. She didn't recall ever – neither before nor since – having seen that colour on a car. Elliði jumped out and loped up the steps to the front door. She tagged along behind. Dóra was stiff after sitting in the car so long. She wasn't as quick on her feet. There was a glimpse of Elliði as he rapped on the door that stood open. Then he disappeared inside before she could say a word. She recalls stopping and looking around the other houses lining the cul-de-sac.

There was a house facing the villa, not as new. She caught sight of an older woman in a nightdress standing in the window, staring at her. She remembers waving to her, but the woman didn't move. Normal people generally take that sort of thing, a uniformed police officer waving at them, as a signal to make themselves scarce. Then she heard a shriek from inside the house. An ear-splitter. Something deeply primal about it. It sounded like a woman. She took the steps at a run and into the house.

There was a raw stench of puke in the hall. There was a sour smell further inside. Like spoiled milk. That was it, soured milk. She was totally sure.

The house was opulent yet bare at the same time. She looked to her left, into the living room. There was a white leather sofa, a glass table and two white Chesterfield armchairs. A deep white carpet covered the floor. The whole place was pretty much white. Straight ahead she could see into the kitchen. There was a white table and white lacquered furnishings. Not a piece of crockery to be seen. Three chairs, and she was sure they were a Danish design. Were these called ant? The chairs, that is. All of a sudden the idea popped into her head that this sour stink wasn't milk, but the house itself. Like it had been made of milk. This was a milky house, whatever that was supposed to mean.

She was just tired and the adrenaline was flooding through her, triggering weird flashes of thought.

Glancing to the right, she noticed a half-open door. Sobs came from inside. She crept towards it. There was nothing hard about that space. The thick white carpet muffled her footsteps. Inside the bedroom, also white, it was dark. An erotic monochrome print hung over the headboard and a small white Moses basket stood at the foot of the bed.

Elliði stood over a woman sitting on the bed. She could see the look of concern on his face. The only light came from a bedside lamp. She approached and took a closer look at the woman. She was wrapped in a dressing gown and there was a newborn baby in her arms. It was blue in the face. Elliði caught her eye and shook his head.

'Dóra, her husband's in the office. In the next room,' he murmured. 'I've called this one in. Can you check on him?'

She nodded and hurried from the room, away from the source of the sour milk smell. She could hear Elliði speaking to the woman in a soft voice. He was doing his best to persuade her to let him hold the baby. He needed to check if it was dead. Not that there could be any doubt.

All the same, he had a duty to check. He had to see if he could perform first aid. Not that he'd be able to. They'd arrived too late for that, and she remembered their ridiculous haste and the speed they had driven to reach this house. There was nothing they could do here.

She hadn't been in uniform long. This job was still new to her, but she understood why the woman resisted handing her child to Elliði. As soon as she did that, then it would all be over. In every sense of the word. As long as it remained in her arms, it would still be a part of her and she wouldn't yet have lost everything. Her arms weren't yet empty. She understood the woman. In her place, she'd most likely have done the same.

She went into the next room, an office with its door standing open. This was a wide space, but just as empty as the rest of the house. A man of around thirty sat at a glass desk, in front of a large picture window. A silver computer monitor stood on the desk, a keyboard lying in front of it. He was bony, hair awry. He wore underpants and a blue woollen sweater. A half-empty bottle of whisky and a glass stood on the desk.

Dóra padded towards him, as if cornering a wounded animal. The man, who stared down at his hands, realised she was there and lifted his head to watch her. His face was blank. He was good-looking, with startlingly blue eyes.

'Hey, well,' he muttered as Dóra went to the picture window and folded her arms. She felt suddenly exhausted and she had no idea what to say to this man. From what she could see of the circumstances, she could figure out what had happened. Cot death is rare, but it happens. No blame attached to anyone. It's a tragic cost of bringing children into the world.

'He just stopped breathing,' the man said and hunched forward.

Then he slipped a hand under his sweater, pulled out a pistol and put the muzzle to his lips.

Dóra recalls stepping in and catching hold of the man's shoulder. Then the weapon went off. She doesn't remember the explosion. Just the pain in her eye.

2

It's the pinging of the old Braun travel alarm clock that wakes Dóra, and she's as surprised as always when she opens her eyes. Considering the doses of medication she takes every evening to help her sleep, she doesn't usually expect to wake up in the mornings. But she does. Mouth dry, her eyes sting and her headache starts behind her forehead and seeps into her brain.

She's alone in bed. She doesn't remember exactly where things are with Jafet, the guy she lives with. She has some recollection of an argument the night before. Then the brooding silence that always follows. Maybe he went out after she went to sleep.

It's getting on for seven. That's enough to tell her that he hasn't slept by her side, because he's rarely up before noon. It's not as if there's anyone else. Jafet isn't like that. He's probably crashed on some friend's sofa.

It's still dark outside. This winter has been a hard one. She's ashamed. It's all her fault, she can't hold herself back. Their relationship has always been on the rocky side, but over the last few months it has twisted itself into an increasingly steep downward spiral, coming to a head with a bang as he takes himself off. Not for long, usually just overnight. Then they talk things over, there are tears and they fuck and the everyday routine returns with promises of tenderness and understanding and intimacy. Until everything goes wrong again. But it's her fault. Jafet is starting to get on her nerves way too much. There's nothing she can put her finger on. It's everything and nothing in particular. She just keeps scratching and scratching until everything blows up in her face. Maybe it's just to give herself some peace.

There's no phone on the table. There's no iPad, smartwatch or computer for checking messages. Dóra has no smart electronics in the flat. The phone and laptop are stored in a Faraday cage that she bought online. This cabinet, which is out in the hall, is supposed to absorb ninety percent of the electromagnetic signals that these devices emit. She also has no Wi-Fi. That's why she uses this ancient alarm clock. When its battery gets low, the ping feels a little softer. Not as piercing. She has no evidence of this, it's just a feeling.

She drags herself to her feet and into a dressing gown. This flat is one open space with a Japanese screen in front of the double bed. This used to be a storeroom for ball bearings and spare parts.

There's a little toilet and shower along the corridor. There's a bathtub against one wall and a kitchen island unit with a gas hob in the middle of the room. They practically never use the bathtub and right now it's overflowing with books. This first-floor flat is in an industrial district on the outskirts of the city. To get to the flat, you have to go through the carpentry workshop downstairs that's run by an old man called Rúrik. He's at work at seven every morning and is gone around five. Rúrik's a little over eighty. He refurbishes old furniture, in between cooking up lacquer to some old recipe that he sells to other people who also refurbish furniture. Dóra's grandfather was Rúrik's brother. He owns the whole building, and although she doesn't feel she's done anything to deserve it, Rúrik adores her.

She packs coffee into the moka pot and screws it together. Her hands tremble a little. The way she is these days means it takes a little while for the world to swim into focus.

She turns on the gas and finds a clean cup almost by

touch alone. She opens a drawer in the island unit where all her medication is kept. She wakes up and starts the day with painkillers. She opens the pill bottle and counts them by feel. There's an expectation about this that has a strong resemblance to addiction.

She holds on to two tablets and crushes them to a mush between her teeth before swallowing. Soon enough the coffee starts to bubble up in the pot. She picks it up, pours a cup and switches off the gas. Sipping the hot coffee breaks down the layer of slime left by the drugs at the back of her mouth and throat.

Next she goes over to the bench with the turntable, amplifier and mixer. She doesn't need to see to be able to switch the system on and drop the needle onto the vinyl. These last few weeks she's been listening to Arca's latest. She has a Technics SL-1200 turntable that was produced as a fiftieth anniversary special edition. It's matt black and cost a fortune. Enough to bring tears to her eyes. But worth it. The record collection that has been expanding year by year is under the turntable bench.

Dóra finishes her coffee and the headache seems to be receding. There's a pain in her right eye that she's learned to live with. That's a stinging pain that's never going away. How heavy it gets depends on how her day shapes up. In some ways it's like the phantom pain that people experience in a limb that's no longer there. After the accident she wore an eye patch for a while. The remnants of the old eye were behind it. That was while the doctors still thought there was a chance of saving it. Then there was a glass eye. All the same, the pain never went away. It's only when she falls asleep that she forgets it.

Dóra pulls on clothes and shoes. She picks a thick winter coat from its hook and at the door she unlocks the Faraday cage. She takes out a slim computer and puts it in her backpack. Then she picks up the phone and glances at the screen. There's an endless string of messages from Jafet.

They're all on the same lines – *sorry* – *talk to me* – *we can fix this*. She can't be dealing with this. Not now. This is a merry-go-round that'll have to stop.

Dóra goes downstairs to the workshop that smells of timber, oil and coffee. Rúrik's at the desk in the office going through invoices and receipts.

She can't help noting that his hands shake. Dóra suspects that he's starting to show symptoms of Parkinson's. The effects of stress and anxiety that go hand in hand with dropping dopamine levels are starting to show on Rúrik. He's so absorbed in paperwork that she decides against disturbing him, goes through the workshop and out through the big doors that stand half-open.

Outside is the Volvo that's pretty much the same age as she is. No doubt it would have been crushed into a little metal cube years ago if Rúrik hadn't taken it upon himself – unasked – to keep it in running order.

Dóra gets behind the wheel and starts the engine. She looks up and sees Rúrik standing in the doorway, nodding at her. She can see his lips move and can read what he's saying. Man is a mechanism. He means her. She nods acknowledgement and backs the car out of its space.

She drives along the street that's lined with cars in every state of repair. Hardly any of them roadworthy. There's all sorts of small-scale business done here: from jeep rebuilds to salad production. Sometimes Dóra refers to this as Snacks-and-New-Boots-Street. There's a crunch at the back of her head. No doctor has yet been able to explain where it comes from. In her imagination it's the two sides of her brain grinding against each other.

Like a pair of little icebergs or tectonic plates.

*

She turns in through the gate at the police station on Hverfisgata, coming to a halt in front of the Special Unit that's getting ready, along with bodies from uniform and CID, the drug squad and the prosecutor's representative. There's a raid scheduled for today. Taking on the Eastern European crims who've been taking over the city recently.

Dóra parks the Volvo in an empty space and goes into the station. She nods to colleagues who are adjusting stab jackets and tool belts. There's a spark in the air. It's still there inside.

This raid has been in preparation for a few weeks now. It's a co-ordinated operation focusing on several companies that the gangs use to launder money, and on the homes of some of the kingpins. Every effort has been made to keep this operation secret. Dóra knows very little about it, despite being part of CID, and she's not interested. She has another important case to think about that has demanded all her attention recently. This had been dropped in her lap, as so often before, as a case to put to bed, since it had already been investigated and the prosecutor didn't feel it was worth pursuing.

This was the death of an old woman, which Dóra's colleague Gunnthór had investigated. The old lady, Lovísa, had been sixty-eight years old and lived in the western part of the city. She had been found dead in bed. The cause of death was respiratory failure. The problem was there was no reason for her death, apart from the strictly medical explanation. The post-mortem showed nothing out of the ordinary. Going by a medical check-up not long before she died, she'd been in robust health.

Gunnthór had made no progress on the case. There were no witnesses. Lovísa had lived alone and there were no marks on the body that indicated anyone had done her harm. Gunnthór, who was up to his ears in preparation for the sweep, had asked Dóra to put this case to bed. That was just fine. Sometimes people do die for no apparent reason, and the world shrugs its shoulders and carries on. But there was something about this that made Dóra stop and think. In particular, a photograph of Lovísa in bed where she'd been found. In reality it was just a minor detail in the picture that nobody seemed to have noticed. Except her.

She wasn't exactly looking forward to summoning Gunnthór to a conference room to go over this with him.

The thing is that Dóra had acquired a reputation within the force. Now and again she'd notice something other investigators had overlooked and few police officers appreciated being pulled up on cases they'd decided couldn't be resolved. No doubt it was much the same as being scolded by a teacher after failing a test. Not that this had ever happened to Dóra during her school years, but she'd witnessed it.

She had noticed particularly that female investigators tended to be more open to discussing cases that had proved to be beyond them. Their male colleagues were less willing, and frequently she would have to go to greater lengths to prove her point. That meant getting them to swallow their obstinacy and pride.

She expected just such a response from Gunnthór. She had spent the best part of a week mulling over this minor detail in the picture and had dug deep enough that she was satisfied she was right. There was nothing wrong with the conclusion regarding the cause of death. That was correct. But Lovísa hadn't died just like that. There were circumstances surrounding her death that couldn't be overlooked.

Dóra goes into the department's open-plan office space and there's the same tension in the air as in the garage at the back of the station. She walks straight into a knot of her colleagues kitted out in tool belts and stab jackets. There are concerned looks on some faces, while others look completely impassive, but it's the same story. They're all tense ahead of what they know is coming. Battering their way into the enemy's home turf. This gang has a reputation for heavy-handed violence. This little Iceland of ours has changed so much. Dóra nods to her colleagues, and some of them return the gesture with an acknowledgement. Others are too absorbed in their own thoughts to notice. She realises that they're all armed. Gunnthór is in charge.

'Can we talk afterwards?' Dóra asks and Gunnthór looks at her in astonishment.

'Sure,' he says, slipping a pistol into its holster. 'Anything in particular?'

'About Lovísa,' Dóra says.

'Who's that?' Gunnthór asks.

'The old lady who suffocated.'

'I don't know when all this is going to be over,' Gunnthór says, glancing at his colleagues, looking serious and standing by the lift doors in the corridor.

'Or in the morning,' Dóra says, and Gunnthór nods like a schoolboy who already knows he's failed a test, and hurries off.

Dóra sighs and heads for the kitchenette in the corner. It looks like a bomb has hit it. The table is littered with coffee mugs and soda bottles, along with wrappers from protein-chocolate bars, sandwiches and ready meals. It's obvious that her colleagues have spent half the night preparing for this sweep operation. She tries not to think about the office's Wi-Fi system and the electromagnetic pulses it beams out.

She opens the dishwasher and to her amazement it's full of clean crockery. She takes a cup, holds it under the coffee machine's spout and presses a button. The screen informs her that if she wants coffee, then she'll have to empty the waste drawer first and fill up the reservoirs of water and coffee beans.

She opens the cupboard above the machine and reaches for a bag of coffee beans. That's when she notices her old partner, Elliði, who's now running this department after his predecessor's burnout. Elliði is as pale as a ghost and looks exhausted. He nods to her with a shadow of a smile. Then he's gone. He slips away from her. That's the way the relationship between them has developed.

By rights, Dóra should be part of this operation with the rest of the team, but there's no question of that. After she was promoted and appointed to this department, Elliði took care to ensure that she barely set foot outside the building. His stance on this is underscored by the regular sick leaves she has to take. Dóra hasn't been out on active ops since they went into that house, back in the day. Elliði blames himself for the way things turned out. He should have checked out the man properly first. He read the situation wrongly, and that mistake cost Dóra dearly. She doesn't see things that way, but there's no arguing with Elliði. He's the head of this department and what he says goes. That call-out is something Elliði never mentions. Only when he's drunk. When that happens, Dóra gets a phone call from him and he goes through it in every detail. Either that or he just cries. At the station he avoids making eye contact. He keeps to himself in his glass-walled cubicle at the far end of the office space. If Dóra's colleagues ever ask about her duties and what exactly she does within the department, that's a mistake they make only once. Although Elliði will moan at her, he's the boss nobody wants to be at loggerheads with. He's a tough opponent, as sharp as a knife, and a good cop.

By the time Dóra has complied with the coffee machine's demands and a thin, brown stream of coffee trickles into her cup, there's a tap on her shoulder. She turns to see Gunnar, the duty inspector.

'You'll have to respond to a call-out for me,' he says, yawning.

'Yes, but …' Dóra hesitates.

'There's no but. There's nobody else.'

3

Rado comes home to his three-room flat in the Urriðaholt district. He shuts the door carefully behind him and slips off his shoes and jacket. It's seven in the morning.

For the last few weeks he's been seconded to the drug squad. They're on the trail of dubious lawyer Thormóður Óli, who's also behind a large-scale cocaine smuggling operation. The problem is that they don't have anything on him. They have grasses, drug mules collared in another operation, pretty much by chance, and there's a forty-year-old woman who knows Thormóður and is certain there's a serious shipment on the way.

Every morning Rado shadows the lawyer from the detached house in Kópavogur where he lives alone, to his legal practice on Borgartún. Around midday Thormóður Óli might go to the gym or for lunch at a restaurant downtown. Occasionally he'll make an appearance at the district court, normally defending some face familiar to the police, the types who call regularly at his practice.

Weekends are the worst. That's when our guy lets his hair down and there's always a hell of a party at the house in Kópavogur. The drug squad makes sure that uniformed officers respond to complaints from the neighbours about the noise. There have been two occasions, a couple of weeks apart, when he collected two children, around six and eight years old, a boy and a girl, and takes them to the movies or the petting zoo. Thormóður Óli is divorced, and the mother of his children lives in the western district of the city. She lives in the basement flat of her parents' house. According to official documents, it's been six months since the divorce.

He has a few female friends who visit regularly. Most of these are familiar to the police in one way or another. They generally have form for minor theft or narcotics offences. Some of them are his former clients. It's almost certain that he's paying them for sex. A couple of times the lawyer has paid a visit to a young woman who has a child about a year old, where he stayed overnight.

This was the case again while Rado was on night shifts. To start with he was simply told this would be his last shift for a while. Everything about this surveillance operation has been weird, to his way of thinking. He has conscientiously tracked Thormóður Óli for weeks, and always solo. He files a timetable of events but isn't required to file reports. He has no idea if the drug squad has a court order allowing them to tap Thormóður Óli's phone. If that's the case, Rado hasn't got to listen to any of the tapes.

Rado tiptoes into Jurek's room. This is his three-year-old son, who has only recently started sleeping in a room of his own. He has a racing car bed. That might have had something to do with his decision. His nightlight, shaped like a strange plastic monster, glows on the bedside table. Jurek is still fast asleep.

He tiptoes back out of the room, and into the bedroom where his wife Ewa is also asleep. Rado undresses silently and slips under the duvet. He hasn't slept for more than twenty-four hours, but he's not tired. There's something that's disturbing him, some kind of hunch. He feels as if there's something vital that he's forgotten. It's the feeling you get when you go out, not sure if you blew out candles or switched off the iron. He tries to close his eyes and concentrate on his breathing, but it doesn't do any good.

He slips out of the room again, picking up his clothes on the way. In the kitchen he glances out of the window, where there's a view of the whole Kauptún area. Costco, IKEA and a Toyota dealership. He switches on the percolator and a moment later is aware of movement in the living room, so he goes to check. Jurek's standing there in his pyjamas, holding the remote control for the vast flat-screen TV that Rado's father-in-law brought them and fitted – unasked – a few days ago.

'We're not watching TV right now, little one,' Rado says gently, and Jurek jumps.

'OK, Dad,' Jurek says, placing the remote on the little glass table and turning away. Rado watches him. He's often pleasantly surprised at how quiet and sensible the boy is. There are never tantrums of the kind Rado has seen other children throwing at nursery. Jurek seems to be an old soul. Not that Rado has mentioned this to anyone. He's been a placid, gentle child from the day he was born. He doesn't get that from his mother, whose moods can change in the blink of an eye, with a temper to match. And Rado has a temperament similar to hers. Maybe two minuses do make a plus.

Rado picks Jurek up, carries him to the kitchen and puts him in a highchair by the kitchen table. He gets out cereal and oat milk for the boy. The percolator wheezes, and Rado pours coffee into a cup. It's a long time since he gave up trying to bring Ewa coffee in bed. That never does any good. Next to his little percolator squats a chromium Italian monster that he wouldn't dare touch. All the same, it's just a dwarf compared to the one behind the counter in the coffee shop Ewa runs in the Smárinn shopping centre.

Sitting opposite his son, Rado sips coffee. The caffeine seems to amplify the disquiet deep inside him. It could be simply because the lack of sleep has left him dazed. There's another feeling that's often there in the background, especially when he's tired. That he doesn't completely belong here. The feeling that he has no part in this home, or this wife, or this little boy who sits opposite him and fishes pieces of cereal from the milk in his bowl to put in his mouth. It's as if he doesn't belong in this arrangement; not quite. All the same, it's not a question of love or devotion. He loves his wife and son with all his heart, even though Ewa isn't always the easiest person to live with. He can't imagine any other life. And yet, in this life, in this place and at this precise moment, there's a wretched thing that lurks within him. That's his big secret. Sometimes when his little boy looks at him, he expects him to mention it.

'It's all right, Dad,' he'll say simply. 'You can go.'

Rado often gets the same nightmare. It always starts with Jurek giving him permission to go. He nods, pulls on shoes and a coat and opens the door. He always wakes up as he steps out into the passage. It's as if that's as far as his mind will take him. Beyond the stairwell there's nothing but a void.

Rado hears Ewa going to the bathroom and shutting the door. He hears her run the shower. He turns to the Italian coffee machine and switches it on, so that it'll be hot by the time she makes her appearance. He tries to push aside his dark thoughts.

He glances at Jurek, who has finished his cereal, and asks him if it isn't time to get ready for nursery. Jurek nods his agreement, without any change to his expression. Rado has no idea if this is normal for such a small boy. He gets to his feet and follows his son along the corridor, past the bathroom from which he can hear the sound of Ewa singing in the shower. That's an indication that she's in a decent mood. If not, then there's silence from the shower. Their relationship had always been a brittle one, but after Jurek's birth they came to a truce of some sort. Rado was a good father. People around them and the family agreed on that. But it didn't feel to him this was any great effort. Quite the opposite, this was effortless. The stress that came as part of his work evaporated the moment he looked into his son's eyes. As clichéd and sentimental as that might sound. There was nothing especially puzzling as to why he was married to Ewa. He's reminded of that as he catches a glimpse of her stepping naked from the bathroom to get dressed in the bedroom. She's a stunning woman. It could be that the root of his doubt lay in the fact that he had no idea what she saw in him. He suspected that she was fully aware of that, and this was something she'd not hesitate to use against him.

It's almost eight by the time Rado takes Jurek into the nursery and says goodbye to him in the cloakroom. He plants a kiss on the top of his head and goes out to the car. It's an old Toyota 4x4 that he bought cheap from a friend. It guzzles fuel but it's reliable and never lets him down. Ewa drives around in a Tesla that was a present from her father.

Ewa knew better than to ask Rado what he was working on, and this morning's no exception. He had told her he was finishing an assignment and wasn't sure what would come next. He was owed a few days off and planned to use them sorting out the garage and seeing if he could fix up the indoor charging point for the Tesla that Ewa had been asking for. They agreed that he would fetch Jurek from nursery at the end of the day.

Ewa was going to go over her accounts at home, deal with orders, and then go to the café later in the day. Rado said that he needed to go to the station to finish a report – a white lie on his part. The bad feeling inside was something that wasn't going to let itself be shaken off easily. It just grew and grew. He felt that he was losing consciousness. There was no chance that he'd be able to sleep. He'd go down to police headquarters on Hverfisgata and clock in for a while. Chat to the guys he hadn't seen during the weeks he'd been seconded to the drug squad. See if Elliði had a case for him to take on.

There's a white Volvo that cuts him up just as he's about to turn into the yard behind the police station on Hverfisgata. Rado swears under his breath and shakes his head. He knows who the Volvo's driver is. The weird woman from CID. The one who's an investigator, but isn't. Some sort of office droid. Rado doesn't quite understand this. But he knows better than to ask. There's a bond of some kind between her and Elliði. Maybe they're having an affair? For a long time he was convinced that she was Elliði's secretary. Which in some ways she is. She's as smart as hell, but also crazy. She cornered him once in the coffee room and ripped to shreds a case report he'd written. That was a kind of grammatical flogging. She went through poor sentence construction and ungrammatical use of the dative, all of which she considered undermined the weight of the case. She'd eventually offered her help in redrafting the text. Rado had immediately accepted.

As Rado turns into the yard behind the white Volvo, his jaw drops at the sight in front of him. They're all in the yard. Literally everyone. The drug squad, the Special Unit and support. All of his colleagues, plus a good chunk of the city's beat cops. Everyone's been called in. Except him. That can mean only one thing. Rado parks away from the group and takes a deep breath. His heart beats faster. Then he opens the door and gets out of the car. He paces slowly through the group as they get themselves ready. Tasers, guns, stab vests. There are representatives of the economic crime unit. Sævar, the head of the SWAT team, grins at Rado and nods his close-cropped head in his direction as he catches his eye. There's no special affection between the two of them. Anyone with eyes in their head knows that. Anyway, his old classmate from the police college is a first-class wanker.

He encounters Elliði, who stares as he notices Rado. Then he sighs. The feeling of disquiet takes complete hold of Rado. He feels faint. He's struggling to keep his balance, but there's nothing to catch hold of. He's alone and all at sea, stranded in the middle of his very own desert.

'Now you know,' Elliði grunts.

'So secondment to the drug squad was to ...' Rado says, and can't find any more words.

'We're bringing Jurek in,' Elliði says. 'The whole crew. I had to keep you away from all this.'

Rado nods. He's about to correct Elliði, but stops short. The Jurek that a large part of the police force is gunning for isn't his son, but Jurek Senior, as he's always known. But Rado keeps quiet.

He can't say anything. There's no response he can make to Elliði's explanation. In his position, he'd have done the same. If one of his team were married to the daughter of the chief of an Eastern European crime gang who'd been allowed free rein for far too long. Especially just as a new Minister of Justice has promised voters an energetic crackdown on organised crime.

'Rado?' Elliði puts a hand on Rado's shoulder. 'Don't do anything stupid. Your phone's tapped.'

'Of course not,' Rado says, watching his colleagues all around him, who look away and avoid catching his eye. 'Just take care.'

Rado feels that he makes it to the back door of the building on autopilot. Once inside, he summons the lift. It takes him up to the cafeteria, which is deserted, and he sits down at the table at the far end.

He fumbles for his phone. He feels it's as hot as if it's on fire. It could burn a hole through his trousers and into his skin. Fuck fuck fuck. He has to call Ewa. He must ... what? What must he do? His phone's being monitored. If he makes a single call within the next hour, he has a good chance of finding himself in a cell. There's a buzz in his ears. His eyes flicker back and forth. He can feel a pain in his chest. He's not having a heart attack. Right now there's more of a chance that he'll drop dead of shame.

4

'It can't be that complicated, surely?' Gunnar asked. He was the duty inspector and shrugged as he spoke.

Callouts can turn out to be anything. Some aren't much more than storms in teacups. That's in the plural, because there are so many of these. The service economy has accustomed the public to having its arse kissed. People call for the most bizarre reasons. Discourteous pizza delivery drivers, waiters who don't speak Icelandic, drunk neighbours (sometimes good enough reason for calling the cops), to cadge a lift, and the list goes on. The Covid calls are pretty much a thing of the past. Back then it wasn't just the nutcases who called, but people who should know better. They were calling to snitch on their fellow citizens, or to complain about the contagion regulations. The pandemic confused people. It was just a way of letting off steam.

This callout that Gunnar wants Dóra to deal with, because there's literally nobody else available, is about a person reported missing at Thingvellir, the national park an hour's drive from the city. Dóra doesn't like the sound of this. There are good reasons she's hidden herself away behind a desk for years. After that fateful shot, if that's the right term for it, she's been plagued by a horde of ailments. After being brought round from her coma, she went through surgery during which the last shards of the bullet were teased out of her eye and brain. She doesn't class these ailments alongside the deep-seated pain that she regularly numbs with drugs. These don't present her with physical pain, but a variety that's mental, and even existential, if you prefer to put fancy words to it. It's a cocktail of all kinds of symptoms, from PTSD to depression, ultra-sensitivity and obsessive behaviour. The doctors told her that the damage to her cerebral cortex would become apparent in changes to her brain activity. These didn't necessarily have to be negative — although in general, they were — and that she should be able to live a normal life, something that she found extremely difficult.

The changes in her were barely discernible to begin with, for the first few months. Neither she nor those around her appeared aware of this. Dóra had slowed right down, which many people — herself included — attributed to the pain medication. But it was so much deeper than that. It was as if a weight had settled on her, as if the seriousness of life had dawned on her in a flash. Proximity makes it a tortuous business to understand your own condition until there's some distance there. It was as if a veil had been drawn back from her senses. Her sensitivity was also increased — towards others, or sometimes not at all. It all depended on how she was feeling. Some days there were uncontrollable fits of weeping, and on other days she was ice-cold, unmovable. The worst were the obsessive episodes. These were rare, but she feared them more than anything else. It was as if she were in the grip of a compulsion. The changes in her mental processes following that shot were far more fundamental than the doctors had anticipated. After being discharged from hospital, she focused on regaining her health. She never spoke of the side effects, other than the pain. She was determined to get back to work, and was convinced that if she told the truth about her condition, she wouldn't be considered competent. She'd be seen as insane. That was a label she could do without. Although society's old prejudices concerning mental health were waning, that wasn't the case with the police. Nobody wanted to work with a partner who was close to the edge. It was tough enough for someone pretty well-balanced to keep themselves sane throughout the innumerable crazy situations the job threw at them.

The first indication that she hadn't come out of the coma unscathed was that her taste in music changed totally. She'd never had much of an interest in music. Of course she'd idolised certain pop gods as a youngster, but had never developed any specific taste over the years. She didn't listen to anything in particular, just whatever happened to be popular on the radio. A few months after coming out of the coma, she'd been in the dentist's waiting room and found herself encountering the cornerstone of western musical culture. The dentist liked to have classical music playing in his surgery and she was totally enraptured. This became the first obsessive episode in which she dived so deep, immersing herself so completely in classical music that she barely slept for weeks on end.

*

'Saying it's a missing person is probably overstating the case,' Gunnar says as the colour drains from Dóra's face. 'It's a class from the Hagi School on an outing and there was one missing when they counted them back into the coach.'

'You want me to go to Thingvellir?' Dóra asks.

'I spoke to the teacher who's in charge of this trip. They're not overly concerned. He's apt to do this. I mean, the kid. Goes missing to attract attention. All I'm asking you to do is go up there and check on the situation. Let's see if it sorts itself out,' Gunnar adds, a beseeching look on his face as he extends a hand, palm open, towards her. There's a set of keys there. 'You can take the jeep that's out in the yard. They're not using it for the operation. Too conspicuous.'

Fifteen minutes later and Dóra's behind the wheel of a brand-new Land Cruiser, heading up Ártúnsbrekka on her way to Thingvellir. Her phone vibrates and she takes an eye off the road to glance at the screen. It's Gunnar sending her the names and phone numbers of the teachers supervising the school outing. It feels like she's doing something wrong, which is sort of true. Elliði would never have allowed this. But he's busy elsewhere.

There's quite a difference between a brand-new Land Cruiser and an antique Volvo. It's not as if the cops are going to stop her, but habit keeps Dóra to the speed limit. She fumbles in her coat pocket for her box of pills. It's where it should be. She feels no pain in her eye or head right now. The car's computer automatically linked to her phone and the dashboard screen tells her that Jafet is calling. The screen offers her two buttons, green and red. She chooses the red one and puts her foot down.

*

By the time Dóra parked at the Thingvellir service centre, Jafet had tried to call her four times. The last time was a text message: *Get in touch.* But Dóra doesn't have time for him right now. The jeep's already attracting attention as she kills the engine and gets out. There are two coaches in the car park. Judging by the age group of one of the coaches' passengers, she has no business with them. They look to be so old that Dóra's not even sure that these people should be out and about, let alone wandering around a national park. A slim man of around forty comes jogging over to her from the other coach. Dóra checks him out. He's wearing a traditional woollen sweater, walking trousers and a newish pair of walking boots. He has a folder and a phone in his hand. He's fair-haired and on the good-looking side. Dóra feels there's a wholesome look to him.

'I'm Marteinn,' he says when he's right in front of her, extending a hand. Dóra takes it and shakes. Marteinn smells unbelievably good. Dóra has to focus so as not to tell him so. That's the damage to her brain more than anything else. She gets these turns. It's a variant of Tourette's, some kind of filter in her head that seems to be out of order.

'I'm Dóra,' she says, sizing him up. 'I was sent about the person reported missing. From the police,' she adds.

'Yes, I figured that out. We're fairly sure that Morgan just hitched a lift back to the city. They aren't answering their phone. It's like it's been switched off.'

'Morgan?' Dóra asks. 'That's his name?'

'No,' Marteinn replies. 'That's what they want to be called now.'

'So Morgan is a nickname?'

'No. It's not a nickname. That's just what they want to be addressed as these days. We have to respect that. There are kids that are doing a bit of searching for themselves,' Marteinn says. 'Last week they were called Ken.'

'We'll need a correct name if we're putting out news of a search for … them.' Dóra shifts a little closer to Marteinn and as unobtrusively as possible takes a deep breath of his scent. She longs more than ever to tell him how good he smells. She feels compelled to do this.

'Guðbjorg,' Marteinn says.

'What?' Dóra can feel the words taking shape on her lips. She'll have to force herself if she doesn't do anything about Marteinn's sweet smell. Hell, this is crazy. 'So Morgan's a girl?' Dóra asks and puts a hand over her mouth.

'Non-binary,' Marteinn says. 'That's the term we use.'

'Listen, Marteinn,' Dóra says. 'I'm going into the service centre for a dump, and when I come back we'll go over all this.'

Dóra marches away, leaving Marteinn with more questions than he had before. She's pleased with herself.

She managed to not mention Marteinn's aroma. Now she no longer has any urge to mention it to him. All this non-binary talk has cast a shadow over him. It's as if, for the sake of his job, he has to kowtow to some lousy kid who's in the throes of a gender identity crisis, or whatever it's called.

There's quite a queue for the toilets at the service centre. A horde of tourists is milling about. Dóra makes out at least four languages – French, German, Spanish and Dutch. She speaks two of these and could teach herself the basics of the others in a weekend. This isn't because she's so smart. This is another of the side effects of that crazy shot. She remembers everything she hears and sees. She's developed a brain like glue. She sits on the toilet and sheds a few tears. There's no special reason for this. She's not weeping over how fate has treated her or anything so dramatic. She just needs to cry a little to defuse the tension.

Beyond the cubicle door a couple argue in Dutch – a language she doesn't really know well. She pricks up her ears and after a minute she finds she understands pretty much all of what they're saying. It's as if a key has been turned in a lock. The argument is about having children. He wants children and she doesn't. Their trip to Iceland has provided him with the revelation that he wants a divorce. Dóra flushes and washes her hands. As she opens the door, the woman is facing her, eyes swollen with tears. Dóra hugs the woman and marches out of the service centre. Her phone's vibrating again. She plucks it from her pocket and takes a quick look at the screen. More messages from Jafet. Time to find that wretched kid. A coach with the *Game of Thrones* logo on its side pulls up just as Dóra leaves the service centre and glances around, looking for Marteinn. She walks past the pale green coach full of teenagers and straight into Marteinn and a woman of about twenty who is tapping something into her phone.

'This is Sandra,' Marteinn says as he notices Dóra. 'She's a student teacher.'

'I'm trying to reach his ... their father,' Sandra says, looking from the screen to Dóra. 'Should we call out the rescue squads?'

'Where did the kid disappear from?' Dóra asks.

'By the Drowning Pool,' Marteinn says with a deep sigh. 'That was where we realised that he ... they were missing.'

'OK,' Dóra says. 'What about the other kids? Nobody else missing? Nobody who knows anything?'

'No,' Sandra says. 'It's a bit complicated. Morgan has a certain status within the group. Or influence, if you see what I mean. They wouldn't take it well if someone were to snitch. I mean, if they had meant to do a runner from the outing.'

'Which is what we think has happened,' Marteinn adds. 'It wouldn't be the first time.'

'It never occurred to you to simply ban Morgan from joining in these outings?' Dóra asks.

'That has never come up,' Marteinn says. 'Every child has the right to be what they are. Excluding them would send all kinds of wrong messages. We don't give up on anyone.'

'Well,' Dóra says after a pause, unsure of how to proceed. 'What do you want me to do?'

Sandra holds up a soaked blue down anorak and a single training shoe. If that's the right word. Dóra can't imagine what kind of sport anyone could train for with shoes like that laced to their feet. It looks more like a weapon from a sci-fi movie.

'We found these by the Drowning Pool,' Marteinn says at last. 'That's Morgan's coat.'

'And one of their shoes,' Sandra adds.

'That's the first thing you should have shown me,' Dóra hisses, heading for the jeep to call out support.

5

Hector was shivering. He probably wasn't wrapped up warmly enough. Access to the laundry room was supposed to be included in his rent for the basement room he had on Kópavogsbraut, but the washing machine was never free. It was running round the clock. Nothing strange about that. There were two single mothers and a horde of kids living on the floor above. Every now and then one of them would stray down to the basement and the braver ones would tap on the door or try the handle. It didn't bother Hector. He had no children of his own but had nothing against them. He had been brought up by a single mother who had always struggled. If there was anything he had wanted or needed, then he'd stolen it. As far as he could make out, that was more or less the way things were upstairs.

He wore jeans, a Garfield tee-shirt and an Adidas hoodie with a bust zip at the front. He had nothing that was clean. The industrial unit that was home to the Sons of the Gods, or the Gods, as the biker club was generally known, was more suited to fish processing than criminal activity. The electric heater that he'd stolen from a building site up in Mosfellsbær and had given to Emmi was enough to keep this echoing, white-painted space warm.

The Sons of the Gods had no links with any gangs in other countries. Hector knew that the leader, Nóri, had tried to get in touch with some of the larger ones with a view to establishing links. But nothing came of it. Iceland was just too small. Too much hassle. Most of the time when the representatives of these overseas clubs turned up at the airport, that was as far as they got before they were dumped on the next flight back home.

It was Emmi who'd invited Hector to the club house and introduced him to the members of the Gods. He naturally recognised a few faces but knew next to nothing about these men. He and Emmi had done time at Hólmsheiði at the same time and had become good friends in prison. All the same, Hector was far from being a motorcycle aficionado. He knew how to ride one. But that was a basic requirement if you want to steal a bike.

He was a thief, first and foremost. He'd sold dope as well and occasionally had a snort, but that didn't do much for him. In fact, he'd sometimes snort way too much. All the same, he didn't quite belong with this gang which was into that kind of business. Most of those on the drugs scene were addicts themselves, and that made them unpredictable, and even downright dangerous. He'd had enough of that sort.

Emmi had talked endlessly about the club when the two of them had been inside, and Hector gradually began to see certain advantages. The problem was that being a solo operator didn't work. He always ended up being robbed by gangs who took a dim view of competition. Especially the fucking Poles. They didn't just steal his loot, but his own stuff as well, even things he'd bought. Hector would steal anything that wasn't nailed down. There was no system he couldn't find a way around. He often had hauls worth a million krónur a day, when he was on a roll. But there are few things that hurt a thief like being robbed. Hector wanted an arrangement with the club that would give him protection in return for a certain outlay. If someone stole from him, they'd even the score in his favour. Hector knew that his word alone wasn't enough. He'd have to come up with the cash. That's the way it always was. But before striking a deal, he wanted to get to know them a little better, find out what they were made of.

There was a little bar, and a small chiller cabinet of spirits in the corner, by the spiral staircase that led up to a closed area that had been offices back when this place had been used for its original purpose. The club's framed logo hung on the wall behind the bar, next to a hammer that Hector was sure was plastic. At any rate, that's what it looked like. It brought to mind the hammer that the thunder god Thór wielded in the Marvel movies. Emmi's brothers, as he called them, were bulky guys, with long hair and beards. Hector stood at the corner of the little bar beside Emmi, who slid a large draught beer along to him. A Harley-Davidson with long forks stood in the middle of the room, and the Gods sipped beer as they admired the motorcycle. Rock music pumped from a wireless speaker tied to the handrail of the spiral staircase. In a nook below the space upstairs was a corner sofa, next to a bench press and a stack of weights. The place reminded Hector of the metal fabricator's workshop where he had worked for a while after a two-year stretch out east for a pick 'n' mix of offences more than a decade ago. He had genuinely made an effort to turn over a new leaf. He'd even finished college at Selfoss. It showed that he could learn if he wanted to. All that had been needed was prison discipline. It had turned out that he was more than averagely bright, as one of the teachers out east had put it, as well as good with his hands. He'd even started reading books without being forced to. His essay about Snorri's Edda had earned a decent grade from that same teacher, who had a knack for getting the best out of the lads on day release from the old prison at Litla Hraun. He didn't judge, and paid them attention. To start with, they were wary. But those who wanted to learn didn't go away disappointed, and that included Hector.

Somehow, he'd been offered a job at the steel fabrication place. That was a good job, and there were good guys working with him. He'd got to know Gústa through a mutual friend, and moved in with her. Gústa was just out of long-term rehab and was also trying to get back on track. He had stopped all that stuff completely while he'd been inside. Sometimes he even went with Gústa to meetings, even though he wasn't going back on the programme himself.

They rented a little place in Hafnarfjörður and Gústa got a job in the bakery nearby. Her six-year-old son Benni spent weekends with them, and there was a good chance he'd be able to stay permanently if Gústa could keep herself clean. Which in the end she couldn't. Hector had established a relationship with the withdrawn lad who sometimes cracked a smile and laughed when they joked together. Sometimes he took the boy with him to work if there was something they needed to finish on a Saturday morning. Then Benni would make himself comfortable on the sofa, similar to the one over there in the nook, playing games on his phone while he waited for Hector. Maybe he'd drink a Coke or an orange juice.

This was when Hector experienced a strange feeling, that he was a man, just an ordinary guy. He was as ordinary as anyone could be. Hector didn't know what became of the boy after Gústa's overdose. Benni stopped coming at weekends to the flat in Hafnarfjörður, and eventually Hector stopped as well and the memory of this experiment with change merged into all the other craziness in his head. He took a deep dive back into the chaos that his life had always been.

Hector was half-way through his beer when Emmi disappeared up the stairs to the space up above. He came back with a man of around forty, with an aquiline nose and a scar low down on one cheek, dressed in the same gear as the others, except for the word *president* in a crescent above the club logo on his leather waistcoat. Hector assumed this had to be Nóri, the top guy. The Gods all glanced in his direction as he descended the stairs, with Emmi trailing behind him. Nóri scanned the room until he caught sight of Hector at the far end of the bar, then took unhurried steps over to him. His eyes were red, no doubt thanks to a joint or two, and he ran a hand though his long, greasy black hair.

'Emmi tells me you're looking for something,' Nóri said in a voice that was barely above a whisper, nodding in Emmi's direction but without taking his eyes off Hector. 'Shall we see if we can figure something out?'

Nóri leaned against the bar and his eyes flickered down to Hector's chest.

'Cool,' Hector said, doing his best to adjust his hoodie to cover Garfield's giant grin. He was certain that this was going to be yet another colossal mistake and he'd spend the rest of his days stealing to pay off this debt.

6

The fishing lodge couldn't be seen from the road, and hardly even from the rutted track that led down to it. If he hadn't got the jeep stuck in the soft ground then he wouldn't be standing here in a pair of rubber boots and a shovel in his hands, trying to fill in the deep tyre tracks. It was as well there was nobody about. There was a farmhouse on the far side of the ravine, but he was fairly sure it had been long abandoned.

Shovelling was tiring, but he didn't mind that. The cool air was invigorating. It was April and the snow was melting, freeing water to stream down from the highlands. It was difficult to see where the meltwater was going, until you put a foot on the ground and the gravel gave way into the slush beneath. This aroused his interest more than anything else. It didn't trouble the Groke in the least. He had never seen any point in letting himself be angered by nature or its laws. In fact, he lived closer to nature than most people − close to the border with death and decomposition. He was a ferryman of a kind, leading all sorts of people, understandably not always willing, to that border and across it.

The two corpses he had conscientiously buried behind the fishing lodge were prime examples. This couple lived in Reykjavík, in one of the new districts that had sprouted up over the last decade. In these sprawling, soulless boxes where vast flat-screens cast their blue glare on the walls and the big picture windows. The couple had stolen money. This was an amount that would have been worth negotiating, if only they'd showed a little inclination. But they hadn't. They thought they would get away with it. They hadn't realised that this was too much money to simply shrug off. Their attitude had been such that threats, beatings and even torture hadn't done the trick. Some people had to have their hands held to the border between life and death, while others failed to understand that their own behaviour brought the border to them. Their deaths would serve as a warning to others. He knew that wasn't true. Man as a species is too cross-grained for that to be the case.

Neither of them had been able to say a word before they died. The man had been coming out of the bathroom. The Groke sank the needle deep into his neck, and he sank down against the wall of this house that looked as if it had been cut from the pages of a piece of property porn. They had great taste, which perhaps was the reason for their downfall. In the end it had all been too costly, all the beautiful art on the walls, the expensive furniture and wardrobes crammed with designer goods.

Just moments after the man slipped to the floor, his wife parked her new electric car in front of the house and wondered who owned the jeep with tinted windows standing in the drive, and which she didn't recall having seen before. She went indoors, called out, but didn't get a response.

The Groke waited patiently in the corridor upstairs. He heard her potter around the kitchen, putting groceries away and calling her husband. The low hum from the man's phone carried from the bedroom. He eventually heard her come up the stairs. When she appeared in the corridor and saw her husband lying there, she was about to scream. But the blow he gave her to the solar plexus punched all the breath out of her. He didn't like this. It felt amateurish. But there was no other option. Then he grabbed her by the back of the neck and sank the needle deep into it. A few seconds later she lay on the floor beside her husband. If anyone were to wonder about them, then border control would inform them that the couple had left the country on a charter flight to Portugal. Their social media accounts had been hacked into. There would be a few pictures posted of landscapes and Southern European cuisine before their trails would disappear for good.

The Groke descended the stairs and went into the kitchen, where he opened the fridge and checked out the contents. The same luxury was on offer there. He glanced at the clock, and sent a Signal message from his phone. 2-0.

It was almost spring. It wouldn't be dark until around eight. It wasn't safe to carry the two comatose bodies out to the jeep until after nightfall. So he could cook himself a light meal. He could catch up on something on TV. They weren't going to wake up until long after he had filled in the grave.

This wasn't the first time he had done this. Of course, it could always happen that someone would regain consciousness along the way, so he always took the precaution of taping their mouths shut if there was a long drive ahead.

He yawned and looked out of the kitchen window. No callers were expected. Those who knew the couple had long since cut them off. It was simply too dangerous to be in touch with those who danced so perilously close to the line.

7

7

Rado reckons he's been sitting in a daze in the canteen for a good hour when she finally calls. He answers on the second ring.

'You have to come home,' she says, voice steady. 'Right now.'

'I'm coming,' he says and hangs up hurriedly. He has no idea who could be listening in.

The drive gives Rado plenty of time to think. Ewa was just a child when she came here from Poland, just like Rado and his Serbian parents. The old home countries, Poland and Serbia, always echoed faintly throughout their lives.

The story, or the little of it that Rado has got to hear from Ewa, is that Jurek, her father, had no choice but to flee under cover of darkness from an Albanian gang. It had been something to do with smuggled goods coming in through the port of Gdansk.

According to Ewa, the move to Iceland had been both an escape and an opportunity to start afresh. The family ran a couple of Polish corner shops in the city, and a tyre workshop. But Rado was no fool. He knew that his father-in-law dipped his fingers in affairs that wouldn't stand up to scrutiny. But he had been certain that none of this was anything serious. Some petty theft, tax evasion and suchlike. It hadn't occurred to him that the scope of the old man's business could be enough to trigger a major police raid.

Ewa's Tesla is nowhere to be seen as Rado pulls up outside the house. He parks his old Land Cruiser a little way off, marches briskly across the driveway and sees a familiar car there. The brand-new BMW 520 belongs to Ewa's brother Artur. *What the hell's he doing here?* Rado wonders as he opens the street door of the block with his key. Ewa and Artur aren't exactly close. Artur's a complete loser who's constantly in some jam or other. Rado's pretty sure he's driving illegally, as he's been pulled so many times drunk or stoned behind the wheel. Rado's close to boiling point. He can feel the anger well up inside him as he goes along the corridor. He's worked so hard and achieved so much; so much more than many other Icelanders of foreign origin. All the way to CID. And what for? So that some small-time Polish wide boy who steals cars and sells cut speed can wreck everything for him?

As Rado holds out his key to open his own front door, he can see that there's no need for it. The door has been kicked in. A hole gapes where the handle should be. One of the doorstops hangs loose to the floor. Rado gingerly pushes the door open and steps inside. All his senses are working overtime. There's no knowing what to expect.

He tiptoes into the flat, fists balled. The closet in the hall is open and their outdoor clothes – little Jurek's hats, his and Ewa's coats – are strewn like wreckage across the floor. There's been a break-in. *Fuck*, Rado thinks. They could still be here. He glances around for anything that could serve as a weapon. He frantically snatches up a long metal Ikea shoehorn and storms into the living room. Ewa and her mother, Marta, are sitting there, with a vodka bottle and two shot glasses on the table. As always, Marta is dressed to kill, in an outfit that's totally wrong for a woman pushing seventy. She's showing far too much of what nobody wants to see anymore, and she's overdone the war paint. It crosses the line and works against her, she's almost like a clown. The smeared mascara does her no favours. Ewa carries herself well. But Rado knows her, he can see she's in shock.

'They've gone,' Ewa says, looking at Rado.

'Who?' Rado asks, understanding nothing. The flat has been completely trashed. 'Was there a break-in?'

'It's your mates,' says Artur, slouching into the living room, a bottle of Heineken in his hand and a cigarette smouldering in the corner of his mouth. He looks like a rapper in a singlet, tracksuit trousers, Nike Air Force-1 shoes and tattoos up to the neck. He tries to be tough, but it's a front. He's an idiot, as soft as butter.

'Put that thing out. If you want to stay healthy,' Rado mutters and Artur starts. Then he smirks and drops the half-smoked cigarette into the beer bottle. 'Which mates of mine were these?'

Rado picks up a photograph in a frame, its glass broken, and drops it silently to the white living-room carpet. Ewa's mother leans over to her and whispers in her ear in Polish. Not that there's any need for that, as Rado understands precious little Polish.

All of a sudden, reality dawns on Rado and he glances around properly. The place has been turned upside down, but nothing's been stolen, as far as he can tell. This wasn't a break-in. No housebreaker would work like this. Too noisy. Why take a chance like that in an apartment block?

'Who's the registered owner of the flat?' Rado asks. Ewa's reply is to look down at her hands. Before they lived together, Rado had his own place in Breiðholt. He sold it to move in with her. As far as he knows, it was her place. Ewa has always looked after the finances and is smart with money.

'It's a holding company that Dad and I own,' she eventually whispers. That means the flat is a perfectly valid target for the police raid. It's no surprise his colleagues avoided his eye at the station that morning.

'And the Tesla as well, I suppose?' Rado asks, and Ewa nods. 'You've wrecked ...' Rado doesn't finish his sentence.

Artur sniggers and his mother hisses something at him in Polish.

'Rado,' his mother-in-law says, her Icelandic thick with an accent, and she sits up on the sofa. 'You're part of this family. Now we need to stand together. Now you need to ...'

Ewa interrupts her mother with sharp words in Polish. Marta nods, shrugs and leans back on the sofa.

'They found nothing here because there was nothing to find. They took my computer. But they were polite,' Ewa says.

'Polite? They smashed the place up!' Rado says, his hands high in the air.

'The forensics people and the one called Elliði. It was the Special Unit first. They hunted through everything before Elliði came and quietened ...'

'And what the fuck have you done?' Rado yells at Artur. 'Tell me!'

Artur looks hesitantly at Ewa and their mother. He's like a little boy caught pranking the neighbours. It would be funny if only their whole existence hadn't been totally trashed.

'No, don't tell me. I don't want to know.' Rado makes for the kitchen, elbowing Artur aside. The situation's the same. There's smashed crockery and every drawer and cupboard is wide open. Rado finds an unbroken glass on the floor and picks it up. He turns on the tap, fills the glass and drinks. His heart hammers in his chest. He's got to calm down. *What next? What now?* He must get a grip on all this. *Think of Jurek.*

Ewa sidles into the kitchen and places a hand on his shoulder. She appears remarkably calm, in spite of all this. But she must know what she's done, and what all this is going to cost.

'Mum says they've arrested Dad,' she says in a low voice.

'And not Artur?' Rado says.

'He was with some girl last night. They must be looking

for him,' she says. 'I don't know any more than you do, my love.'

'We'll have to clear this up before we fetch Jurek,' Rado says at last. 'We can't let him see this.'

'No,' Ewa says and turns to Rado, pulling him close and looking into his eyes. 'They don't have anything. This is a storm in a teacup.'

'Sure, but we're in the teacup,' Rado says, pushing her away, but she pulls him back and catches his eye. The fire he knows so well is burning in her eyes. He has no chance against her in this mood.

'Listen to me,' she snaps. 'We're in this together. Me and you. This is no time for sulking. I need you.'

'Meaning what?' Rado asks and the feeling of dread deep in his belly makes itself felt. He's losing to her yet again. She's stronger than he is, the dominant partner in this relationship. She knows it. This is the way they've always been.

'I mean, we're in this together,' she says.

'Stop,' Rado says, trying to pull away by backing off, but she holds on to him – not tight, but firmly.

'You need to find out where they're holding Dad,' she says.

'And what?'

'He needs his medication,' she says.

'He's ill?' Rado asks, peering past her into the living room where Marta has taken out a red vape and pulls at it while tapping at her phone.

'It's his heart,' Ewa says.

'They'll look after him in custody. If he asks for a doctor, they can't refuse,' Rado says, fairly certain that he's right about this, even though he knows the custody cells are no kindergarten and nobody gets waited on hand and foot.

'That's no good. You'll have to go and take him his medication without anyone, y'know, realising it.'

Ewa holds a little white paper bag and pushes it against his chest.

'Why?' Rado asks, instinctively taking the bag.

'Dad doesn't want anyone to know he has heart problems,' Ewa tells him. 'He's scared others will see it as weakness.'

'Others, who?' Rado asks.

'Don't talk like a fool,' Ewa says, turning on her way out of the kitchen.

Rado follows and drops the bag into his jacket pocket. They can't argue this out here, in front of Marta and Artur.

'You fetch Jurek and clean up here. I might be able to sneak the medication to him if he's being held by the police at the Hverfisgata station. But if he's been sent to Litla Hraun or Hólmsheiði, then there's nothing I can do. Understand?'

Rado glares at Ewa, who nods and picks up her phone from the living-room table.

'Yes,' she whispers, giving him an enigmatic look. 'I'll have to walk to fetch Jurek. The child seat's in the Tesla.'

Rado nods and leaves the flat. He walks straight into three women in fleeces marked with the logo of a cleaning company. They mutter together in Polish.

Rado gestures for them to stay where they are and goes back into the flat where Ewa and Marta are still sitting on the sofa. Artur appears in the kitchen doorway, with a fresh cigarette lit.

'These women,' Rado snarls. 'Are they here to clean our flat?'

'Yes,' Ewa sighs and nods.

'Send them home. This time you can clean up your own fucking mess.'

8

'There's nobody available right now.'

Gunnar's voice echoes inside the jeep where Dóra is sitting outside the service centre.

'I have a blue anorak and a shoe belonging to the kid,' Dóra tells him firmly. 'I need a diver and we need to call out the rescue squads for a search.'

She hears Gunnar sigh into the phone. It's as if the sound comes from the glove compartment.

'None of the Special Unit are available because of the raid. Do you think she's in the water?' Gunnar asks.

'The kid was last seen by the Drowning Pool. So we need to search Silfra and Davíðsgjá. Those pools are much deeper,' Dóra says. 'The Drowning Pool's too shallow for anyone to actually drown in it.'

'Didn't you say there had been all kinds of trouble with this girl? Sneaking off from school trips, and so on? Any substance abuse? Maybe you ought to head back to town and see if she's turned up at home. If not, then start trawling the dope dens. Uniform has a list of these places I can send you.'

'Does that sound likely? She's not wearing a coat and has only one shoe,' Dóra says.

'Look, in the meantime I can call out the Selfoss rescue squad and get them to search the national park. They might have a diver as well. Get a picture of the kid and I'll circulate it. I can put out an alert online as well,' Gunnar says. 'Today's just so fucking difficult because of the raid.'

'I'll head back to town,' Dóra says drily. She looks past the jeep's windscreen to the coach, where Marteinn is standing at Sandra's side, eyes fixed on her. Dóra gets out of the jeep and crosses the car park to them.

'The rescue squad's being called out,' she announces to Marteinn as calmly as she can manage. 'And a diver,' she adds, noticing that he reacts to the word as if he had been punched. Bringing in a diver rarely bodes well.

'Jesus,' Sandra whispers. 'Do you think they …'

'At this stage we don't think anything,' Dóra says, as if the police force as a whole is focused on a teenager going missing. It certainly isn't. The force has other fish to fry at the moment, an Eastern European crime cartel. 'It's time you took these kids back to town,' she says, glancing up at Morgan's classmates who are pressed to the coach windows, watching. 'I need information on Guðbjörg's parents. Phone numbers and suchlike.'

'Morgan has a complicated home life,' Marteinn says, scrolling through his phone. 'They live with their father. There's no mother in the picture. Morgan also spends time with their paternal grandmother. I'll send you the numbers and addresses.'

'What's complicated about that?' Dóra asks.

'Well, who knows? Child protection has been … involved. Morgan's dad is … Let's say there have been some problems there, if I can put it like that.'

'Understood,' Dóra replies. 'And the mother? You don't imagine there's any possibility Morgan could be with her?'

'Morgan moved here from Sweden two years ago. That's all I know. Except that she's not in the picture,' Marteinn says, handing Dóra his phone.

On the screen she sees a photo of Marteinn, Sandra and a dark-complexioned teenage girl outside the visitor centre.

'That's Morgan. The photo was taken earlier.'

Dóra uses two fingers to enlarge the image until the teenager's impassive, beautiful and unhappy (in her opinion) face fills the screen.

'Send me this picture,' she says, handing the phone back to him.

*

On the way back into the city, Dóra's thoughts go to the Drowning Pool. According to the annals, eighteen women were supposed to have been drowned there, for immorality of various kinds. This was the infanticide or the exposure of a bastard child, or else incest that could result in a woman, sometimes with the man's connivance, committing the first of the two crimes that were punishable with death. A chicken and egg situation, so to speak.

It was after 1565, when the Grand Judgement had become law, that men spat on their hands and got to work. Every summer saw an execution at Thingvellir, well into the eighteenth century. The place names carry a strong insight into how matters were conducted. The national park was home to Brennugjá, Kagahólmar and Höggstokkseyri, places where people were either burnt, had their bones broken, or were beheaded and their heads stuck on spikes. *To instil terror in others*, as it was put. Or they were drowned.

She recalls that women were tied in a bag woven of horse-hair to be drowned. She once saw a picture of such a bag. Now she's overwhelmed with the feeling of what it must be like to try to draw breath in a bag like that, knowing what was to come. The emotion surges so strongly that she seriously starts to wonder if she has suffered such a fate in a former life. But that's a ridiculous notion. She has no belief whatsoever in life beyond the grave. To her, it's a selfish and imbecilic anthropomorphism of nature. If that's the correct word. She ought to look it up when she gets a moment. *Anthropomorphism – to humanise things.* Maybe she could make the word fashionable. But first she has to get out of this damned bag.

Eventually she pulls into a bus stop and hauls open the driver's door. It's just as well the bus shelter's deserted. She has to perform a ritual to shake off the feeling that she's about to be drowned. She recalls that she felt the bag was so small. Were the Icelanders of olden times really such midgets? All those heroes who raped their sisters and daughters who then bore their children just to end up in a bag? Men were beheaded. That's a cleaner exit than being drowned in a bag like a stray dog.

Dóra pulls off her top. Her nipples instantly harden in the chill. She takes a deep breath and comes properly to her senses. She stands behind the jeep to avoid the curious of eyes of passing drivers. She's driving a marked police car, which isn't ideal. Some prude could decide to call the station, instead of calling the scandal phone-in on Radio Saga.

She pulls on her singlet and sweater, ignoring gawping faces, and gets back behind the wheel.

Suddenly her heart skips a beat. It simply hasn't occurred to her that there could be anything suspicious about Morgan's disappearance, that there could be a crime behind it. Surely, it wasn't as if Morgan's classmates would decide to drown them in the Drowning Pool? That thought's too terrible to pursue to a conclusion. But that's precisely what Dóra does as she drives through Mosfellsbær. If that was what happened, would Marteinn have noticed? The whole class couldn't be guilty? Could they have stuck to their story the whole time? Children are more than capable of murdering other children. Even if they don't have an understanding of what an act like that means.

Dóra curses herself for not having even gone into the coach to take a look at the class. Too late now. Elliði would forbid her from making an appearance at the station if she started with the assumption that Morgan had been murdered. She feels a new pang as her thoughts go to him. It's practically certain he'll hand the investigation to someone else as soon as he finds out that Gunnar had sent her to the scene. There's a fluttering in her stomach that she can't explain. She wants to solve this case. But she's racing against the clock. She's determined to get as far as she can before Elliði stops her. His logic for doing so will be straightforward. Either she trusts herself to investigate cases, with everything that goes with that – or not. There's no middle ground other than what he's marked out for her within CID. That's the crux of it. She isn't sure. Today she can cope well enough with this investigation. Tomorrow might be another story, and no certainty she'll be able to get to the station. That won't solve any cases. They need to be followed up. Every effort has to be made. That's maybe asking too much of someone who still has bullet fragments deep in her head.

Dóra finds the police headquarters on Hverfisgata in turmoil when she shows up there. There are dozens of men in handcuffs lined up at the yard entrance and her colleagues are trying to work out where to put them all. All of the cells are already full. They'll have to be held elsewhere. Elliði takes control in his usual unflappable manner, directing them to be taken to various regional stations around the city, while some are sent out east to Litla Hraun to be kept in isolation.

Most of the arrested look much the same. They're dressed in tracksuits of the kind most Eastern European men seem to favour. Dóra wonders whether it's racist to say they all look like Poles. Some of them are from Poland and they mutter together in their own language, even though the cops threaten to gag them if they don't keep quiet.

Elliði's too busy to notice Dóra. That's fine. Her errand here won't take long. She's here simply to drop off the jeep and pick up her Volvo, oh, and grab a carton of skyr and a banana from the canteen. She shouldn't take medication on an empty stomach. She has to eat something, otherwise the whole world could end up on its head.

In the corridor she runs into Gunnar, and he tells her that the rescue squad from Selfoss is expected to be at Thingvellir later in the day to start the search. They're bringing a dog, which makes everything more manageable. But there's no news of a diver.

'If the kid had fallen into Silfra or Davíðsgjá, then we'd see. The water's so clear. That's what the rescue squad guys say. But we'll still get it checked as soon as possible. Search until there's nothing open to doubt,' Gunnar says. 'There's a press notice gone out with the photo you sent.'

'That's good,' Dóra says, making for the lift and pressing the button.

The canteen's lively. Dóra hears her colleagues talking about how the raid went like a dream. They sit and let the tension seep out of them. It seems nobody has been hurt, which is always a relief, and they encountered little resistance. A tall guy in the Special Unit, whose name Dóra doesn't know, says that the gang had been caught in bed. He holds a submarine sandwich that looks like a canapé in his shovel of a hand. Dóra spies out Gunnthór at one of the tables. Katrín, one of their CID colleagues, sits opposite him. She's still wearing her stab jacket. Dóra can't stop herself, and heads over to them. Gunnthór's instinct is to stand up. There's no need for that with a full plate of food in front of him. Katrín nods to Dóra and glances at Gunnthór, who's forced to sit down again.

'The old woman who suffocated,' Dóra says.

'What about her?' Gunnthór asks, prodding his food with a fork.

'I blew up a couple of the pictures forensics took in her

flat. In the bedroom there's a weird green line running down the wall. It's not mould, or paint, or water damage. Any guesses what it could be?'

Dóra stretches and her neck cracks.

'I'm trying to eat here. It's been a long day,' Gunnthór says calmly, and that's presumably because Katrín's sitting there.

'Was the bedroom window open or closed?' Dóra asks, leaning forward over the table towards Gunnthór.

'I don't remember.'

'In the photos it's open. Did you open it when you arrived at the scene?'

'I suppose so,' Gunnthór says after a long pause.

'OK. Was there a smell out in the stairway?' Dóra asks.

'Yes, of course. That's why the neighbours called the police. The old lady must have died in the flat, which was locked from the inside. The same with the bedroom window. That was locked as well,' Gunnthór says, as he forks chips into his mouth.

'So you take a deep breath, rush in and open all the windows?'

'Most of them. That's what you have to do at a crime scene,' he says, and Dóra's sure that's a barb directed at her. She lets it pass, but it's high time for her to take the medication she keeps in the Volvo's glove compartment.

'It's plant food. On the wall,' Katrín says suddenly.

Dóra's so excited that she instinctively claps her hands and then sits on them so she'll have to stop.

'Exactly. There was a dope farm in the flat above. I checked it out. The upstairs neighbour has a record for that stuff,' Dóra says. 'I got the landlord to let me in. The guy upstairs made himself scarce as soon as old Lovísa died. And he was quick about it. He didn't manage to clear up completely. That flat on the upper floor is almost airtight. That's so the smell doesn't get out. He also used very powerful, very quiet fans. Much too powerful. They sucked all the air out of Lovísa's flat as well. Because of the smell of the body, and as you held your breath and opened the windows right away, you didn't suspect anything.'

Gunnthór's jaw hangs open.

'You're a freak,' he says at last, shaking his head in astonishment.

'Great work,' says Katrín, patting Dóra's shoulder.

She marches out of the canteen, gulping down the skyr as she waits for the lift. She wants to vomit, weep and scream. All at the same time. Sometimes she can be so clueless. What had she expected? That they would finally accept her as a member of the gang? The two of them at the table had the same expression, just in different versions. They maybe had some opinion of her, but their primary emotion was pity. That hurts. But it's not as painful as not having seen this coming.

Stupid cow, she mutters to herself as she steps into the empty lift, presses the button and gets a jolt of static. A cutaway vision of the police station comes suddenly to mind, like a schematic of electrical cables and network connections. She wants to march back into the canteen and answer right back.

I'm not just a freak! I'm a freak who's right! is what she wants to yell at them. But she doesn't. Now she has to shelter from these billowing waves of electricity and data. Instead, just as the lift door is about to open, she calls out, 'Morgan, I'm coming! I'll find you! I promise!'

9

Dóra opens the Volvo's glove compartment and takes out a pill bottle. She fishes out two tablets and swallows them down. She gazes through the windscreen at the yard behind the police station. Gang members are being herded like sheep. They're put in cars that drive off, one after the other.

There's a break in the line of vehicles and then it's Dóra's turn to drive away. Her phone vibrates on the seat beside her. Jafet's calling. She ignores it. She's turning onto Sæbraut when she feels the medication's effects pass through her body. Finally, there's a moment's silence in her head. At last, she can think. Or rather, not think. There's quiet. Not a dead silence, but enough for her to be able to consider through the next steps in the search for Morgan.

She'll start at her – or their – home. According to Marteinn, Morgan lives in a rented flat in the Laugarnes district with her father. His name's Hákon and he works as a builder. The last thing Dóra did before leaving the station was to look him up on the police system. He has a few fines and convictions behind him for possession, a few fights and generally being unruly. It's all trivial stuff. She wonders if she ought to have someone with her to speak to him, in case he turns out to be trouble. But she's not expecting anything like that. He needs her, not the other way around. She's searching for his child. That's an argument that usually holds water. But not every time. In this instance she has no idea of the nature of the relationship between father and child. Maybe it's a relief that she's gone. It might be the medication talking, but she's hoping for the best, hoping that he misses her and that his dearest wish is for his child to be found unharmed, as quickly as possible.

She parks the car outside a house that looks like it was built in the middle of the last century using poor quality materials. That applies to the whole street, and some of those houses look as if they're dying from some kind of wasting disease. The feeling is that they've been sick from birth and the kind thing to do would be to let them crumble to nothing so the street can start again from scratch.

Dóra walks around the house and knocks at the door of the basement flat. No response. She hears movement and turns. There's a woman emerging from the garage that's built against the side of the house. She's wearing a thin, threadbare cotton tee-shirt and plastic slippers. They look like Crocs, but are most likely a cheap knock-off version of that legendary footwear. Dóra reckons she looks to be around sixty.

'Are you from child protection?' the woman asks, hands on hips. She's chubby, with a freckled face, green eyes and a sharp nose.

'No.' Dóra says.

'Social services?'

'No,' Dóra repeats.

'Are you ...?'

'Let me stop you there,' Dóra says. 'I'm from the police.'

'Really?' the woman asks. She frowns and picks up a tub of washing by the garage door. She's about to go back inside, then pauses. Curiosity has the upper hand. Dóra notices a blurred tattoo on her left forearm. She's not sure but thinks it might be a poodle.

'What do the police ...?'

'This isn't a quiz,' Dóra says. 'Do you know the people who live in this basement?'

'I've seen them about,' the woman says hesitantly. 'I know them a bit.'

'What's that supposed to mean?' Dóra asks.

'You're from the cops, you said? Has something happened?' The woman tilts her head a little to one side, as if trying to peer past Dóra at the basement flat door. It's as if she suspects there's something terrible in there.

'We're looking for the daughter, Guðbjörg.'

Dóra can't be sure this person's aware of their change of name.

'If you're looking for her, then it's worth your knowing that 'she' is now 'they' and she doesn't call herself Guðbjörg,' the woman announces, taking a couple of steps towards Dóra.

'Exactly. They call themselves Morgan.'

'Could be. The name changes all the time. Like they're trying them out for size.'

'Do you know where I can find her ... their father, Hákon?'

'He looks after her. He drinks a bit, but the kid's always turned out well, y'know. It goes without saying he's not perfect. But who is?' the woman gabbles in Hákon's defence. 'When there was mould in my place, he ripped out all the tiles and put new ones in the bathroom. And he only charged me for the materials. I can tell you, my uncle's over ninety. He's in a home. Last year I bought him a TV, and a man came from a company the manager strongly recommended. They sent a lad to fit the TV on the wall and the bill was ninety thousand! The telly only cost thirty thousand. Isn't that disgraceful? Billing him like that? This country's going to the dogs.'

'He's a helpful type,' Dóra says.

'Who?' the woman asks, suddenly deflated.

'Hákon.'

'Yeah,' she says with emphasis, as if she's anxious to protect him, or else she's aggrieved with herself for veering off track.

Dóra makes out a faint smell of booze behind the scent of a perfume that's both piercing and sickly. It's clear the woman has been drinking. That explains why she's so garrulous.

'Where do I find him?' Dóra asks, backing away slightly from the woman to catch her breath.

The neighbour explains that Hákon is working on a new high-rise that's taking shape on the city's outskirts. This is on a piece of land that over the last few years has been the subject of inheritance and planning disputes. This tower block is supposed to be made up of luxury apartments, no expense spared, including a round-the-clock concierge in reception, where there's also a wood fire burning, presumably also day and night. There's a private road leading to the place, which is behind a gate, and security round the clock. The ground floor is for a restaurant, coffee houses and a variety of services.

The maintenance and management of this building is in the hands of a company that picks and chooses buyers at its own discretion – normally on a financial basis. The apartments in this place are roughly the size of an average detached house. This is where the rich can live in peace among other wealthy people. There's even a nine-hole golf course in the grounds at the back, as well as a swimming pool and a spa in the basement.

As far as Dóra is aware, the construction is in its final stages, with most, or all, of the apartments already sold. Dóra gets back in the car and switches on the radio before reversing out of the drive. A presenter is in full critical flow about the European Union's demands, while also giving the Progressive Party a beating. Dóra smiles absently and drives through the city towards the tower.

*

Dóra pulls up by the gate on the private road leading up to

the tower, which can't be missed, even from a distance. It's a building that reminds her more than anything of the rainbow artwork outside the Leifur Eiríksson airport terminal through which every visitor to Iceland passes. Except that this isn't bow-shaped, but stretches as straight as an arrow to the heavens. At first glance it's not reminiscent of a conventional skyscraper. The design is more daring than that. It's closer to the Gherkin that forms part of the London skyline, but Dóra's feeling is that it's more stylish. She winds down the window and shows a uniformed security guard her identification, telling him that she's looking for one of the workmen inside the building. The guard barely glances at her warrant card and waves to his colleague in the security office, and the gate opens with a low hiss. Dóra drives up to the building, which is surrounded by sheds and a variety of machines and vehicles. The groundwork has yet to be done around the tower, while the road leading up to it dog-legs through an expanse of lava. There are a couple of lifts running up and down the outside of the building, ferrying materials up or helmeted men down. Dóra has the feeling that they began building this place starting at the top and working downwards.

Dóra gets out of the Volvo and checks her surroundings. She walks over to one of the cabins that serves as an office and knocks on the open door. This is a noisy environment, so she puts some muscle into her knock, and the door swings open a little further. A man sitting at the desk with a helmet on his head looks up from an open laptop. There's a thin layer of cement dust coating every surface of the office, where plans of the construction, graphs and charts, inexplicable to Dóra, hang on the walls.

'Good day,' the man says. He has an outdoor complexion, is on the good-looking side and looks to be around forty.

'Hello.' Dóra approaches the desk. 'I'm looking for Hákon Sigurðsson. I understand he's working here.'

'And who might you be?' the man asks, closing the laptop.

'Police.'

'I see.' He gets to his feet, and Dóra notices he has a paunch and there are rolls of fat around his hips. She wants to ask why he's so oddly shaped. Most guys have a belly. But there aren't many who are so broad across the rear end. She wants to ask him about his diet. She suspects that this is the result of eating genetically modified meat, imported ribs and suchlike. Maybe that boosts the production of female hormones? But she keeps quiet. It's no business of hers. She catches herself staring and has the feeling that the man notices.

'He's in the top-floor apartment,' the man says, as if avoiding Dóra's curious eyes.

'How do I get up there?' Dóra asks.

'I can take you up. Is everything all right?'

'Am I all right?' Dóra says without thinking, eyeing the diagram of the tower on the wall next to the desk.

'No, I mean Hákon,' the man replies, stepping around the desk.

'Yes. I just need to speak to him.'

'This way,' the man says. 'I'll take you to him.'

Dóra follows though the construction area that echoes with the sound of hammer blows and purring diesel engines. It's cold, and there's a stiff breeze blowing. He leads her to one of the goods lifts on the outside of the building. This reminds her of a barred cage for a wild animal. The man puts his back into hauling the gate open, and gestures for her to step inside. She goes into the narrow space and her heels click on the steel floor. The man deftly shuts the gate and presses a button. The lift jerks into movement and makes its gradual way upwards. The small mesh of the wire cage makes it almost impossible to admire the view, but Dóra does her best. The wind makes the cage shake and Dóra locks her fingers around one of the bars in the corner.

'It's perfectly safe,' the man calls to her over the whine of the lift motor and the whistling of the wind. 'Just try to relax.'

Dóra sneaks another look at the man's hips. He's misunderstood her. She's not suffering from vertigo. She's just struggling, cooped up in this small space with him, to not mention his physical shape. She's so desperate to ask the question about his possible consumption of genetically modified meat that she can hardly contain herself. She tries to form the question in the most innocent possible way, before it pops out of her mouth. But that's not possible. She senses that her mind won't allow it. In an effort to find some kind of middle way, she decides to whisper, hoping that the man won't hear her over the hum of the motor.

'Do you eat a lot of fast food?' she mutters as she looks in his direction.

'What did you say?' the man asks out loud. *The fucking state of her head!* he thinks, grimacing as he cranes his neck towards her.

Fortunately, he hadn't heard the question. But her head's not letting go. Just asking isn't enough. Her head wants to see reactions to the question, and an answer. Dóra looks up through the mesh. There's still some way to the top. She's not sure she can keep herself in check. She needs to do something to change the tune (as she thinks of it) playing in her head. The feeling is of having to overpower a slippery speed freak – something she has had to do. She and Elliði were once on a callout to a house in Garðabær where they encountered a man in swimming trunks in the living room. He had been awake for the best part of a week. This was in a house he had been asked to look after during the owner's absence. By then he had comprehensively wrecked everything. A neighbour, who had found the dog wandering near a busy road, was the one who had alerted the police. The speed freak had rubbed himself down with olive oil and stripped down to swimming trunks, ready for the coming struggle with the aliens he was terrified were coming to abduct him. It was a hell of a struggle to get the cuffs on him. Dóra often thinks of that callout as she struggles with her own subconscious. Elliði had started singing to him as they made unsuccessful attempts to pin the man down. 'You are not Alone' was the song. Neither Dóra nor the speed freak knew what was going on. Elliði paid them no attention as he sang louder, and danced closer to the man, managing to catch hold of his arm and snap the cuffs on.

'I just had to do something to distract him,' Elliði said at the end of the shift as they sat in the squad car outside Hlölli's snack bar, putting away New York-style submarine sandwiches. 'Junkies don't see the world like we do. Nothing matters to them. At the same time, everything matters. I had to throw him a curve ball. Break the trance and put another tune on the turntable.'

Dóra always felt this demonstrated Elliði's remarkable insight. He was in fact a deep thinker with a capacity to read people. And now she was standing in this life and could just as well be smeared with oil and stripped down to bathing trunks. This was why she was welling up, because she was such a freak. But also over what a good man Elliði really was, who didn't deserve her breaking the delicate arrangement between them by going out on a shout as if nothing could be more normal. The tune hummed in her head.

The man can't avoid noticing that Dóra's singing with tears in her eyes. He pretends to see nothing, gazing out through the wire mesh over the city beneath them. A moment later the lift lurches to a halt and he opens the gate. The first thing Dóra notices is the whine of the wind that catches and gnaws at flapping sheets of industrial plastic.

'Hákon's working in the big bathroom,' the man says. 'Take care not to go past the rails. It's not safe. Hákon will put you back in the lift to come down again.'

Then he shuts the gate.

'Sorry,' Dóra calls through the mesh. 'What's your name?'

'Eiríkur,' he hesitates and replies.

'And what's your job here?'

'I'm the site foreman,' he says and presses the button. His face disappears as the lift starts its unhurried descent of the skyscraper's side.

Dóra looks around the top-floor apartment. It's vast. She sees that the handrails have yet to be fitted to the balcony that appears to run all the way around the building. The apartment is on two levels, connected by a central spiral staircase. The parquet floor has been laid in some places, and there's bare concrete in others. Those are the areas that are to be tiled. Dóra goes into a large living room with a copper fireplace in the middle. The inner and outer areas of the living room are partitioned from each other by narrow, patterned columns. This place puts Dóra in mind of a Disney castle. Glancing around, she tries to figure out the layout. All she can hear is the moaning wind, and sheets of plastic stretching and snapping. She ventures up the spiral staircase. There's no handrail yet. Looking up, she catches sight of a multi-coloured skylight window that casts a mesmerising array of coloured light. At the top of the stairs she finally hears some movement at the far end of a corridor. She passes two huge bedrooms before finding herself facing a massive bathroom.

She spies Hákon on his knees. It looks like he's praying to Mecca, but in fact he's squeezing tile adhesive from a tube. He stops when he notices her and looks at her questioningly. Hákon is drop-dead good-looking. But there's also something tragic about this man. It's something soft and vulnerable and helpless which only makes him even more attractive. That is, in the eyes of those who are looking for a man to save.

'Who might you be?' he asks gently, as Dóra had anticipated. There isn't a trace of suspicion in his voice.

'I'm from the police. We're looking for your daughter. She disappeared from a school outing to Thingvellir today.'

Dóra feels a pang of guilt for not having checked with the rescue squad. As far as she's aware, she's the only one searching for Morgan right now.

'I understand.' Hákon sighs heavily, puts aside the tub of adhesive and gets to his feet. Dóra almost steps forward to help him but stops herself. There's this magnetic aura about him, a charm. She's only just met the man and already wants to help him to his feet. She's going to have to be careful with him.

'It's not the first time,' Hákon says, putting a cigarette between his lips and lighting it. He has pale blue eyes and full lips. Dóra notices the dark blue patches beneath his eyes. She suspects that he's high. She recognises the beats, and knows a thing or two about being buzzing at work.

'Have you heard from her today?' Dóra asks. Hákon doesn't seem to be bothered by the pronoun she uses.

'Not a thing.'

'Any idea where I could find her?' Dóra asks, losing herself for a moment in his eyes.

'Is her phone offline?' Hákon asks, scratching the stubble on his chin.

'Yes.'

'Should I be worried?' he asks and sounds sincere. 'Considering you're here, I mean. Doesn't there have to be twenty-four hours or something before the police take an interest?'

'Yes, but these are particular circumstances. She disappeared from a school outing,' Dóra says.

'She has a temperament that can be difficult. Hormones,

y'see. She's becoming a woman,' Hákon says. 'Sometimes she takes herself off as a way of punishing me. But she always comes back.'

'Is she using anything?' Dóra asks.

'Nothing serious. Not really,' Hákon says, catching her eye.

'Any idea where she could be?'

'None at all. Which is shit. I haven't given her all the attention she needs recently. Been busy here,' Hákon says, gesturing at the bathroom that looks to be half-way to being finished. A vast bathtub and a shower cubicle have been fitted, but the toilet and basin are still missing. Dóra looks down at the floor where Hákon was on his knees. He's tiled a small section, but if she's not wrong, there's a lot to be done. There are boxes of tiles piled in a corner.

Dóra gives Hákon her number and he promises to call if he hears anything. She thanks him for his time and makes for the spiral staircase. Then she turns and goes back to the bathroom where Hákon is busy placing tiles.

'Two thousand, three hundred and fifty-eight,' she blurts out.

'What?'

'Nothing. You'll have to show me back to the lift,' Dóra says, and he gazes back at her without a word. She can feel an electric rush of arousal in her crotch. This guy's just too much.

10

The Groke usually spends this time of year in Thailand. The temperature suits him, not too hot, not too humid. He didn't feel the food was anything special, but he wasn't exactly a gourmet. He hadn't had that kind of upbringing. But Thailand is relaxing in its own way. It's an opportunity to catch his breath.

The south of Spain had been a good place as well for a while. After his service in the Norwegian army and work in North Africa, where he had been in the security detail at an oil refinery, he often spent his leave in southern Spain. But now the Costa del Sol was crawling with criminals. Too much chance of running into someone he knew, and he didn't have the patience for that.

A few times he had holed up in white-painted villages up in the mountains. He liked it there, but it wasn't going to work long-term. There were too many people around, eyes everywhere. People wanted to settle scores. It was easier to keep his head down in Asia.

They had sent three men to look for him when someone had noticed him in Cadiz, and without him noticing, they'd followed him up into the mountains. One of them was Irish. The other two from Montenegro. They knew what they were doing. But not well enough. Nowhere near good enough.

He had lost them in the village's myriad of tiny streets. Then he let them sniff out his trail again, leading them to the forest just as the sun was setting behind the mountain. He knew those woods like the back of his hand. They never had a chance. They made far too much noise.

He buried them as deep as he could in an abandoned chalk quarry, the place that had given the village the white of its houses. This was so that the vultures and the wild dogs wouldn't sniff out the corpses. The quarry had thousands of years of history behind it. He recalled the chalk dust whirling into the air as he dragged the lifeless bodies down there in the darkness. *Red on white.* That's how the memory of all this stayed in his mind.

The evening sun just managed to send its dying rays down into the quarry. By the time he clambered back out over the rim, it was pitch dark.

After the job in North Africa came to an end, he had picked up this other line of work by chance. The first one he rubbed out was a Moroccan hash dealer who refused to pay for a shipment that had been taken off him in Andalusia. The Spanish cops had stopped him for breaking a speed limit, so it had been his own fault. The Groke had slit the man's throat in a Marbella night club. Right next door there was a football match being played. Finding a parking space had been a nightmare.

This was the first person he murdered on his own initiative. Up to then he had never deployed a weapon without being ordered to.

The Groke epithet had come from his time in the Norwegian army. He knew this was the name of some cartoon character. The joke – if it could be called a joke – was that anything the Groke touched would freeze. That wasn't true, but was close enough. Anyone he touched was inclined to be dead before long. The Special Forces guys he was with were a great gang. This was all well-meant. Everyone had a nickname. It's a way of bringing the group together, forming a brotherhood.

He wasn't exactly insane. And he wasn't immoral, not

exactly. He wasn't a monster. He wasn't like some of the ghost-like people he had encountered along the way, cold through and through. He understood the difference between right and wrong. Weaklings don't get as far as he had in the military. But whether it was all that time, or the solitude, or the nature of the job, he wasn't entirely stable and he was fully aware of that – somewhere deep inside.

He'd stopped counting how many people he had rubbed out over the years. After North Africa he had lost track of time in the sense of how people experience it in dealings with others. He was always alone and always on the move. He went from one job to the next in between dropping off the radar at intervals to recharge his batteries. He was always busy, constantly in demand. If the Groke was on someone's trail it was as well for them to say their prayers. He had been close to being caught a couple of times, but had always managed to fade away, to disappear into the shadows. He had done what was expected of him in Iceland and was checking flights to Asia when a request dropped in for him to stay a little longer up there in the north. There was a situation, another assignment, if he wanted it, before heading back up to the lonely mountain.

11

Jurek Senior sits in a cell at the police station on Hverfisgata. Around him the place buzzes with activity. There's the hum of electricity in the air that always comes with a big operation. Rado keeps his head down, as much as he can. It helps that there's hardly anyone who wants to meet his gaze. For them he's invisible. Worse than that. He's a ghost. Perhaps there are some of his colleagues who regret keeping the raid from him. But that's their problem. Whatever angle you want to look at it from, he's finished as a cop.

So smuggling cardiac pills into his father-in-law's cell is just adding fuel to the fire.

The warder hesitates when Rado asks which is Jurek Senior's cell.

'I'm giving you a direct order,' he snaps and the warder fumbles for the keys.

'But you're ...' he stammers.

'I'm what?' Rado demands. 'I rank higher than you, so do as you're told.'

It's stuffy inside the cell. Jurek Senior sits on the bunk, wearing his shellsuit and patent leather shoes. He looks up as Rado turns to face him, first shutting the cell door in the warder's face.

'You here?' he mutters in Icelandic, with the same heavy accent as his wife.

'Yes,' Rado says, relaxing, and for a moment it's as if the despair he can see in the old man's eyes fills the cell like poison gas. He's no longer angry. The sermon he was going to deliver, the one he'd composed in his head on the way to the station, has vanished.

'Do they have anything on you? Anything serious?' Rado drops the white pharmacy bag onto the mattress at Jurek Senior's side, and it disappears into his broad hand.

'That's my problem,' the old man mutters, hanging his head. 'But yours as well, I guess. That's a shame. You so wanted to be a cop.' The old man's Icelandic is excellent, despite his accent. In spite of his appearance and his stature – he's built like a bull – Jurek is a natural leader and as smart as they come. In another place and at some other time he could have had a great future on the right side of the law. That's assuming he'd have wanted to.

'You didn't have any concerns about me, or what? I mean, when you did whatever it was that landed you in here? Hadn't you stopped all the dodgy business?'

'It's about not leaving food on the table,' Jurek Senior says, slipping the white paper bag inside his jacket. That has to be some Polish expression he's translated into Icelandic.

'These people who live here, these Icelanders. They are so innocent. Far too ... soft and gullible,' the old man says, eyeing the graffiti on the cell walls.

'All the same, they managed to bang you up in a cell. You should see the state they left our place in,' Rado says and Jurek Senior flinches. It's slight, but Rado notices.

'Was my grandson there?'

'No.'

'That's good. Don't worry about me. I've seen worse cells than this one,' Jurek Senior says.

'I don't doubt it.' Rado is on his feet, ready to bang on the door to let the warder know that this highly irregular visit is at an end.

'Hold on a moment,' Jurek Senior says. 'They all know you're here in my cell. If they don't, then they soon will. So the damage has been done.'

'I've nothing to say to you,' Rado says, arms folded.

'Then can I tell you something? To end with?' the old man asks. Rado sighs and nods.

'Fair enough,' he says, leaning against the wall.

'There was a sailor. His ship sank in the Caribbean, he was the only survivor. He washed up on a desert island. Years later, a ship passed by. He managed to light a fire and attract attention. The ship stopped and they sent some men in a little boat to the island. When they got to the shore, the castaway told them that he had been there for many years. They look around the island, which is little more than a bare rock. There's no vegetation, and hardly any animals. How did you manage to stay alive? they asked. I ate my own shit, the castaway said. Wasn't that disgusting? they asked. No, he said. Eating your own shit is fine. But the shit that comes from shit is fucking horrible. Shit of the shit, y'see?'

Rado can see Jurek Senior grin. This is the closest his father-in-law will ever come to admitting the error of his ways. Rado snorts, and smiles. He stands upright, and bangs on the cell door.

This visit is over. He doesn't need to spend a single minute longer on the desert island that this cell is.

Rado glances back inside the cell before the overstressed warder bangs the door shut. The smirk has disappeared from the old man's face. He looks impassive, distant. It's like he's been carved in stone.

Wherever a man goes, he takes his true self with him. That's something Rado has heard somewhere before. That's all he can recall of the sermon he had composed in his head on the way down to the station. But he'd decided to leave those words unspoken. The sound of the key turning as the warder locks the door is enough.

Rado walks silently out into the yard, straight into Sævar. Rado catches hold of his stab jacket and headbutts him straight between the eyes.

'Next time you break into my home, I'll be waiting for you,' he rasps, without letting go of the stab vest. His Special Unit colleagues come rushing across, but Rado uses Sævar, who can barely stand on his own feet, as a shield.

'Calm down! All of you!' Elliði shouts, rushing to place himself between Rado as he releases Sævar, who collapses onto the floor, and the Special Unit guys, who hesitate when faced with Elliði's authoritative tone. He takes the initiative and hustles Rado along the corridor and into an empty office, locking the door.

'What the hell are you doing, boy?' he demands, wiping the sweat from his brow.

'These are the fuckers who broke into my house and trashed the place. That's just fine, is it?'

Rado quivers with fury.

'No, of course not. But this is a complex operation. I couldn't be everywhere,' Elliði says, perching against the edge of the desk. 'Of course they were wrong to do that. But the flat's owned by your father-in-law, or a company he owns.'

'So what's this operation all about? I reckon I have a right to know,' Rado says. He can hear the commotion on the far side of the door as Sævar's colleagues attend to him.

'You're no fool,' Elliði says. 'You must have some idea of what your father-in-law and his goons get up to.'

Rado says nothing.

'It's about a shipment. The drug squad has been busting people with pills left, right and centre. It's something similar to oxy, but much stronger. They reckon this stuff's produced in Albania. Jurek has been importing it. Covid generated a vacuum, and he jumped in. The Ministry gave us more or less carte blanche to put a stop to it, using whatever methods,' Elliði says, as someone hammers on the door.

BROKEN

Elliði stands up and opens it a crack. Sævar is outside.

'Let me in,' he snarls.

'Forget it,' Elliði retorts. 'Try making an effort not to be such a wanker. Then people might stop wanting to punch you.' Then he slams the door in Sævar's face. Rado can't stop himself sniggering.

'We'll have to find some solution here, Rado,' Elliði says, running fingers through his thin hair.

'Did you find any gear?' Rado asks.

'You know I can't tell you. I ... There's pressure to suspend you.'

'Fuck.'

'You're a good officer and you've done well in this department. Go home for a few days. Let's see how this works out.' Elliði glances awkwardly at Rado, who realises that Elliði is giving him the answer to his question – maybe without meaning to. With no drugs, they have no direct evidence. Old Jurek's too smart to say anything on the phone. Too smart to get anywhere near the gear himself. His colleagues' jubilation over the outcome of the raid is premature. Rado doubts that they'll get anything of any use out of the gang members. Their loyalty to Jurek runs far too deep. Maybe he's not as near to being finished as he had thought. That's yet to become apparent.

'Then I'll go home. If you can get that gorilla out there off my back,' Rado says at last, and Elliði nods.

He can do that.

12

The goods lift bumps to the ground and Dóra steps out. Hákon offered to accompany her but she decided she'd be best off on her own. There's no knowing what kind of awkward clanger she might drop on the way down.

She feels she's losing her grip. In all honesty, considering the way today has worked out, that's how it feels.

She's had far too many *scenes*, as she thinks of the moments when she's not in control. It feels like she's going backwards. She has no idea if this is the result of the stress that inevitably accompanies such an investigation, or if it's something deeper. She wants to just go home and put the day behind her, curl up under the duvet and find out if tomorrow turns out a better day. There's every chance that this missing person case won't be her responsibility tomorrow morning. She can already hear the conversation in her head, with Elliði clearing his throat and explaining clumsily that he desperately needs her to deal with some urgent paperwork. She'll nod and hand over all the phone numbers to one of her colleagues in the department, give him all the details. Then she'll sense her own inadequacy burn her face into a flush of shame. She'll do her best to keep her theories to herself and refrain from giving any suggestions on the next steps to take.

As much as she longs for the safe cocoon of home, there's plenty of the day left. The adventure – as she allows herself to call it – isn't over until the day is done.

She finds the number Gunnar had given her for the rescue squad guy, and calls. It rings for a long time before there's an answer.

'Sumarliði,' a strong voice announces. He's puffing, short of breath. That bodes well, Dóra feels, an indicator that they're fine-combing the national park in the search for the missing teen.

'Hello,' she says. 'Dóra from the police in Reykjavík. How's the search going?'

'Well, it's ...' she hears him say. There's more, but the snapping wind drowns out his words.

'You dropped out there.'

Dóra goes over to the Volvo and opens the door. There's a constant flow of vehicles in and out of the construction site.

'It's going all right,' Sumarliði says. 'But we haven't found her.'

'How about the diver?'

'We sent down an underwater drone. Nothing to be seen. And it'll be getting dark soon. So we'll have to make a decision whether or not to continue the search in the morning. The dog didn't find anything either. The officer who called us out said that the girl might be using drugs. Couldn't she have hitched a ride to town, or got someone to come and get her?'

'We can't be sure,' Dóra says, getting into the Volvo.

'Shall we see how it looks in the morning?' Sumarliði asks.

'I'll call you,' she says and hangs up.

Dóra drives down the dog-leg road from the skyscraper, down to the office by the gate, and follows a truck through the open gate. Dusk is falling. Her phone buzzes and she can see it's yet another message from Jafet. Instead of opening them, she heads home by the most direct route. There's a large van outside the workshop. Dóra spies Thrándur, Jafet's best friend, coming through the big doors with a box in his hands, placing it in the van. Rúrik is nowhere to be seen.

Dóra gets out of the Volvo and locks it. She sighs. She knows perfectly well what's happening. This is confirmed when she opens the most recent of Jafet's messages.

I'm moving out. Please pick up.

Dóra goes over to the van and walks straight into Jafet and his friend Tommi, between them manoeuvring a green Chesterfield into the van. Tommi and Thrándur stand in embarrassment, glancing from Jafet to Dóra and back.

'This is awkward,' Dóra says at last with a thin smile.

'Is that everything?' Teddi says, peering into the van that's only half-full. Dóra sneaks a glance inside.

'Guys, could you wait in the van? I'll be right with you,' Jafet says in a resignation. Tommi and Thrándur nod.

'See you,' Thrándur says, catching Dóra's eye, and they get into the front seat of the van, leaving Jafet and Dóra standing behind it.

'I didn't want it to be this way,' Jafet says, his voice quivering. 'I can't do this anymore. It's too difficult.'

'I'm too difficult,' Dóra says with certainty.

'Not ... Am I getting it wrong? Aren't you tired of us as well?' Jafet asks at last.

'I should have replied when you called,' Dóra says, although it sounds as if she's speaking to herself and not to the man who's leaving her. This is the guy who has had enough of them, enough of her. She understands perfectly. She's pretty much in agreement with him.

'I didn't take the vinyl,' Jafet says. 'Go through the records yourself. Take your time. No rush. You know better than I do which ones are yours. If there are any there that are mine and you want them, then that's fine.'

'Where are you moving to? Can I ask?'

'Of course. My cousin has a little flat downtown. I can stay there until I find somewhere else,' Jafet says and there are tears in his eyes. 'Are you going to be all right without me?'

'Sure,' Dóra says, nodding. 'Just go.'

She shuts the van's back doors. She doesn't slam, just shuts them carefully, almost lovingly. But not fully, since she's naturally a long way from being perfect.

*

She drives out to Thingvellir. It's too dark to see anything, but she stops at Hagkaup to buy a head torch and a battery. This isn't because she's expecting to find Morgan, for whom the rescue squad with dogs and the underwater drone have searched unsuccessfully through the little daylight that winter allows at this time of year, but because she can't face sitting in a half-empty flat mourning a broken relationship. This has taken her totally unawares. But the same can be said of everything else she has experienced over the course of this day and the search for the missing teenager. It hasn't been easy, but she has been busy with police work all day, and not hidden away behind a desk at the station on Hverfisgata.

Jafet, who is normally completely predictable, finally pulled his socks up and said enough's enough. Maybe she's − more than likely unconsciously − been pushing him out these last few months. But he's always come back, always given her another chance. That's because she's not like most people. She's sick. Not that he uses that word out loud, not in her hearing.

She feels a sob rising and turns up the radio. Booming techno. After a little while she turns it off. This was the music that brought them together. Jafet runs a small record shop in the city centre and there's the occasional gig there. That was where they got to know each other, when Dóra's taste in music broadened. That was after the accident. Jafet assiduously fed her new music. She spent so much time in the shop that there was nothing for it but for them to get beyond just fooling around, as old Rúrik put it.

It's as dark as hell at Thingvellir. As Dóra gets out of the Volvo, she feels the winter cold like slamming into a wall. It's as well she's dressed for it. She had to root through drawers to find woollen underwear. She pulls on gloves and a balaclava she found in a cupboard in the workshop. There's a smell of smoke about it. She puts on the head torch she'd already tried out in the car and makes for the Drowning Pool. The snow crackles underfoot. To begin with, that's all she can hear. Then her rapid breaths add to the mix. The head torch casts a ghostly light over the snow-covered ground. She left her phone in the car, in case Elliði happened to be on the case. That's mad. What if she has an accident? Nobody knows she's here. But sometimes you have to squeeze out the self-pity that's on offer.

It can be tough to be in a bad way.

By the time she gets to the Drowning Pool she can no longer feel her toes. She stops, directing the beam of light at the surface of the water. There's no snow at the shoreline. She wanders aimlessly and tries to think of what could have happened to Morgan. If they're in the midst of some teen rebellion phase, why join in this school trip? Why not just play truant? No, something must have happened. The most likely scenario is that the youngster sneaked off from the group, to maximise the whole drama, and hitched a ride back to the city. If something had happened here in the national park, then the rescue squad would have found them. The kid would certainly have shouted for help. Is that a given? That's assuming this is all about attention-seeking?

Dóra finds a flat rock by the Drowning Pool and sits on it.

It's not long before her buttocks are frozen cold. First it smarts and then her arse goes numb. Just like her toes.

She uses the head torch to search to the left and right. She sees the lights of a car in the distance. Then the light catches something a few metres away. She points the light back to the spot. The light catches it again. She stands up and feels her way cautiously closer. The light pools on the ground until she catches sight of something. Her heart jumps. She picks up the phone in its pink case and examines it. A little metal letter hangs from the case on a leather thong:

M

13

Hector's basement room on Kópavogsbraut is stacked with stolen goods. He's been going through the city these last few weeks like a one-man crime wave. He's done everything from shoplifting to housebreaking. He's on a roll. Yeah, of course he's buzzing on speed but there are moments, sometimes whole chunks of the day, when he's not had a snort. The kick stealing gives him is so much more powerful. There are four scooters stashed under the bed, in addition to the ones he's already given to the bigger of the lads upstairs, as well as all sorts of clothing, tools he's spirited away from building sites – all he needs is a helmet and a hi-vis vest – and stuff from a load of break-ins at houses and apartments. There are laptops, tablets, games consoles, phones, watches, Bluetooth speakers, foreign currency, one vibrator that'll fetch a good price online, and all sorts of other junk that he needs to go through carefully to check its value.

He knows it's just a matter of time before the cops are on his trail. Facebook must be buzzing. He knows he has to cool things down. For him that's the tricky part of it. It's a struggle to stop when you're on a roll like this. Once the cops are part of the game, then it becomes a chase. He'll have to be more careful and he'll have to avoid places like the shopping centres. So Kringlan and Smáralind are off limits. Too many cameras there.

The Polish guys have left him totally alone. He hasn't run

into them.

He's also heard that the drug squad has collared most of them in some major dope bust, and they're all cooling their heels in cells.

Emmi has tried to call him a few times since he went to the biker hangout to ask for protection. Hector hasn't been dissing him, not exactly, nor the club. But these last few weeks he's been as if in a trance. There's been no time for anything else.

He looks around the basement room. Nobody knows he lives here. Only Emmi, and that's who's standing outside the building on Kópavogsbraut as Hector hauls the heavy scooter out through the basement door, on his way to case a potential break-in at a computer company in Hafnarfjörður.

'They want to talk,' Emmi says, jerking his head towards a black Escalade 4x4 further up the street. He has a purple black eye.

'Going to beat me up?' he asks, almost flippantly.

'You ought to pick up when I call. I'm calling on their behalf,' Emmi says with a sigh.

Hector puts the scooter aside by the basement door. He doesn't even bother to lock it. Then he follows Emmi over to the black jeep. One of the gods is behind the wheel. The rear windows are tinted, so he has no idea what to expect as Emmi gestures for him to sit in the back.

He opens the back door and gets inside. Nóri's sitting there, wearing dark glasses. That doesn't come as a surprise.

'So,' Nóri says, and the god at the wheel starts the engine and pulls away. Emmi's left on the pavement, hands spread wide. That doesn't look promising. There's a better than even chance this is going to end with physical injury. Maybe things can be squared before it gets that far.

'You came to us,' Nóri says. 'Nobody twisted your arm. I didn't.'

'I know what the deal is,' Hector says, trying not to

sound as though he's whining. 'Maybe I should just pay the drug squad? I mean, they've pulled the Polish guys off the street. You didn't need to do a thing.'

Hector knows this isn't going to be a free ride. But he can't give too much away.

'You're getting things round your neck.' In a flash, Nóri's fist closes around Hector's throat and squeezes. He's pinned down in the back seat. 'You run around and thieve because I allow you to.'

By the time Nóri releases his hold, Hector's eyes are ready to pop out of his head.

'OK, OK,' Hector whispers, between gasps for air. He's dizzy with lack of oxygen. 'I'll pay what we agreed.'

'That deal's no longer on the table,' Nóri says, lighting a cigarette. Hector looks up and out through the windscreen where the god at the wheel of the Escalade turns into a street in an industrial area of Kópavogur. His mind's working full speed. He has no doubt Emmi has broken into the basement room on Kópavogsbraut. It won't take him long to clear it. That's a bastard. But he'll have to live with it. All the same, Hector is no fool. The more valuable stuff and most of the money has been stashed somewhere else. If they're going to work him over, then he'll just have to live with that. As long as he can still get about. A balaclava will hide any facial injuries. He can always find something to kill the pain. The worst part's the room on Kópavogsbraut. He won't be able to go back there. He'll have to find somewhere else. That could take a while. He might have to go to a guest house or a hotel for the time being. But then he'll have to look out for the cops, who are no doubt watching. Maybe he can find a summer cottage somewhere near the city where he can lick his wounds. But that's tricky as well. Fucking cameras everywhere.

'Now pay attention,' Nóri says as the god brings the jeep to a halt outside a meat processing place. He catches hold of Hector's head and presses his face tight to the window.

14

Dóra's early at the station on Hverfisgata. It's been a hell of a rough night. That's not just because Jafet has left her, but because, despite not being a believer in predestination, she's convinced this is an investigation she has to pursue all the way. She tossed and turned, composing a mental list of what she would need to do right away, and what she had done well or badly on the first day.

The rescue squad will have to be called out again, with an expanded search area, there'll have to be questions asked of the kids on the outing, and any CCTV cameras at the service centre will need checking. There'll have to be a round of the city's dope dens and they'll have to circulate Morgan's picture to all the media and ask for the public to come forward with information.

Dóra's the first of CID to turn up and fetches herself a coffee. She's already spoken to the night shift's duty inspector and there have been no reports of Morgan overnight.

She can feel how tired she is. There's a nervous tic tapping at the back of her head, and that makes a change from the itch and sting in her eye. Her subconscious – if brain and thought can be separated, which she's not sure about – is remarkably calm. If she can maintain this placidity for the next hour, or until Elliði shows his face, then there's no certainty that he'll take the investigation out of her hands. The raid and the arrests that came with it are going to stretch the department to its limits. Elliði simply doesn't have the manpower to be able to say no to her.

It's not as if she needs to be on the scene the whole time. She can easily manage the investigation from her desk in the corner. She's not going to be striding around the national park at Thingvellir. There's a whole rescue squad for that. The uniform branch can comb the dope dens while she sits by the phone. Simples. It's so simple that she goes ceaselessly over her sales pitch to Elliði as she sips hot coffee and waits for him.

Gunnthór's the next to turn up at CID. He acts as if he hasn't seen her sitting at her desk, and goes to get himself a coffee from the machine. Then he hesitates, scanning the open-plan space as if to be sure they're alone. Then he goes over to her.

'Hey, sorry about yesterday,' he says, and clears his throat. 'Let me take a closer look. You might be onto something.' He marches back to his desk and switches on the computer.

'No problem,' says Dóra, who really wants to cry. Instead she gets up and hurries to the toilet along the corridor, locks the door and allows herself a silent celebratory dance. It's certainly something for Gunnthór to offer an apology. She takes off her sweater and holds it over – and in – her mouth as she whoops in delight. Then she regains control of herself and checks her face in the mirror. She doesn't see herself as all that ugly. She's on the slim side – that's thanks to the medication – and there are only a few grey hairs to be found in her thick blonde mop. The bad eye is naturally weird, and it's the first thing people notice, but it doesn't bother her today. Her tits have dropped a little, and she could do with a shower. Leaning closer to the mirror, she wonders if there's some spark coming to life inside her. There's a pink flush to her cheeks. This looks good. The cleaner, who has been standing stiffly at her side since she came bustling in, meets her eye in the mirror. Dóra would ask her opinion, but isn't sure she speaks Icelandic.

The department's fully manned by the time Elliði makes his appearance. He scans the faces present, and nods to Dóra, which means she's to come to his office.

He closes the door behind them and takes a seat behind his desk. He gives Dóra a look that invites her to take a seat, but she stays resolutely on her feet, arms folded.

Dóra inspects her old friend and colleague. There are deep black smudges under his bloodshot eyes. His face is grey, his fingers are yellow with nicotine and he could do with losing a few kilos. She wonders quickly which of them is in a worse condition as far as health goes. In society's eyes, it's her. But there's no knowing how that'll pan out if Elliði doesn't get a grip.

'Gunnar made me take on that missing person case,' she blurts out before Elliði can say anything.

'What's the situation? Has the kid been found?' Elliði asks as he leans back in his chair. Dóra gives him a rundown of the investigation so far, finishing up with finding the phone by the Drowning Pool that she's almost certain is Morgan's. She tried to call Hákon, the teen's father, an hour ago. But he wasn't picking up.

Elliði is silent for a while. Dóra's sure she can sense the cogwheels meshing in his head, as if his thought processes are steam-powered.

'What are you going to do?' Dóra asks, once she's given up waiting for a response.

'Has Jafet moved out? Have you split up?'

'How the hell did you know that?' Dóra snaps. 'And what makes it any business of yours?'

Her subconscious placidity is rapidly ebbing away.

'He's worried about you. So am I. You know that,' Elliði says quietly, as if asking her to lower her voice as well.

'There's nothing wrong with me!' Dóra says, even though she doesn't believe that herself. The words just tumbled out of her. 'I mean ... I may be ... But I can manage this investigation,' she adds with all the grace she can muster.

'Yes. Sure. The missing person. Or the missing teenage girl. It's a hell of a mess. The chief superintendent called me into his office just now. He'd somehow heard you were running this case. Did you tell anyone?' Elliði asks, his voice dropping to a whisper, as if his office is bugged. His eyes wander to the open-plan space beyond the glass.

'I haven't told anyone. I wouldn't do that without speaking to you first,' Dóra says.

'Well, someone blabbed to him, and he took it straight to the boss. People here aren't fools. We are detectives, after all. If you screw it up, I get the blame. The office politics in this place are merciless. You get it? So I'm asking, straight out. Do you trust yourself to take on this case?' Elliði's fists are clenched tight. Before Dóra can respond, there's a knock on the door. 'Come in,' Elliði calls out and the door opens. Rado's standing there.

There's as much surprise on his face as there is on Dóra's. Rado stands hesitantly in the doorway.

'Come in. Shut the door,' Elliði says, and Rado obeys. He steps inside and closes the door behind him. Elliði points to the empty chair facing his desk. Rado sits down.

'It seems this is trending,' Elliði says.

'What is?' Rado asks.

'This girl's disappearance.' Elliði glances at Dóra. 'Or what?'

'It's true. It's trending on social media. But it's not been picked up by the mainstream media yet,' Dóra replies. 'The word is that we're dragging our heels on this.'

'Who's saying that?' Rado shifts in his seat. There's a narrow bruise on his forehead, from head-butting Sævar. He's a long way from being a bruiser. He's short and slim, and the only exercise he gets these days is a run or a game of indoor football with old school friends. He has a brown belt in Jiu-Jitsu, but gave up training around the time his son was born.

'Some online smartarses,' Elliði says. 'I want the two of you to handle this case.'

'I can manage this on my own,' Rado says, eyes fixed on Elliði.

'No. The chief wants a female officer running it. It looks better. So you're on the case together,' Elliði decrees.

'But with all due respect ...' Rado looks doubtfully at Dóra. 'Is she ...?'

'Says who? Isn't your father-in-law in a cell here? Right here in this building? Are you sure *he's* up to this?' There are sparks flying from Dóra's eyes.

'Cool it!' Elliði hisses at them as if he's scolding a dog. 'I promised to find you a niche,' he tells Rado. 'You can say no and take time off. This is how I can keep you in the department. Do we understand one another?'

'Perfectly,' Rado says, and glances at Dóra, who swears under her breath.

'And you!' Elliði turns to Dóra. 'There's a shitload of data concerning the raid that needs inputting for the prosecutor. Most of it's so dull that it's off the scale. Aren't your typing fingers itching?'

Dóra and Rado leave Elliði's office. Dóra spies Gunnthór standing by the coffee machine and gives him a wink, a smirk on her lips. She knows who's been telling tales. She's certain he's the one who went running to Chief Superintendent Bjarki Freyr. Dóra just smiles and looks over at Rado.

'The press statement and the picture have gone out to the media. I was going to go down to the school to talk to the class. Coming?' she asks.

'You can fill me in on the details on the way.'

Rado's putting on a brave face.

They take the white Volvo, as Ewa is using Rado's old Land Cruiser today, and head for the Hagi School to interview Guðbjörg's classmates. They agreed in the lift to stick to using their given name – or rather, *her* given name. The Reykjavík police must surely carry more weight than the pronoun police.

Dóra drives and Rado sits in the passenger seat. He's tired. He didn't sleep well last night. When he came home, after smuggling the heart medication into his father-in-law's cell, everything was fine. Everything had been cleared up and the place was orderly again. Everything that had been damaged or broken in the raid had been removed. Ewa had been in touch with her lawyer, who assured her that she could continue to live in the apartment, and that he would make every effort to get her laptop returned. The lawyer wasn't confident that would happen anytime soon – if ever. Her father's fingerprints were all over the whole business.

Ewa had fetched Jurek Junior from school by the time Rado came home. He was sitting on the living-room sofa eating pizza. A children's programme was on the big flat-screen TV, which had escaped unscathed, and Ewa was folding laundry. At first glance everything appeared so normal, even the expressions on Ewa's and Jurek Junior's faces. She handed him a cold beer from the fridge and the cheerful Cocomelon song that filled the living room helped with the impression that everything was the way it ought to be, that there hadn't been a massive upheaval and breach of trust in their relationship. Rado was too tired, didn't have the energy to quarrel with Ewa. She had a knack of shrugging off anything that related to her father's life of crime. It was as if it was no business of hers. This was a woman who didn't let herself be knocked off balance. So he let it lie. He accepted the beer, sat down next to Jurek and reached for a slice of pizza from the living-room table.

Afterwards he went with the lad, watched him brush his teeth and got him ready for bed. When he came back, Ewa was sitting at the kitchen table, but he made no attempt to start a conversation. He was aware that the climate had changed, this wasn't anything like a normal disagreement between them. This went much deeper. An uncanny premonition made itself felt. This was when he made the connection and took the full force of the blow. This was certainly a bright, beautiful three-room flat in the Urriðaholt district, a family's home, and the only home their son had known in his short life. But now it was more than that. Now it was also a crime scene.

'What about her stuff, the coat, shoes and phone?' Rado asks as Dóra drives over the Tjörn Bridge.

'All with forensics,' Dóra replies, squinting. The low winter sun glints on the lake. All the windows of the houses along Tjarnargata seem to her to glow. That could just be a mirage. *Best not mention that to the new partner.*

'What did the father say about the phone? Does he know the code for it?'

Rado's trying to not sound pushy. This case is less than twenty-four hours old. There's every chance the kid will show up in some dope den. Or have a boyfriend nobody knew about. Likely someone older. It's a story that's as old as it is new. Normally these kids come to their senses when they see their own picture in the media. That's when the guilt complex kicks in. That's as long as they aren't too far gone. Or it's when the dope runs out. Then they're collared for something, theft or public disorder.

'I haven't got through to him this morning,' Dóra says. 'He's not answering his phone. But I know where he works.'

Rado grimaces. What kind of parent whose child has gone missing has their phone switched off?

'What about the rescue squads?' he asks.

'They should be at the scene. They're widening the search area. Abseiling into crevasses.' Dóra takes the turning off the roundabout by the National Museum in the direction of Hótel Saga. 'They arrested your father-in-law,' she says suddenly. 'That must be tough. Are you going to separate from your wife? I'm asking because my boyfriend was packing all his stuff into a van when I got home yesterday.'

'Let's stick to business,' Rado says firmly, and Dóra nods. His response is reassuring. He's clearly not the type to be easily ruffled. But no doubt he's heard tales about her. Nothing's safe from the station gossip.

Dóra parks outside the Hagi School and they both get out.

'Marteinn is Guðbjörg's class teacher and he's expecting us, and so's the deputy head,' Dóra says as they walk into the school hall, as the main entrance is closed for building work. To their left, under the stairs, is the canteen. The hall is reminiscent of a community centre somewhere out in the countryside. There's a raised stage at one end, long tables and plastic chairs that Dóra thinks would be more at home in a Swedish prison. It's as if they're the spawn of kindergarten furniture and eighties brutalist outdoor benches, and perfectly fit the image Dóra has of Sweden – none of which is based on anything remotely realistic.

A plump woman of around sixty in an African-patterned trouser suit almost runs over to them as soon as she sees them. Dóra notices Marteinn and Sandra sitting facing each other at one of the long tables next to the entrance. They get to their feet.

'Good morning. My name's Guðrún and I'm the deputy head teacher here,' the woman says, offering a hand. Rado takes it and announces that they're from the police. Marteinn nods to Dóra, who gives him a nod of acknowledgement. She's decided to let Rado take the lead for the moment.

'Can we talk here?' Rado asks, looking around the hall.

'Any news?' Guðrún asks, hands clenched tight.

'No,' Dóra says. 'Not so far.'

'Who are Guðbjörg's friends in the class? We want to start with them,' Rado says, planting himself down at one of the long tables.

'Her class teacher,' Dóra says to Rado, pointing at Marteinn.

'Hello,' Rado says, nodding to Marteinn and taking out a small notebook and a pen. He gestures for Marteinn to come over to him. Dóra watches with interest. In a matter of moments, Rado has taken control. He's effortlessly become the focal point, with everyone hovering around him. It's clear to Dóra that there's much she can learn from this new colleague.

'Marteinn is more up to speed on who she ... they spend most time with,' Guðrún says, her hands still tightly balled.

'Sonja, Eydís, Birgitta,' Marteinn says. 'They're the ones who are closest. To Morgan.'

'Start with Sonja. Get her, would you?' Rado says. Marteinn nods, and leaves the hall, with Sandra trailing behind him.

'It's lunch at twelve,' Guðrún says. 'And there's a break in half an hour. We normally have the hall open.'

'But not today,' Rado says amiably.

'No, of course. I'll leave you to it.'

Guðrún catches Dóra's eye, and leaves the hall with slow, hesitating steps. It's as if she doesn't want to leave.

It's not long before Marteinn escorts a teenage girl into the hall. Dóra sits at Rado's side and sneaks a closer look at him. There's black stubble on his cheeks and he has a dark complexion. She looks down at the open notebook. One of the pages is covered in small, neat script.

The girl takes slow steps towards them, as if she's being led in front of a court. Marteinn hesitates in the doorway.

She's tall, bony, with hair so fair it's almost white, and her looks are unusual. Dóra feels she reminds her of an alien, but keeps quiet. The girl stops at the table and looks at Dóra and Rado in turn.

'Sit down,' Rado prompts softly, and she does so. 'You're Sonja?'

'Yes,' the girl says, as if wondering why she's there.

'And your patronymic?' Rado holds the pen and makes notes.

'Like ... Kjartansdóttir,' Sonja says. 'What, like ... What do you want?'

'The school trip yesterday,' Rado says. 'How do you feel Guðbjörg was?'

'You mean Morgan,' Sonja says, as if correcting a mistake.

'Yes. Morgan,' Rado says and Dóra watches him write down the girl's full name in his notebook.

'Just ... I don't know,' Sonja says and looks to one side at Marteinn, who stands in the doorway. 'We hang out together sometimes. But not all the time.' Sonja's eyes are on the table and she rubs her hands together.

'And yesterday?' Dóra asks and Sonja turns her pale blue eyes on her.

'Are they dead or something?' Sonja asks suddenly and looks appealingly at Marteinn, who jogs over to the long table.

'No. She's simply missing,' Rado says. Sonja's trembling.

'Listen, Sonja,' Marteinn says, coming over to the table. 'They're just lost.'

'They're just too much!' Sonja blares, and stands up. 'I mean, they just want all the attention ... that cunt.'

Marteinn extends a hand to Sonja, but she brushes it aside and storms out of the hall.

'That's the way teenagers can be. Sometimes the fangs come out without a moment's notice,' Marteinn says, scratching one ear. 'It was Sonja's birthday yesterday. She felt that Morgan took her special day hostage.'

'Hostage?' Dóra asks.

'Morgan had an anxiety attack just as we were leaving in the coach yesterday. Sonja brought muffins for everyone, but the panic attack got all the attention. Sonja's sure that Morgan staged it. Could well be. There's often a struggle between them for attention.' Marteinn's face slips into a half-smirk.

'Let's have the other two,' Rado says. 'We'll talk to them at the same time.'

Rado catches Dóra's eye. She's not sure if he means they'll take one each or talk to the two girls together. She puts her hands on the chair and sits on them, as she has a sudden urge to stroke the stubble on Rado's face to feel how rough it is.

Eydís and Birgitta don't have much to tell them. It complicates things that the two girls insist on speaking English – which Dóra knows is a current fad among youngsters of this age. At one point the conversation becomes a parody of a bad TV cop show, with both of them speaking in exaggerated American accents. Rado finishes it by thanking them, when it's obvious they have no idea why Morgan made an exit from the school outing. All they can confirm is that Morgan – or Guðbjörg – is a loose cannon and they're sure she planned to go missing.

After a few words with Marteinn and Sandra, who had accompanied Eydís and Birgitta to the hall, they go back out to the car. Dóra's trying to call Sumarliði at the same time as unlocking the Volvo, when Rado's phone buzzes in his pocket. He answers, giving his name. Then he puts the phone down without saying a single thing, and meanders away, as if in a daze. Dóra hears Sumarliði pick up, but she hangs up. Rado loses his balance and drops to sit in the snow outside the school. Dóra hurries over to him.

'What's up?'

'It's Jurek,' Rado whispers. His face has turned grey. 'He's dead.'

'Who's that?' Dóra asks, sitting down beside him in the snow.

'My father-in-law.'

15

Elliði's standing there as the white Volvo pulls into the yard. Rado is out before Dóra. He's been silent all the way from the school up to the station. He slams the car door and storms over to the entrance. Elliði heads him off, raising a hand to halt him in his tracks.

'He's not here,' Elliði says. 'He's been taken to the mortuary.'

'What happened?' Rado is unsteady on his feet. 'I have to call ...'

'Calm down.' Elliði gently takes the phone from Rado's hands and hugs him in an embrace that's almost a restraint. 'Come inside and sit down.' Elliði looks over his shoulder at Rado and Dóra, as if he's checking on her as well.

She nods acknowledgement, expressionless. It's as if this has lightened her mood. She feels sympathy for this man, this new partner of hers. But not in a way that means she's a direct participant in his tragedy. She didn't know the guy's father-in-law. But she's lost so much of her own over the years; sometimes herself, as well as other people.

She follows Elliði and Rado into the station. They make for the same empty office where Rado had his disagreement with Sævar and the Special Unit. Elliði plants Rado in a chair and is about to shut the door when Dóra slips into the doorway. Elliði hesitates for a moment, then gives way and gestures for Dóra to step inside.

In any case, they're all in the soup together.

Elliði extracts a can of Coke from his pocket, pops the tab and hands it to Rado. He takes a sip from it. It's an old trick to knock back the adrenaline and calm the nervous system.

'I'll have to call my wife,' Rado mutters.

'Nobody knows yet,' Elliði says.

'What happened? Wasn't he in custody?' Dóra asks.

'He was found dead in his cell this morning. Most likely a heart attack,' Elliði says and lights a cigarette. He takes a puff and offers it to Rado. He shakes his head.

'Is there anything you need to tell me?' Elliði extinguishes his cigarette in the drops of coffee in the bottom of a paper cup. The smell fills the office and reminds Dóra of her first years on the force. This was the smell of the job. That, and booze and vomit – which is still the case.

'I went into his cell yesterday,' Rado says.

'Fuck!' Dóra says, unable to restraint herself.

'I didn't do anything to him, if that's what you're thinking.' Rado's hands twist into knots. Neither Dóra nor Elliði read anything into that. The man's distressed and isn't trying to hide it. 'He had a heart condition. I was asked to take him his medication.'

'Which you should have declared. It's not as if he would have been banned from taking it. He could naturally have seen a doctor if he'd asked.'

'He didn't want anyone to know he was sick,' Rado whispers after a long pause.

'I checked the log. You were probably the last person to see him alive. How stupid can you be?' Elliði glares at Rado.

'I wasn't exactly thinking straight. I wanted to look into his eyes. He wrecked my ...' Rado coughs and looks around the walls of the empty office, as if a rational answer might be found somewhere there.

'Now what?' Dóra asks.

'What's the situation with the missing girl?' Elliði asks.

'Still missing,' Dóra says and reaches for the can of Coke on the desk. Rado and Elliði both stare as she drinks from it. 'But there's progress. Sort of. We didn't get anything out of her classmates. I'll check with the rescue squad, and then we need to take a look round the dope dens.'

'We?' Rado asks, wide eyes on Dóra.

'Yes. We,' Dóra replies in an encouraging tone.

'I don't for a moment imagine that you had anything to do with your father-in-law's death,' Elliði says, lighting another cigarette. 'What I can tell you is that I've had four calls from upstairs this morning wanting to know about this girl and whether she has been found. This is becoming a problem in their eyes. They're terrified the media are going to screw them, without any lube. There's a crowd online convinced we're dragging our heels because she's dark-skinned. That's the latest. What I need from you is to find this girl right away. Then we can assess the situation. There'll no doubt be an inquiry of some sort, because he died in our custody, but to start with I'd like to ask you to inform the family of your father-in-law's death. But I can't give you any time to be with them right now. This girl has to be found. If it's too big an ask, then I'll find someone else to take it on. But I need an answer right now. There's a press conference in twenty minutes. The suits want you there. You're the faces of this investigation.'

'What did you see?' Dóra asks, catching Rado's eye.

'What do you mean?' Rado shifts in his chair.

'When you went into the cell and looked into his eyes.'

Rado doesn't answer. He sighs and gets to his feet.

'Let's find this girl,' he says. 'The devil's snapping at my heels, whatever I do.'

The press call – or the information event, as the press officer prefers to call it – takes place on the police station's front steps. That's good tactical thinking. The biting winter wind should cut short any extended rambling or further questions. Dóra and Rado are told to take two or three questions, and then call it a day.

There's a gaggle of journalists, photographers and TV crews standing in a knot in front of the station. In the lobby Dóra reads through the prepared statement but struggles to concentrate as Chief Superintendent Bjarki Freyr – otherwise known as Gorbi when he's out of earshot, thanks to the birthmark on his forehead – and Superintendent Gunndís Ósk, stand talking quietly with earnest expressions on their faces. The press officer hovers around them.

Elliði goes over and exchanges a few words with them that Dóra and Rado can't hear. Then he comes over to them and ushers them outside to start the press conference. Dóra is to read a short statement that sounds as if the force has dropped everything else in its search for Morgan, and then it's Rado's turn, to field questions.

Dóra takes up a position on the lowest step with the press pack in a semi-circle facing her. She's hit by both flashes and lights. She clears her throat and reads a short statement, setting out the facts of Guðbjörg's disappearance from the school outing to Thingvellir and the investigation's progress so far. The statement is short and to the point. She ends with a request for anyone with relevant information to contact the police immediately.

Dóra senses Rado at her side and when she finishes, he takes a step forward.

'Any questions?' Rado scans the faces.

'She's of mixed heritage?' This is Unnar asking, a guy of around thirty who runs a popular crime blog that covers both old cases and new. His website is called bransi.is, and it has a strong following among younger people.

'Yes,' Rado replies quickly. 'Any more questions?'

'Hold on,' Unnar says, edging closer. He's holding a camera with a microphone.

'Has the rescue team made any progress?' asks a woman journalist from the state broadcaster.

'The search has been in progress at Thingvellir since yesterday,' Rado replies.

'Is this a hate crime?' Unnar asks.

'It's a missing person inquiry,' Rado says to Unnar, whose camera is practically in Rado's face. He's not looking at him directly, but at the little screen. There's an odd pause in the exchange.

'There was a major police operation yesterday. Is there sufficient manpower available to cope with this case properly? There are rumours that the victim's skin colour ...'

'That's all the information there is at this point,' Rado says calmly. 'Thank you all for your attention.'

Rado catches Dóra's eye and they turn to go up the steps into the station.

They're just inside the door when they hear Unnar's voice behind them. 'The gang that was arrested yesterday. Are you linked to them?' He's followed them inside.

Rado steps back a little, blocking the camera's lens. Then he takes a nimble sidestep, catching hold of the hand holding the camera. Rado gives it a twist and the camera drops to the floor. Rado steps on it, cracking the lens. But he manages to do this in a manner that can be interpreted as clumsiness or an accident. Not that it is.

'What the fuck are you doing?' Unnar demands.

'So sorry,' Rado says, releasing his hand. 'You took me by surprise.'

'You saw what he did!' Unnar says, looking at Dóra.

'He tripped,' Dóra says. 'Now get lost and leave us alone.'

It's as well that the senior ranks, Elliði and the press officer are nowhere to be seen. They've no doubt retreated to their offices to watch the press conference on their computer screens, from a safe distance.

'That was deliberate!'

Unnar picks up the smashed camera from the floor and Dóra takes hold of him, shepherding him out of the station and slamming the door behind him. He turns to face her.

There's a smirk on his face that Dóra knows doesn't bode well.

'Want me to drive you home?' Dóra asks, as they sit facing each other in the canteen. She feels a chill, in spite of the fact that the place is well heated, almost overheated.

'I suppose so.' Rado has barely touched his coffee or the pastry on a plate in front of him. Dóra wonders if it's all over. She practically had to lead Rado to the lift and from there to the canteen after that altercation with the lad with the camera. It's as if all the air has been sucked out of him.

'Hey, talk to me. What's on your mind?' Dóra asks, swiftly snatching his pastry and taking a bite from it.

'Everything, and nothing. Am I really that stupid? Everyone knew that my father-in-law is ... was a criminal. Was everyone aware that people trod on eggshells around me? I mean, that lad down there. He knew.'

'Someone's leaked to him. I can't speak for others in the department, but I knew there were family links there. But this is Iceland, and with all due respect, it wasn't as if your father-in-law was a big fish. Not recently, at any rate. Hell, don't worry about it. This was a protected workplace long before your arrival here,' Dóra says, finishing his pastry.

'Why? I mean ... why don't you take on investigations? I mean, direct involvement?' Rado asks suddenly.

'You ought to ask instead what's wrong with me. That's what you really want to know. Isn't it?'

'Since you mention it,' Rado says with a shrug.

'It's a long story. Come on, I'll drive you home. You can have the rest of the day to take the sad news to your family. In the meantime, I'll get back to searching for the girl,' Dóra says, getting to her feet. She feels a moment's giddiness. 'And while I remember, my condolences.'

'Thanks,' Rado says, standing up with a sharp sigh. He can feel a chill as well.

16

Rado declined the offer of a lift and decided to take a taxi home. The driver, who had been standing beside his vehicle and smoking, makes no attempt at conversation on the way. He has the radio on, and Rado can hear people discussing Guðbjörg's disappearance and the rumour – thanks to the flood of conspiracy theories in circulation – that institutionalised racism within the police force is the reason the girl hasn't been found. The chat's abruptly cut off by adverts, and Rado hears one for lamb chops that immediately triggers a memory of his late father-in-law. Once Ewa's and Rado's relationship had become serious, when they had moved in together, Jurek Senior and Marta invited them over for dinner. This was in the middle of summer and as they drove up to the detached house, in a cul-de-sac in Hafnarfjörður, the garage doors stood open. Jurek Senior was there with a lamb carcass chained up by its hind legs. He had already skinned it and was busy dressing the carcass. Blood dripped from it and hit the white-painted floor like raindrops. A few hours later they sat on the veranda behind the house, with a whole roast lamb. Artur was there as well, turning up late, drunk and probably stoned, then argued with his parents in Polish and stormed out in a sulk.

Later that evening Ewa told him that her father was apt to go out into the countryside and snatch a sheep or a lamb. This was when Rado was still in uniform and they joked about whether he ought to haul his father-in-law down to the station and charge him with rustling sheep. Maybe he should have been more critical back then, but he was blinded. Ewa was everything.

As the taxi pulls up, Rado sees no sign of his Land Cruiser. He asks the driver to wait while he goes inside. Nobody home. Checking the time, Rado sees that it's a while before Ewa fetches Jurek from play school. He takes a deep breath. There's nothing for it but to call her. He selects the number and she picks up right away.

'*Hæ*, where are you?' he asks.

'With Mum,' she says, with a chill in her voice.

'Is Jurek with you?'

'He's at nursery,' she replies.

'When will you be home?'

'Don't know,' she replies and Rado can hear Polish voices behind her.

'I have to talk to you.'

'We've heard about Dad,' she says.

'What?' Rado demands.

'We know he's dead,' Ewa tells him.

'Who told you?' Rado says.

'That doesn't matter. You'll have to fetch Jurek. I don't know when I'll be able to get away,' Ewa says.

'Do you want me to come over?'

Rado's heart is beating faster.

'That's not smart. I think the house is under surveillance.'

'Who's that?' Rado asks.

'The cops. Do you know when I get the Tesla back?' Ewa asks.

'You know I don't have anything to do with that,' Rado replies and with that Ewa says she has to go and hangs up.

Rado can hear movement by the door, and goes towards it. The taxi driver's outside with a card reader in his hand. Everyone has to pay.

BROKEN

Down in the basement storeroom Rado hauls out the pushchair that's no longer used, mainly because the boy no longer wants to sit in it. It's jammed next to the freezer and it's an effort to drag it out into the narrow corridor. He has to carry it up folded, as it's too wide to open out down there.

It's warmer and the snow's rapidly becoming slush. Rado splashes through it to the play school and leaves it outside. He's too early, as he couldn't face staying alone in the flat a moment longer. The children have finished their nap and are sitting in the classroom having a snack. As soon as little Jurek sees his father, he gets to his feet and pads over to him. Rado suddenly has a vision of all these children that are being born, all the time, into this world. They're woken and put to sleep, dressed, fed, scolded and kissed. He feels a flood of emotion as this little body folds itself into his embrace, arms outstretched. He's never loved any person as he does this little boy. He lifts him up, even though the lad's not fond of being held when there are other kids around, and looks into his eyes. He has the same enigmatic look to his face. Rado, who believes in nothing supernatural, wonders if the collection of genes his family has carried through the centuries, all the way up here to this cold northern country, is beset by some curse. Could the child know from somewhere deep in his subconscious that joy is in such short supply that it doesn't pay to give yourself over to it? Or is there something called childhood depression or infant sadness? No, the boy isn't exactly gloomy. Maybe steadfastness is closer to the mark? At any rate, he behaves as if the world was no business of his – not exactly. And Rado envies him that more than he can put into words.

Rado pushes the little boy home. Although he wouldn't admit it, his son's excited by splashing through the slush. Rado hadn't expected that the day would turn out like this, that the two of them would be together and disconnected from mourning Jurek Senior's death. He's decided that it'll fall to Ewa to tell the boy about his grandfather's death. This is the first death the boy will experience of someone close to him. Rado mentally runs through the names of all the relatives he lost in the war in Bosnia, and how it affected him. But the answer evades him. When his parents applied for asylum in Iceland, he was much the same age as little Jurek, just a little older. Rado is certain that his parents had decided between them never to discuss the old country or the war within earshot of him or his brother Zeljko. Sometimes, when their parents thought they were asleep, the boys would hear them speaking in hushed tones. Occasionally he would encounter his father, who was no longer working, outside the block where they lived in Árbær, sitting on a bench. He was as thin as a rail, black-haired, sitting there in a coat that was far too thin, shivering as if he was using the cold to punish himself.

Eventually he spent so much time outside that Rado could practically work out when he would find him there. Sometimes on the way home from school he would pause and watch his father from a distance. It wasn't as if he was sitting there smoking or on his phone. He just sat there on the bench, hands idle, and did nothing, barely even taking in his surroundings. He sat there like a condemned man waiting for the hangman. By coming to Iceland they had become second-class citizens. There was never enough. They just somehow scraped by. At some point Rado wrote an essay at school about the Icelandic employment market, about foreign and migrant labour. Work permits were tied to employers. The immigrant had no rights, no right of residence, wasn't part of society. Rado found this a bizarre attitude. What could be more Icelandic than poverty? Shouldn't there be a beggar on the national crest rather than those weird guardian spirits?

It was much later that Rado understood what had

happened in Srebrenica. How could he, as the father of a boy who had just lost his grandfather, draw some wisdom from the war that his own people had waged and brought home to him? There had to be a way to understand these events clearly.

Rado shakes his head and makes for the Bónus supermarket that's next door to Costco. He has no desire to go home right away and little Jurek appears to be happy to sit in the buggy. He's struggling to get his head around the events of the last twenty-four hours. He feels anger, guilt and loss. But what he's mourning isn't his father-in-law but his own innocence – if that's what you could call the barrier that's in his mind. He's totally unaware of the Groke, sitting in a rental car in the car park outside, watching the two of them.

It's almost seven in the evening. Rado's cooking cheesy pasta for little Jurek, who sits on the floor, engrossed in a colouring book. The plan is to feed the boy. Then it's bath time, and then getting ready for bed. But first he's calling Dóra to find out what's happened. He has the same feeling of foreboding in his gut. But he tries to come across as positive, so as not to upset Jurek. The boy's sensitive to his surroundings. That's the same as he himself was as a youngster to the overhyped idea of a calm outward appearance, enabling to the bitter end. Rado catches himself counting the days since he last saw his brother as he spoons the gluey pasta onto a plate for the boy.

Just then his phone starts to vibrate on the table. Rado hands Jurek a plastic fork and checks the screen. It's an unfamiliar number, but he answers anyway.

'Sumarliði says they've been over every inch of the national park,' Dóra blurts out.

'Sumarliði?' Rado grinds a little sea salt over the pasta.

'He's in charge of the rescue squad,' Dóra says.

'Anything from forensics?' Rado asks.

'They say there's nothing on the coat or the shoe that's of interest. No blood or other traces. Nothing that indicates a struggle,' Dóra continues. 'Then there's the phone. Forensics are pressuring the phone provider for the activity log. Morgan's debit card hasn't been used for at least a week. The last transaction was at a vape shop on Hverfisgata. I've been in touch already and nobody there has seen Morgan since the appeal for them.'

'OK.' Rado fills a glass with water for the boy, who is already shovelling down pasta. It's disappearing at a great pace. He barely seems to chew as it's swallowed down. 'Nothing from the general public?'

'Nope.'

'OK,' Rado says. 'And the drug dens?'

'Haven't heard anything yet,' Dóra says despondently.

'And the dad?'

'What about him?' Dóra asks.

'Heard anything from him?' Rado asks.

'Nothing.'

'Isn't that weird? Not being in touch at all?' Rado hands the boy the glass and takes the plate of pasta so he won't choke on it. His mouth is so full that his cheeks are swollen.

'Yes. Very,' Dóra says. 'What's your feeling?'

'About him?'

'Yes.'

'I haven't met him,' Rado says. 'But we'll have to get hold of the man. Doesn't he have sole custody?'

'He does,' Dóra says.

'At any rate, he doesn't seem to be too worried about his daughter.' Rado watches little Jurek finish the water and then hand him the glass.

'How are you, anyway?' Dóra asks suddenly.

'Us?' Rado asks sharply, and immediately regrets it. 'As can be expected. Shall we catch up at the station around eight tomorrow?'

'Yes,' Dóra says after a moment's pause. 'I'll be here.'

Then she hangs up.

Once the boy has had a bath and Rado has helped him brush his teeth and get ready for bed, about forty minutes later they go to Jurek's room where he picks the book he wants his father to read for him. Rado lifts the duvet, but the lad shakes his head. That's fine, as Rado has no desire to be alone at the moment. With his son in his arms, he goes to his bedroom and they curl up under the duvet. The room has Ewa's aroma about it. Little Jurek snuggles up to him as Rado reads him the story. The boy is asleep before he's finished.

Rado pads back to the kitchen and clears up the dinner things. He hasn't eaten anything himself. Couldn't face it. There's that feeling of dread deep inside that leaves no room for anything else. He wonders whether to call Ewa. But he decides against it. He wouldn't know what to say. He drops his phone in his pocket, switches off the kitchen lights and lies down beside his son in the bedroom. He's exhausted and soon asleep.

He stirs just once, when Ewa crawls into bed beside him. Her face is wet with tears. He holds her close. But he doesn't speak. His dreams are aimless. He's outside Bónus with little Jurek in the buggy. Black ravens circle tightly overhead.

He wakes to find little Jurek standing up in the bed. He's muttering the same few words in Polish, again and again.

Ewa notices and sits up.

'What's he saying?' Rado asks, looking at Ewa.

'The shit of the shit.'

17

These are the ones Dóra calls the skulls, the worst addicts. The ones who don't eat, just take drugs. The ones that are so skinny that their bones stick out, their faces like skulls with skin stretched over them.

They're the walking Holocaust victims, one-man death camps. They see her as a beast of their own species that has wandered into their patch of jungle. That's because she's an addict herself. But she's a socially acceptable addict. She doesn't ever have to come to places like this. She meets doctors who prescribe medication for her without asking too many questions. But those drugs are such that there's no way to build up a dependence. That's the big lie.

She's spent the night going round the dope hangouts with two experienced officers. They're practically identical, like bears or chubby Vikings. They're on a comfortable wavelength as they go about their work, conscientiously but with an understanding of human nature.

These two (mostly) amiable guides take Dóra around every nook and cranny of the city where the hardcore druggies hang out. These are the ones who are worst off. Sometimes they're in apartments they've managed to hang on to. These are maybe the homes of those who are still a little higher up the pecking order, not quite on the bones of their arses yet. But they lord it over a court of skulls who exchange stolen goods or a fuck for dope. These two plainclothes cops in their stab vests and gloves knock at the doors of one dope den after another, on Dóra's behalf.

But there's no sign of Morgan.

Sometimes they don't need to knock, because there's not even a door. In one place there are four boneheads sitting on a sofa in a dingy living room, playing a computer game on a huge flat-screen. They're all wearing hoodies. *Hoodies, hoodies, hoodies.* It's as good as an unofficial uniform; it goes well with trackie bottoms and either trainers or laced-up Docs. The four on the sofa put Dóra in mind of patients in rehab. There's no way to gauge their ages. That could be anything. Dope makes people old long before their time. They all have the same expression, as if there's some new Insta Skull-Face filter that's been used for all of them. They don't even look up as Dóra and the two cops make an appearance. Their attention's on the flat-screen. A skeletal lad with a Chinese symbol tattooed on his neck grips the controller, swaying to and fro as if he's not on this filthy sofa but in the bright and colourful world beyond the screen. His long hair is tied in a knot at the back of his head.

One of the cops kicks the sofa, gently but enough to snap the four of them out of their trance, and they stare in some kind of wonder at Dóra and the two cops.

'What?' hisses a blonde woman of around thirty with acne scars on her cheeks and a constant tic.

'Looking for this girl,' Dóra says, holding the screen of her phone out to the woman, who snatches at her wrist and pulls her closer. The two cops are ready to intervene, but Dóra signals for them to back off.

'Is there a reward?' the woman demands suddenly, peering at the photo of Morgan. 'I'm really good at finding ... y'know ... all sorts.'

It's as if the search is some kind of game or contest. The cops smile and shake their heads.

'Haven't seen anyone,' the lad with the Chinese tattoo says, without taking his eyes off the screen. His voice is startlingly deep. The woman lets go of Dóra and looks down at her hands.

'Not seen anyone,' she mutters and scratches her forearms.

Dóra scans the flat and decides to take a closer look. She creeps along the passage, without hearing a word of protest from the four boneheads on the sofa. She stops and picks up children's toys from the floor in front of a closed bedroom door.

Putting her shoulder to it, Dóra opens the door. At some time this had been the bedroom of a child, or children. There's a colourful poster from the National Theatre on the wall, showing Pippi Longstocking. Dóra's sure that the actress playing Pippi has to be at least sixty by now. She saw an interview with her in some newspaper.

There's a little IKEA cot, some bedclothes but no mattress. The head of an inflatable pelican swim ring on the floor droops as the air leaks out of it. On a white chest, with all the drawers pulled out and gaping open, there's a triple photo frame showing children of between two and about five years old. Three girls. On the shelf are a few twisted soft drink bottles with necks distorted, production defects. Dóra recollects that an older cousin of hers used to collect these bottles. At some time in the past they were collector's items, back when people collected pens, serviettes and matchboxes.

'Please ... Not in here,' the woman's voice begs behind Dóra. But there's something menacingly casual about her.

Take it easy, Sibba,' one of the cops warns her.

Dóra turns but there's nobody there. She steps out of the room and shuts the door.

On the way down the stairs the two cops tell her that the woman with the pitted cheeks had lost custody of her children.

'She was apt to drop them on the floor.'

'And against the walls,' the other cop sighs. 'These people.'

Dóra recalls the deformed bottles in the children's room up there. In those few square metres of misery.

At around five in the morning, Dóra's had enough. The cops tell her there are plenty more places that would fit the bill. But they can't just barge in. Those are places where the inhabitants are either too canny or too high up the pecking order. That's where authority isn't welcome. Some places are off limits without the Special Unit backing them up. But the chances of Morgan being in those places are slim. Dóra longs to take a shower and wash the night off her. She wants to scrub herself until the skin bleeds, find someone who can wash the whole thing off her. But that'll have to wait.

The last call on this whistle-stop tour of the underworld is Morgan's (or Guðbjörg's) home in the Laugarnes district. Her father, Hákon, still hasn't picked up. His phone's switched off. The chances of him losing his phone on the day of his daughter's disappearance are astronomically small. Dóra's been half-expecting to stumble across him in some drug den.

The house in the Laugarnes district is in darkness as the patrol car comes to a halt in the slush and puddles of the driveway.

'Is he the registered owner of a vehicle?' asks one of the two cops.

Dóra's in the back, the two cops in the front. She has the feeling she's being given an induction, rather than being responsible for investigating the teenager's disappearance.

'No. He lost his licence,' Dóra says. 'Lifelong ban.'

'What do you want to do? You reckon he's home?' asks the cop behind the wheel.

'Knock. We have to knock. We have to be able to get hold of the man.' Dóra unclips her seat belt and gets out. The two cops follow, squelching through the slush on their way around the back of the house to the door of the basement flat. It's wide open.

They all notice at the same moment, and the two cops practically sweep Dóra aside before they make a move to enter the darkened flat, torches aloft.

'Police!' one of them calls out, loud enough to make Dóra flinch. She feels for a switch and turns on the hall light. Dóra goes down the steps into the flat. She takes care to touch nothing. She feels in her pockets for gloves and pulls them on. There's a tension in the air. Something's happened here. But Dóra has no idea what.

The cops switch on more lights and Dóra follows along a corridor that's narrow, with plastic tiles on the floor. She stumbles and grabs the arm of one of the cops, and he spins round, ready for a fight. As soon as he realises there's no danger, a look of disgust appears on his face.

'Try and stay on your feet, will you?' he hisses.

They open the two bedrooms. Look inside the little bathroom and finally check the living room. The place is deserted. There's a smell of lemon in the air.

'Is this guy a speed freak?' one of the cops asks suddenly.

'What?' Dóra asks.

'It's that clean in here,' the other cop says, nodding.

Dóra scans the flat, goes from one room to the next. Everything's clean and neat. She doesn't understand the question.

'What do you mean, it's *that clean*?'

'Let's take a look,' the other cop says with a sigh. He goes into the kitchen and looks around. He opens the oven. It's so clean it sparkles.

'Take a look at that,' the cop says. 'It's practically like new. Even though it's an old stove.' He opens the fridge. 'Same here.' The elderly fridge is pristine, like new, almost. There's nothing in it. Just a jar of pickled cucumbers and a bottle of Valur tomato sauce.

'That fridge is textbook,' the cop says. 'Totally clean and nothing to eat. That's not normal. These people pop pills and start cleaning. No oven's ever that clean. No fridge, for that matter. We've been on shouts to total slums where everything's as clean as an operating theatre. These people get so wired up by speed.'

'While they stay filthy and sweaty themselves,' the other cop adds, going into the bathroom that's so clean it shines. 'And they reckon we don't have a clue. Nope, whoever lives here's definitely on speed. That's for sure.'

Dóra shuts the fridge and goes out of the kitchen, over to one of the bedrooms. She sees in a moment that this is Hákon's room. There's a double bed in there, and work clothes are strewn on a chair. She opens the wardrobe. There's a black rubbish bag, open, full of men's clothes. A dark suit hangs there, along with one shirt. Dóra shuts the door and goes back out into the passage, to the room opposite Hákon's. This one clearly belongs to a teenager. Plastic figurines, in plastic-windowed boxes, stand on a shelf above a single bed, covered with a purple throw. There's a small desk under the window, strewn with all sorts of things. Manga posters hang on the walls and there's a stack of Manga comics by the headboard of the bed. Dóra switches on the desk lamp. She examines the desk minutely, notices grooves in its surface, splashes of paint and drops beneath textbooks and other stuff. Two framed drawings look pretty good, and even though they aren't up to the standard of the Manga pictures, they bear witness to a certain talent. Dóra has no idea whether that gets any encouragement in this home. She reckons they have to be by Morgan.

Dóra takes a step back and surveys the desk. At first glance it looks shambolic. That doesn't fit with the rest of the room, which is tidy, but not as clinically tidy as the other rooms in the flat. It looks to her as if Morgan has emptied their school bag onto the desk, pulled out a few items, and then made an exit.

She opens the wardrobe that stands against one wall and gets the same sense as she scans the contents. Nothing has been folded, and it looks as if half of the clothes are missing. If not more. But Dóra can't be certain. There's just the instinct that Morgan has run for it – in a hurry. Just the essentials have been taken. She opens the desk drawers and finds a few used drawing pads.

She flips through them, which isn't easy with gloved hands, and that gives her an overview of the teenager's development as an artist. But there's a common theme throughout these pads. All the drawings are sketches or unfinished. Dóra looks at the two framed pictures. One is of a woman with dark skin. She's not dissimilar to Morgan, if the pictures she has come across of them on social media are anything to go by. The other is a lava landscape. There's a full moon in the picture. It's shaped like a heart. This gives the picture, which is otherwise competently executed, an amateurish feel. It's like something you'd buy from IKEA already framed.

Dóra runs a hand over her forehead. She's getting a pounding headache. She needs to take her medication again. But she hangs back, thinking it over. It seems too much of a jump between what looks to be the most recent work on the pads and the pictures on the desk. It seems that at least one, or more, drawings are missing from the series. That supports the theory that they took these with them. *Wouldn't she do that herself?*

'What's the plan?' asks one of the two cops, yawning in the doorway of the teenager's bedroom.

'I want forensics to check this place. We need to know if this has been cleaned to hide something.'

Dóra puts the pad gently back in its place. She's starting to feel a fondness for this kid. Almost silently, she curses the world for being the way it is.

*

The child seat is in the Tesla, which is still being held by the police. Ewa tells Rado, while they sit over coffee, that she'll walk Jurek to play school. It's still dark. It's six in the morning. Ewa's face is puffy with weeping and she trembles.

'You want me to stay here with you?' he asks.

'No. Go on. They need you. I saw a picture of the girl in the papers. You have to find her. Her parents must be in such a state,' Ewa says. 'Your position ... your work ...'

'Is just work. Your father just died,' Rado whispers, and eyes the bedroom door.

'What are they saying at the station, about you?' Ewa asks. 'I mean, about you and us?'

'I think they feel sorry for me. Some of them, anyway. I was led on a wild goose chase while the operation against your father was being planned.'

'How was he? When you saw him?' Ewa asks, covering her face with her hands, and moving them aside, over her ears. It's as if she doesn't want to hear.

'Just ... As normal. His usual self,' Rado says after a moment's pause.

'So he got his medication?'

'Of course,' Rado says. 'There'll be an inquiry. Elliði says it's a formality. I mean, he had a heart attack. Then there are all kinds of things that affect my position.'

Rado picks up both their phones and takes them to the bathroom. He puts them in the cabinet and shuts it. Then he comes back.

'I need to have some idea of the damage,' Rado says as he sits down. 'What was your father up to?'

'I don't know anything. Mum knows nothing. If Artur knows anything, then ... he's not going to say a word.' Ewa shrugs. 'All the accounts have been frozen. The café is sealed off. The lawyer is trying to get some kind of overview. I mean ... I don't even know what assets he's left behind. And Mum knows practically nothing at all. You definitely gave him the medication?' Ewa asks.

'Yes,' Rado says, watching her face intently. 'Hold on? Why are you asking me this?'

'I'm sorry.' Ewa grasps Rado's arm. 'It's just stress. Everything's in chaos at Mum's place and … people are coming out with all sorts of weird stuff. Not thinking straight.'

'Surely you don't believe I had anything to do with your father's death?' Rado gets to his feet.

'No. Of course not,' Ewa whispers. 'It's just the sorrow. It fucks you up.' She brushes away tears. 'Speaking of which, we'll have to pay out for the funeral. There's no money anywhere.'

'Nothing?' Rado says in surprise.

'No. When they took everything, they took everything,' Ewa grates, and then flashes up a convincing smile as their still sleepy son wanders into the kitchen. She hugs him tightly.

Rado gets up from the table.

He gives Ewa a kiss, and the boy gets one as well. The little guy seems tired. That's understandable after the night's bad dreams. Rado's surprisingly calm, considering she's virtually accused him of murdering her father. But she's always said exactly what comes to mind. It was enough for her to say the words out loud to be able to write that idea off. It's a side of her he's always loved. There's a filter missing somewhere. That's the same as his new police partner, but not on the same scale. Rado's feeling is that he's going to have to hold her hand to some extent through this investigation. That's to keep her from going off the rails. But he's used to that; too used to that. Dóra reminds Rado chillingly of Zeljko. He's been through all this before with a sick individual. There are two years between them. But Rado never managed to save his brother. He was too sick. It was a rollercoaster of his crazy thoughts when they were youngsters. Rado normally managed to calm his brother by holding him in his arms, sometimes tight. That depended on the circumstances. But then Zeljko got too strong – and too sick. Later on, when Rado trained in Jiu-Jitsu he was forcibly reminded of his brother when he lay bathed in sweat and in someone's lock on the training mat. Sometimes he closed his eyes and sensed his brother close by.

They'd shared a room in the little flat in Árbær. It was dangerous to be around him. Their mother's feeling was that this came from the paternal side of the family, that fury. She was adamant that Zeljko had to be locked in at night. Rado was supposed to sleep on the sofa in the living room. But he refused. He had her lock him in with his brother. He wasn't frightened of him. He was more nervous that the fury was deep inside him as well, that he'd also lose direction. But that never happened.

Rado had always been more like his mother, much calmer. He was ashamed for his brother's excesses. He was so tired of coming up with excuses for him at school and among their friends.

Rado hasn't seen Zeljko for five thousand, four hundred and seventy-five days. He doesn't know if he's alive or dead. When he closes his eyes, he struggles to visualise his face, other than twisted with fury and pain.

He brushes aside these thoughts as he turns into the yard behind the police station on Hverfisgata. Today he needs to be sharp. Today he needs a clear mind. They have to find this girl.

18

Hector sits in the upstairs room of the Sons of the Gods' headquarters, one side of his face swollen and caked with blood. With his hands tied behind his back, he's losing the feeling in his fingers.

Emmi stands in a corner, arms folded, while Nóri sits behind the desk that was probably already there when the biker gang took over the place, and peers at the plans of a building. The other gang members are busy with the stolen goods they're ferrying from the place on Kópavogsbraut in a little van. The window provides Hector with a fine view of what they're doing.

They examine everything. Some of them even try on for size shoes and clothes that Hector had stolen for his own. In most cases these are too small.

'Are these all kids' sizes?' one of the gods calls out to the room upstairs, waving a hoodie, and there's a gale of laughter from the others.

Nóri signals for them to be quiet, and they obey. They continue to carry in stolen goods from the van, like ants at work.

Once again Hector experiences the depths of betrayal.

Having the fruits of his own crimes stolen from him.

'You don't need to tie me up,' Hector mumbles. His tongue's swollen.

'Yeah?' Nóri looks up at Hector. 'You tried to do a runner from the jeep just now.'

'I panicked.' There's resignation in Hector's voice. 'I'm not going anywhere.'

'Well, then.' Nóri glances at Emmi and nods. He goes over to Hector and cuts the ties with a pair of wire cutters. The blood flows back to his fingers and he feels nauseous.

'Going to behave, are you?' Nóri asks.

There's a large, incredibly ugly painting on the wall behind him, of a Viking riding a motorcycle, under a dark sky, with flowing lava and the fires of a volcano behind him. Next to it there's a framed piece of some skin, with lines in flowing script. Hector peers at the words.

The True North will never die.
See as it rises from the deep!
See the Men of the North.
The one, true white race!

This must refer to the club, a position statement of a kind.

'Understood?' Nóri grunts.

Hector nods.

'So, you're more than just a thief. You're also a craftsman,' Nóri says, his mouth twisting upwards into a slight grimace. 'Right now you're crafting something. Putting something together in your head. Some plot or other. Castles in the air. You can stop that right now.'

'OK?' Hector says, as if has no idea what Nóri means by all this. That's not true. He's doing exactly as Nóri described, trying to figure out an exit from the mess he's in.

'I started training to be a plumber. Did you know that?' Nóri says and looks down at the plans.

Hector doesn't reply. There was no way he could have known that.

'May I?' he says quietly. Nóri raises an eyebrow, unsure what he has in mind. But Hector stretches towards the desk and Nóri understands.

'Good man,' Nóri says and glances at Emmi, who has no idea what's going on. 'Like I said. I trained to be a plumber, so I know a bit about plans like this.'

Hector looks over the plans of what has to be the meat packing plant they drove past that morning – the one they want broken into. It's not the first time he's used plans like this to organise a job. A few times he's had the opportunity to break into places, having first been able to check them out. Normally that's been with the help of someone on the inside, or simply a company owner looking to cash in on insurance.

'I didn't see any security cameras there,' Hector says.

'That's good!' Nóri replies, nodding approval.

'Not necessarily.' Hector clenches his fists to work the blood into his hands. 'Who owns this meat place?'

'What does that matter?' Nóri flexes his hands and his knuckles crack. Then he dips a hand into a pocket of his leather waistcoat and takes out a small bag of speed, opens it, spoons a little onto the point of a knife and hands it to Hector, who hesitates for a moment before instinct kicks in and the powder disappears into his nose as if by some magic that even he doesn't understand.

'Good man,' Nóri says and Hector nods emphatically as his head clicks into gear. It's as if someone suddenly switched the lights on.

'Good man,' Nóri smiles, nodding repeatedly. Like the monkey he is, Emmi follows suit. Hector's circulation churns as the speed makes its way through his veins. This is the real stuff. But it stings like hell. Not just his nose, but his whole being. His concept of who he really is. His role in life.

Your man.
His man.
Their man.
Always.

BROKEN

Never my own.
Always someone else's.
Just another Nordic Nigger.

19

Arriving at the station, Rado runs into Guðjón from forensics in the yard. He's fiftyish, short and tubby, with a beard that's starting to grey.

'Aren't you coming out to Laugarnes?' Guðjón asks. He's clad in overalls and carrying a case.

'What's going on?' Rado asks and checks the time on his phone. It's just before eight.

'Looks like we might have a potential crime scene,' Guðjón says, and walks away. Rado hesitates for a moment, and then hurries to follow.

Dóra's not picking up, so he gets the address from Guðjón. He pushes his Land Cruiser hard, hoping to get there ahead of the crime scene investigators or forensic team. What does that mean, a potential crime scene? Rado catches himself thinking out the next moves. If this is a murder, then that changes everything. Then the question is whether or not the case will be taken off him and Dóra. Searching for a missing teen is one thing, managing a murder investigation is another. Maybe too much for Elliði to swallow, let alone the guys upstairs.

Rado turns into the street and up the gravel drive of the house. There's a patrol car by the house, but nobody's about. He kills the jeep's engine and gets out. He goes over to the patrol car where two cops sit in the front seats. They're big guys. Rado knows them, Gísli and Friðbjörn. Gísli's behind the wheel and he rolls down the driver's side window.

'You here? Aren't you ...?' Friðbjörn jabs Gísli with an elbow before he can finish his sentence.

'Where's the door to the basement flat?' Rado asks, glancing at the house.

'Round the back,' Gísli says through a yawn. 'But nobody's to go in there until forensics have checked the place out. Are you part of this investigation?' he asks hesitantly. Rado nods.

'Really? Then your partner's here with us,' Friðbjörn says and jerks his head towards the back seat. Rado stoops to look. Dóra's fast asleep there.

'She conked out about an hour ago,' Gísli says in a low voice. 'Understandable. She's a ball of fire. Then she just totally ran out of juice.' It's as if he's speaking about a child, or some kind of innocent abroad, Rado thinks, as he looks along the street to see the forensic team's van turning into the drive.

'The girl hasn't shown up anywhere?' Friðbjörn asks, sounding hopeful. He must be exhausted after a long night.

'Not yet,' Rado says and notices Friðbjörn whisper something to Gísli, who nods agreement.

'Hey. About Sleeping Beauty in the back. We're going to have to wake her up because our shift's over. We need to get back to the station,' Gísli says, sounding awkward.

Rado opens the back door and cautiously shakes Dóra's shoulder.

'Hey, good morning,' he says softly, and then louder, more firmly, but Dóra doesn't stir. She doesn't even mumble anything. Rado leans in close to be certain she's breathing. That's when one eye opens. There are just centimetres between their faces. Rado backs away and Dóra sits up. Her eyes are bloodshot and it takes her a few seconds to work out where she is.

'Good morning,' Rado repeats. Dóra takes a deep breath and wriggles off the seat and out of the car, shutting the door behind her.

'Is it round the back?' Guðjón asks as he gets out of the forensics van. He's dressed in white overalls. The street around them is coming to life and the police presence is attracting attention as people head out to their daily lives.

'Yes,' Dóra mutters, steadying herself with a hand against the patrol car's roof.

'This is where they live?' Rado asks.

'Yep,' Dóra says, and stretches.

'What's the situation? Why call in forensics?' Rado nods to Friðbjörn and Gísli as they reverse out of the drive, past the van. He can see that Dóra is trembling from top to toe. 'Are you all right?'

'Yeah,' Dóra says. 'This flat. It's not right. There's something … something crooked about it.'

'OK.' Rado nods to Guðjón as he disappears around the corner to find the door to the basement flat.

'Don't you want to go home and get some rest? I mean, now that I'm here.' Rado looks into Dóra's eyes. The whites are red. He's already wondering if he shouldn't take her straight to A&E. 'When did you last get some sleep?'

'Don't remember.' Dóra grimaces. It's as if a needle has been plunged through the top of her head and down into her brain, and someone's stirring it. There's a massive pressure behind her eyes. She feels that her brain could just explode at any moment, like in those YouTube videos of people blowing up water melons with rubber bands.

'Do we check the U-bends as well?' Guðjón calls from the corner of the house. Rado shrugs. 'Yes or no?'

'Yes, U-bends as well, please,' Dóra calls out to him and he disappears around the corner to the basement and the potential crime scene that neither Dóra nor Rado are inclined to talk about right now. But there's no getting around it.

'So the theory is that the dad could have harmed her?' Rado hears himself saying. It's not exactly a question for Dóra. He's not certain she's all there mentally, even though she's standing on her own two feet. 'Why would he do that? What's the motive? Anything along those lines about him on the records? Any notifications or charges? Do we need to speak to Child Protection?'

'Not sure what you mean,' Dóra says, putting a steadying hand against the wall behind her.

'She could have threatened to spill the beans and he ... he ...' Rado looks around. He sees a family of four – a man, woman and primary school-age children – standing next to their urban SUV and gaping at him. The woman's holding a small dog and is dressed in camouflage colours, and she's shaking like a leaf. Rado nods to them.

'There's nothing like that about him on the system.' Dóra says.

'Fair enough. You met him. What's your impression?' Rado asks.

'He was just ... normal. All the same, he came across as being on something.'

'Doped?' Rado looks over his shoulder at the family that's reversing out of their drive. They're still watching, as if what's going on is more exciting than the day they have ahead of them. They have no suspicion that Rado would give so much to be in their position, instead of dealing with the problems he's facing.

'Isn't everyone? Yeah, dope. But what dope and where did he get it? From some skullhead in a hoodie, or a smart doctor who signs a prescription because he has symptoms?'

This angry little speech drains Dóra of energy so that she sinks to her haunches, her back against the rough concrete wall to avoid losing consciousness.

'We're not working together if that's the way you're going to be,' Rado says after a moment of silence between them. 'Now you're working yourself up for no reason. Considering the situation here, you should be careful of what you're saying. Otherwise you're no use.'

'OK,' Dóra whispers, abashed. 'You're right. It's just pressure, and when you said something about him being doped up I just took it personally. I'm on medication that I have to take every day.'

'And how's that working out?'

'More or less.' Dóra looks up at Rado, who looms over her.

'Then you'd better take it.' There's a shadow of a smile on Rado's face. 'Come on, I can lean the seat in the jeep back. You can get some rest while we wait for Guðjón.'

Rado extends a hand and Dóra grasps it so he can haul her to her feet.

It's an hour before Guðjón marches around the corner of the house with his case in his hand. It's difficult to interpret the fixed scowl on his face. Rado's sure that's because this man is always the bringer of bad news. Most of the time. Even the good news is bad, and that must affect people. If someone dies in suspicious circumstances, then he's called out. But isn't it supposed to be good news if the person died a natural death? Yet the damage is already done.

It goes without saying that there are exceptions, but Rado hasn't witnessed many of those. No doubt working in the forensic division calls for a special kind of masochism. Or maybe the trick is to have no feelings about anything. But nobody can do that. At any rate, none of the forensics people Rado has encountered can do that. So why doesn't Sisyphus give up rolling that rock up the side of a mountain, just to see it roll back down? One answer is that he's in Hell – the Greek version. *He can't help himself.*

That's no doubt the reason why Rado and his partner, now snoring in the front seat of the Toyota and dribbling from the corner of her mouth, are chasing the tail of this missing person inquiry up here in the Laugarnes district of the city.

Rado gets quietly out of the jeep. There's something

strange about this. Of course he should wake Dóra. But something tells him not to. It's as if he has an urge to protect her. He wants to be the first to hear the bad news from Guðjón, to shield her from this. He feels a need to let sleep cure her ills – as far as that's possible – before going any further.

Guðjón shakes his head as he meets him in the drive, and Rado knows that could mean anything.

'So?' Rado asks.

'No blood. The U-bends are clear,' Guðjón says, producing a vape the size of an old-fashioned mobile phone and taking a puff. As he exhales in the middle of this Icelandic winter, he gives off the vape's sickly artificial smell of melon. 'I hate these basement flats. People shouldn't live buried underground. It's bad karma.'

'Well then...' Rado takes a step back, out of the melon cloud. He'd prefer the conversation to not shift to basement flats that have been crime scenes. He doesn't want Guðjón to start telling rambling stories.

'How are you, anyway?' Guðjón asks, looking at Rado. The vape whines as he takes another melon-flavoured puff.

'Meaning what?'

'You're no fool. You know what they say at the station,' Guðjón says, exhaling and swallowing.

'I've been happier,' Rado says, almost surprised at his own honesty.

'This country's too small. I'll tell you that,' Guðjón says. 'I've seen this flat before.'

'When was that?'

Rado feels a surge of energy.

'That was a different case. There was an old guy who lived here and he died. It turned out he'd slipped on the tiles and broke his neck. It looks like the tiles haven't been changed. I could dig out the pictures. But that's not relevant. Those are the same tiles in the bathroom. It's as weird as hell. I couldn't for the life of me remember what the old guy looked like, but I remember those tiles. For whatever reason, my head's decided to hang on to useless information. But now I'd best be on my way.' Guðjón puts the vape between his lips. 'Don't know if I should tell you, but I will. I'm going to your father-in-law's autopsy now.'

Before Rado can say anything, he hears his Land Cruiser's door swing open. He sees Guðjón's jaw drop, and turns. Dóra's standing beside there, blood seeping from one eye. It trickles down her cheek like tears. Then it drips into the snow.

20

Rado's in the car park outside A&E when Elliði gets out of his car and splashes through the slush over to him.

'What happened?' he asks. He's short of breath.

'They're examining her now,' Rado says, buttoning his coat. It's getting cold. 'Tell me something. What's wrong with her? I know she's something special, but I mean physically?'

'Fuck,' Elliði mutters, lighting a cigarette. 'She hasn't told you anything?'

'No.' Rado puts his hands in his pockets. 'She said she was on medication. Then she started to bleed from one eye.'

'Where?' Elliði drags on his cigarette.

'We were at the girl's house up in Laugarnes when she suddenly ...'

'Has she shown up?'

There's a glimmer of hope in Elliði's eye.

'No.'

'OK.' Elliði stamps out the half-smoked cigarette. 'Hell. What about the dad?'

'Can't get hold of him. I gather from Guðjón the flat isn't a crime scene. Maybe just bad parenting. But that's not illegal,' Rado says. 'But what's the score with her?' Does she have something on you?'

'Dóra?' Elliði stares at Rado through narrowed eyes. 'We were on a bad shout. She was injured. It's not as if she's at any point been classed as not competent to do her job. She has good days and bad. I gave her a chance. Gave her space. She's not the only one ... to get that sort of treatment.'

'Elliði, there's blood dripping from her eye!' Rado says, shaking his head.

'But she's smart, isn't she?' The gleam of hope is rekindled in Elliði's eyes.

'But this isn't ...'

'This is what it is now. Let's see where it goes. I'll go inside and check on her. Find out what the doctors have to say. What you can do for me right now is find this girl.'

Elliði lights another cigarette.

Rado tries to read something from the agitation of his boss, who acts as if nothing's that important, at the same time as he's ready to sacrifice anything for a colleague who was injured so long ago that nobody really remembers what happened. Rado finally just nods and saunters over to his Land Cruiser. As he drives out of the A&E car park, Elliði waves to him.

The man's an enigma.

*

Rado steers clear of CID when he gets to the station. Instead, he goes to the vacant office on the ground floor where Elliði read him the riot act and told Sævar from the Special Unit to shove it up his arse and slammed the door on him. He doesn't ask anyone's permission. The person whose permission he should be asking is turning a blind eye to police work. Or rather, a bloody eye.

It's stuffy in there. Rado slides a hand through the blinds and opens the window a crack. This office has escaped all the renovations of the last few years, decades, even. There's wood panelling and even a cast-iron radiator under the window that has stains Rado would prefer not to think about.

He puts his laptop on the dusty desk. The Coke can Elliði handed him is still there. A 1997 Support for the Handicapped calendar hangs on the wall opposite the desk. There's a mutter of voices out in the corridor, but in here it couldn't be quieter. Nobody's coming in here to trouble him. Back in the day this desk was used to soften people up if they weren't inclined to behave. But that's all in the past. Or mostly in the past. This office is old Iceland through and through. This is the kind of office where the Guðmundur and Geirfinnur cases were 'investigated,' a relic of the brutal way things used to be.

Rado starts by setting out in a document everything he knows about Morgan's disappearance – having decided that he'll use the girl's preferred name, and he'll respect their preferred pronouns as well.

On the way to A&E, Dóra had given him a rundown of her thoughts, not that he'd exactly asked for it, concerning the state of the teenager's bedroom in the basement flat – that they had been moving or fleeing. That's understandable, considering the domestic circumstances. Rado suggested that this could be a suicide. If Morgan had removed anything from the room, then it could be something they wouldn't want to be found after their death, or they could have just given things away as parting gifts – without a word about what they had in mind. The previous day Dóra had been in touch with the juvenile mental health ward to fish for more information about Morgan. According to the senior doctor, Morgan had made an appointment and requested treatment from the transition team. The teenager's father, Hákon, had flatly refused to countenance treatment, and as Morgan wasn't yet sixteen, that was that.

But there had to be a larger network of acquaintances around the teen than just their dad, girlfriends and school, especially in this country where everyone's related. Even though there's no mother in the picture, there must be some paternal family. Rado logs in and checks the breakdown of the teen's phone usage that came from the network provider. There's no way of knowing if or when there might be access to the phone Dóra had found at Thingvellir, and it still hasn't been confirmed that it belonged to Morgan. Despite Dóra's attempts to put him in the picture on the way to hospital, Rado can't escape the feeling that this is revision, that he's walking in his colleague's footsteps. That doesn't work in a case like this. Time's too pressing for that.

Rado goes through the list of phone numbers and conscientiously checks them. There aren't many, and most seem to belong to her classmates. Rado pauses by one number that has been called a few times and looks it up. This turns out to be a retirement home. He decides it's quicker to go there than to spend time looking for Morgan's potential relatives on the computer and comparing these to the names of the residents. It can't do any harm to check if anyone there recognises the teen.

Before getting to his feet, Rado checks the bransi.is crime blog. The clip is there of when Rado broke the camera, and Unnar provides a voiceover to give the confused incident some context. This is Unnar's preferred context. Alongside the video clip is a photo of Jurek Senior being escorted from the district court by his lawyer. His face can't be seen, covered by a plastic folder. There's a logo under the video clip, two revolvers that snake around a candle, which is to indicate that this is a death notice. Rado doesn't click on it. Eighteen thousand people have clicked the *like* button under the clip, and a few more add to the total while Rado watches it. Further down the page, he finds a picture of Morgan and text that's lifted verbatim from the press release about the teenager's disappearance. This has six thousand likes. The online versions of the mainstream media don't even mention the altercation. Unnar isn't popular among real journalists, and most of them have some coverage of Morgan's disappearance. Tragedy always makes fresh news. The teen is disappearing under the mass. Before long, they will have been buried far below the surface. There's always something new that takes precedence. Rado's dearest wish is that the next news of Morgan will be a short statement to the effect that they have been found in good health.

Rado parks the Toyota outside the Droplaugarstaðir retirement home. He has a photo of Morgan on his phone. He checks the time. A major search by the rescue squads should be getting underway about now. Every shed and shack over a wide area will be checked and the whole shoreline will be covered in the search for the missing teenager. The big question is whether the searchers should also have a picture of the father and look for him at the same time. Rado has already checked whether Morgan has shown up at the country's one international airport at Keflavík, but the border control force is adamant they haven't.

There's a relaxed atmosphere in the home's lobby. Rado spies a glass cage by the entrance, but it's empty. Doors that Rado assumes would usually be kept shut stand open as two men between them haul a sofa along the corridor. A coffee table already stands in the lobby, its top in a tiled pattern that contrasts starkly with the institution-style furniture. Sisyphus and his labours are to be found everywhere.

The door to a little room beside the glass cage is open, and next to it a sign announces this is the manager's office. Rado soon finds out that the manager is Birna, a woman of around sixty. He explains what brings him to this place and shows her the picture of Morgan. Birna peers at it and nods. She recognises Morgan.

'You know her?' Rado drops the phone back in his pocket.

'Don't you mean *them*?' A shadow of a smirk appears. Birna comes across as relaxed but authoritative, despite her fleece and white clogs. 'Yes, I know them.'

'How so?' Rado asks.

'They come here sometimes to visit one of the residents.'

'Who's that?'

'Come on. I'll take you to her.'

Rado follows Birna as she – quite literally – works her way along the corridors to the resident Morgan is acquainted with. She has a greeting for everyone she meets and pauses a couple of times to exchange a few words with staff. On the way they come across an older man scolding a young man, barely more than a lad, who is fixing a flat-screen to the wall of his room. The lad wears a cap marked with the logo of an electrical and electronics supplier Rado has never heard of. It's obvious he has little idea of what he's doing. There's a scowl of dissatisfaction on the old man's face as he watches proceedings.

Rado follows Birna through a small open kitchen and into a lounge where several of the residents are listening to the radio. Finally, Birna pauses by a door that's closed.

'She's in here,' Birna says. Rado has the sudden idea that Morgan is behind the door, although that's absurd. 'Want me to come in and introduce you to her? Just so she doesn't get a shock to find the police in her living room.'

'What do you think?' Rado asks.

'No.' Birna shakes her head. 'I don't imagine she'll care either way. I'll be downstairs if you need me,' she adds, and marches away.

Rado knocks lightly, and waits for a moment before trying the handle and cautiously opening the door.

'Who's there?' a deep female voice asks. Rado opens the door all the way and finds himself facing a room that's much the same as the ones he's seen open while following Birna. There's a hospital bed in the middle and not much else. A small chest of drawers stands by the side of the bed and seems to serve as a nightstand. A few pictures hang from wires from a picture rail. There's no space anywhere for anything permanent. The turnover must be too quick for anything like that. A thin woman with a long, grey braid of hair lies in the bed. Her white nightdress seems to Rado to be not of the age they're living in, or even of the one before that.

'Hello, my name's Rado and I'm a police officer with Reykjavík CID.' He shuts the door and turns back to the woman. She has deep lines around her eyes and a sharp aquiline nose. She sits up in bed and reaches for a little remote control that raises the back of the bed so she can sit straight. She smooths the duvet over her lap and looks at Rado.

'You're from Yugoslavia?' she asks, peering at him.

'No,' Rado replies and crosses over to the bed. He's sure he can hear a trace of an accent in her voice. The stresses in her speech are strange. 'I'm of Bosnian heritage. But I see myself as an Icelander. And you?'

'I arrived here in this country in 1956 as a refugee from Hungary, the day before Christmas Eve. I was going to go to Canada, but there was a three-month wait,' the old woman says, and Rado's sure this isn't the first time she's made this speech.

'You know this girl?' Rado hands her the phone, with the picture of Morgan on the screen. The old lady opens a drawer and fishes out a pair of reading glasses that she perches on her nose.

'Yes,' she says after having looked carefully at the picture. 'That's little Guðbjörg.'

'Are you related?' Rado asks.

'I'm her grandmother.'

'How old were you when you came here from Hungary?'

'You're not as daft as you look,' the old woman grins. 'We're not blood relatives. I was twenty-six when I came here. My husband was sent to Siberia. Which means I'm ninety-two.'

'But you know her family? You know her father?'

'I know he's useless,' she snaps with disdain.

'When did you last see her?' Rado's becoming impatient and the old lady seems to sense that.

'Has something happened to her?'

'She's missing. We're ... the police are looking for her.'

'Has she done anything wrong?' the old woman asks.

'No. She's just missing.'

'She visits me sometimes. We got to know each other through some school project. Youngsters are sent to institutions where we old people have been put away. I like her. She's tough. She was the one who made me her grandmother. I accepted that, as I no longer have anyone else. She's alone as well.' The old lady takes off her glasses and replaces them in the drawer. Rado steals a glance at a black-and-white photo in a silver frame above her bed, and the old lady notices. 'That's all I have left of him. My husband. I lost other relatives, and don't even have pictures of them. Don't you have photos of those you lost, Rado?' the old lady asks in a tone that's softer, but slightly accusing.

'When did you last see her?' Rado tries to keep the conversation on track.

'This desolate country,' she replies, looking at the window. 'Here you can hardly tell night from day. How on earth am I supposed to know?'

Rado finally says goodbye to the old lady, once he's convinced that she doesn't remember when she last saw Morgan, and stalks along the corridor towards the entrance. The building is filled with the aroma of fresh waffles and coffee. Going around a corner, he almost crashes into an elderly woman with a walker, and his phone starts to buzz in his pocket. It's a number he doesn't recognise.

'Rado,' he says.

'Can you pick me up?' Dóra asks hoarsely from the other end of the line.

'Where are you?' Rado asks, standing in Droplaugarstadir's entrance hall.

'The City Hospital. I'll wait in the lobby.'

'Fifteen minutes, OK?'

'Yeah,' Dóra says and hangs up.

Rado draws a deep breath and looks around. Something's bothering him. He's forgetting something. When he remembers what it is, he strides over to Birna's office, where the door is half-open.

He taps on the door and she looks up from her computer screen.

'The old lady, the one I was talking to. What's her name?'

Birna glances quickly at the screen and then back at Rado. The shadow of a smirk is back.

'Morgana.'

21

Dóra's outside the lobby when Rado drives up to the City Hospital. She's as pale as a ghost. He pushes open the passenger door and she clambers into the jeep with difficulty.

'Home?'

'No,' she replies. 'Work.'

'A few hours ago you were barely conscious.' Rado tries to sound like it's business as usual.

'I'm fine. Down to the station.'

'Yeah, well. Then I want to know what's wrong with you. Why you were bleeding from one eye. I reckon I deserve to know if we're going to be working together.'

'I was shot in the head. OK?' Dóra shrugs. 'Now can we go to the station?'

'And you survived?' Rado isn't exactly asking a question. The words just tumble out of him.

'Just about,' Dóra mumbles.

'When you and Elliði were ...'

'He didn't see the gun. He sent me into a room with a man who picked it up and shot himself.' Dóra sighs and Rado pulls away. 'Can we stop off on the way?' Dóra asks.

'Sure. Where?'

'Hlölli's stall. I'm starving.'

Rado and Dóra sit in his Land Cruiser, parked illegally on Ingólfstorg, putting away Hlölli's submarine sandwiches.

Rado has never been here before. Dóra can't believe it and orders two New York subs. Rado tells her about the visit to Droplaugarstaðir while they sit there.

'Fata Morgana,' Dóra says through a mouthful of sandwich.

'Which means what?'

'That's what the name means. It's a mirage or an illusion. It's a natural phenomenon. Rising air currents make it look as if there's water or quicksilver in the distance,' Dóra says and Rado holds back from wiping a smear of yellow sauce from her chin.

'That's where Morgan got the idea for the name. Not from Morgan Freeman,' Rado says, in a doomed attempt to be funny.

'No. She's much smarter than that.' Dóra sips soda.

'He shot you?' Rado blurts out suddenly. 'I don't understand what happened.'

'No, he shot himself and me at the same time. He was sitting at a desk and I was standing behind him. The bullet went right through his head and into mine. At any rate, the fragments of it. Some of his brain as well. Bone and stuff ... cranial fluid. They got most of the bullet out of my head. That's apart from some fragments they don't dare touch. That's what causes me ... problems. I mean, in daily life. But I can tell you that a bleed from one eye is something new.' Dóra catches Rado's eye. 'That guy was supposed to be amazingly clever. Sometimes I wonder if I managed to get infected with his intelligence. Considering I'm blonde,' she says with a smile.

'Shit.'

Rado puts his sandwich aside. All of a sudden, his appetite's gone.

'Isn't it time to press the red button?' Dóra asks. 'Broaden the search? Has anyone been in touch about Morgan?'

'No. Nobody.' Rado opens the window a little. 'I say we

see how today turns out. Then ... We press the button.'
'Agreed.'
Dóra swallows the remainder of her sandwich.

*

Dóra and Rado agree to use the vacant office to work on the case. Dóra says the lighting upstairs at CID doesn't agree with her. Rado fetches another chair from along the corridor and places it on the other side of the desk.

'Up to you which chair you want,' he says, nodding at the office chair that's upholstered in some patchwork fabric and strengthened with fake leather. Dóra takes the chair he brought from the corridor.

Rado sits behind the desk and opens his laptop. Dóra's phone vibrates, and she answers it. Rado watches her as she listens, a serious look on her face, says nothing and then hangs up.

'There's someone in reception claiming to have seen Morgan,' Dóra says, getting to her feet.

'When?'

'Last night.'

Dóra and Rado groan in unison as they catch sight of Unnar in the station's reception area.

'Hey, wait,' he calls out, waving. 'I've got something.'

'You'd better not be wasting our time,' Dóra says in an ice-cold tone.

They escort Unnar down the stairs and into the little office, where they gesture for him to take the chair facing the desk.

'Let's hear it.' Rado shuts the door, while Dóra takes the office chair and shifts in it to make herself comfortable.

'What happened to you? You look like a ghost,' Unnar says, staring at Dóra.

'Having my period,' Dóra says without missing a beat. Rado coughs to mask a laugh.

'All right.' Unnar looks lost as he catches Rado's eye.

'What do you have?' Rado takes a step towards the chair where Unnar's sitting, and looms over him. He steps around the chair, so that Unnar has to crane his neck to look at him.

'The girl, there ... the one you're looking for. I ...'

'You what?' Dóra snaps, and Unnar turns to face her.

'I get all kinds of tips that drop in to bransi.is about all kinds of cases. As you well know, some of these have helped solve cases,' Unnar says hesitantly.

'Are you trying to sell us an ad?' Rado asks, and Unnar twists around in the chair to see him.

'I mean ... no ...'

'What, then? What do you have?' Rado leans over Unnar. It's as if this office is infected with all the violence that has taken place here over the years. Rado longs to pick up one of those old phone books and use it to batter the wretched boy's head.

Rado folds his arms and crosses over to stand behind the desk. Unnar takes out his phone and holds it up.

'I was wondering if we could come to some arrangement about ...'

Unnar doesn't get to finish his sentence as Dóra reaches out quickly and grabs his collar.

'D'you think this is a negotiating table? We're looking for a missing sixteen-year-old child.' Dóra's face is inches from Unnar's. Despite Unnar's beseeching look, Rado isn't inclined to go to his assistance. 'You know anything about her?'

Dóra lets go her grip and Unnar sinks back into the chair.

'No,' Unnar whispers shamefacedly. 'But I know where her father could be.'

'Where?' Dóra demands.

'Take a look.' Unnar shows first Dóra and then Rado a picture on his phone. It shows a drunken Hákon sitting at a table with two men. It looks like some kind of social centre with tables with vinyl tablecloths and gold or dark yellow curtains in the windows.

'Where was this picture taken?' Dóra asks.

'I know where we're going.'

Rado opens the door and beckons for Unnar to go with him. Dóra stands up, but Rado gestures for her to sit still by the desk.

'What d'you say about doing a deal?'

Unnar's immediately pluckier out here in the corridor with people about and less chance of Rado roughing him up. But Rado quickly hauls him round a corner and they're out of sight. It's just the two of them.

'I'll do a deal with you,' Rado says. 'The Polish gang that was arrested. You give me everything you have about them, and you'll be the first one I call when I have something for the media. Then the others'll have to quote you. Isn't that the way it works?'

'You mean it?' Unnar asks in astonishment.

'Totally,' Rado says, looking into Unnar's eyes. He's looking for even tiny reactions, any indicators that the boy is serious.

'OK. Cool. I'm up for it.' Unnar rubs his hands together. 'But don't you know everything about that? Wasn't your father-in-law the big ...'

'Or I can just forget any deal and you can go and fuck yourself,' Rado says.

'No, no. I get it. Sorry.' Unnar's hands are up, palms out. It's not a facial reaction, but a universal symbol of capitulation. You don't have to be a cop to understand that.

Rado finds Dóra hunched over his laptop when he returns to the office.

'What did he have to say?' Dóra asks without looking up from the screen.

'Who?' Rado stares at her.

'What went on between you two out there?' Now Dóra's

eyes are on Rado. He hesitates, and there's something about the situation right now, or about Dóra, that disarms him. So he tells her the truth about the deal with Unnar. At the very least this is dubious, and the least he could have done would have been to consult his partner.

'And you're going to honour your side of it?' Dóra asks.

'I don't know. Just closing my eyes and ears to anything connected to my wife's family isn't a tactic that's going to work in the long term,' he says at last. 'That's if it isn't too late.'

'There's one thing I can tell you,' Dóra says. 'If Elliði says he'll back you up if we find Morgan, then that's what he'll do. And why don't you have any family photos on your computer? I can't find a single one.'

'Try and behave yourself,' Rado says. 'We're going for a drive.'

Rado stops the unmarked police car outside a large building on Skeifan that houses a number of business units. There's a dry-cleaner, a chiropractor and an outdoor activity shop, as well as offices and outlets for the unlikeliest things, such as sound therapy and computer components.

'What's here?' Dóra asks as they get out of the car.

'The Golden Hall. Haven't you heard of it?' Rado locks the car.

'Isn't the Golden Hall at Hótel Borg?' Dóra asks, following Rado into the building's lobby.

'It's here as well.' Rado gestures for her to follow him up the stairs, which are carpeted. That's odd for a building like this. Dóra notices that the carpet is so thick that their footsteps are silent. She also notices a security camera bolted to the wall on the landing leading up to the first floor. It's so obvious that placing it there must have been deliberate. Its red light flickers on and off in the gloom of the stairwell. They can't be heard, but she's sure they can be seen.

Rado goes up to a solidly built door with a peephole, where he stands and knocks lightly. It's as if his knock is absorbed by the door. Dóra can barely hear it. But a moment later the door opens and they enter a different world.

They step into a lobby in semi-darkness where a huge muscular man with a slightly dazed expression is sitting on a barstool. He's wearing an Adidas tracksuit and sunglasses, and he looks to be around thirty. Dóra's guess is that he must weigh two hundred kilos. She longs to ask him but holds back. He gets to his feet and peels off his sunglasses.

'What do you want?' he demands as he looks them up and down. It's as if he's assessing whether they could be dangerous.

Dóra wonders if he was able to open the door for them without having to stand up, or if there's some mechanism that opens and shuts it. She gets her answer when the door behind her shuts with a low click without the man having moved an inch. She spies another camera high in the corner of the lobby. The red light on this one also flickers. There has to be someone other than the big man opening and closing the door.

'A word with him,' Rado says calmly, looking the big man in the eye.

'He's not here.'

The big man takes a step towards Rado and Dóra. He uses his bulk to block them off.

'Yeah, sure. He's here.'

Rado smiles at the big man, totally unfazed. He even takes a step in his direction. In this little dance taking place in this small space, someone will have to take the next step. It falls to the big man. He extends a hand and twitches aside a curtain, like an ancient flying dinosaur lifting a wing.

Beyond is a large, dark hall. There's a bar at the far end

where some men sit drinking, talking in murmurs. The hall is filled with covered tables and thick curtains, like the ones that were in the picture Unnar showed them, blocking out any light that might try to get in. Pictures hang on the walls. Dóra goes closer and peers at them. They show farms and people at work in the countryside.

'What is this place?' Dóra whispers to Rado.

'It was a regional association that owned this place, all people from some fjord out in the east. They gave up during Covid. Now it belongs to Gústav Karl,' Rado whispers to her, as he looks over to where the man in question is leaning on his elbows on the bar, watching them.

'Not Karl Gústav?' Dóra says.

'Almost. The other way around.'

Rado can feel his stress level rising as they approach the bar. Gústav Karl is a big fish in the underworld. He looks younger, but he's pushing fifty, has been a criminal since childhood and is probably one of the most dangerous men in the country – if not the most dangerous. He's a genuine kingpin, with fingers in pies everywhere. He was considered a promising handball player in his youth and even had a place on the national team. But his temperament wasn't suited to a lengthy sports career.

Rado is concerned that he's made a mistake by bringing Dóra into this place. Gústav Karl is a powder keg waiting to go off. There's no knowing how he'll react if she comes out with something he doesn't like. He's entirely unpredictable. He's wearing cycling trousers, a singlet and a waistcoat that the untrained eye would connect with a sport of some kind. But as far as Rado can make out, it's either bulletproof or stabproof, or maybe both. Gústav Karl looks fit and healthy, more like an entrepreneur marketing a new app or launching a budget airline than the criminal he truly is.

'My condolences,' he says with a touch of scorn as he

stares at Rado. The story of Jurek Senior's death has clearly been quick to make its way around the city's underworld.

'Thanks,' Rado says impassively. The men sitting at the bar are quick to disappear when they realise that Rado and Dóra are cops. Rado's pretty sure these are men who have been playing poker all night long. They're from every level of society. What they have in common is their gambling addiction. He reckons that these are men who have lost everything and are here for a stiffener before heading out into the daylight and the merciless reality that's the consequence of the night's doings. Neither Hákon nor the men with him in the picture Unnar showed them are present.

'Were you close?' Gústav Karl asks and there's a mocking tone to his voice. Rado shakes his head and says nothing. He's hoping that Gústav Karl will infer that he has no inclination to discuss his father-in-law's passing.

Dóra notices Gústav Karl's knuckles. They're swollen and bloody.

Rado asks if he's seen Hákon, holding up his phone to show him his picture.

'When was this supposed to have been taken?' Gústav Karl asks, glancing at them both in turn.

'Last night,' Dóra says, although she can't be sure of that. The picture could have been taken weeks ago for all she knows.

'OK,' Gústav Karl says. 'What's this about?'

'Missing person. His daughter's disappeared.'

'The darkie?' Gústav Karl's expression doesn't change.

'Any idea where we could find her?' Dóra asks. Gústav Karl straightens his back and rubs his hands.

'He was here last night. He had a bit of cash. There was a fight here yesterday.' Gústav Karl caresses his battered knuckles. 'Then he left.'

This is a place where you can place bets on anything the online gambling sites offer, and with the same odds. You can even bet with money borrowed from the house, within limits and against a collateral.

'OK,' Rado says. 'Where?'

'No idea,' Gústav Karl says, putting his hands behind his back.

'I reckon that'll do,' Rado says, glancing at Dóra to indicate that this visit is over.

'Are we thinking the same thing?' Dóra asks when they're standing outside the building.

'Yep. He could have him hidden away somewhere. Hákon can't be reached. Maybe he doesn't have a choice about that,' Rado says, cursing silently.

'We need the Special Unit to go in there. We can keep the place under surveillance in the meantime.' Dóra looks around to locate other exits.

'The thing is, I'm not exactly popular with them right now.' Rado sighs and pushes his hands deep into his coat pockets. It's cold and there's a sharp wind blowing.

'Do we have any kit in the car?' Dóra goes round to the back of the unmarked car and signals for Rado to open the boot. He does, and she opens it and rummages through the contents.

'What's your thinking?' Rado asks.

'The slob by the door's a big lad, but he's not quick on his feet. He reckons he's too big for anyone to mess with him. Ninety-nine per cent of the time, he'd be right.' Dóra opens a case to check the charge level of the taser it contains. 'If he's not too fat, I'll zap him with this and you tie him up.'

Dóra passes Rado a bunch of cable ties.

'Let's cool it for a moment,' Rado says and looks up at the windows of the old rural association where the curtains are still drawn.

'We can't wait. We have to go in there and get round the back.' Dóra pockets the taser.

'You're certain there's something round the back up

there?' Rado glances again at the windows.

'Wasn't this a meeting hall? There must be a kitchen behind the bar, or a cleaner's closet.' Dóra fetches a stab jacket from the boot of the car, takes off her coat and put it on. Then she puts her coat on again over it.

'How about reinforcements?' Rado puts a hand on Dóra's shoulder. 'Listen to me for a moment.'

'No. You listen to me. If we can take out the slob, then it's Karl Gústav against two of us. I know you were in the Special Unit. You should be able to hold him down if he tries anything. At least long enough for me to taser him.'

Dóra takes a deep breath and adjusts the stab jacket.

'His name's Gústav Karl. The opposite way around to the king, remember?' Rado stuffs the ties in a pocket. 'Slow down. Call this one in. Get some support.'

'I was shot in the head on a shout and survived. What the hell should I be frightened of up there?' Dóra says and Rado doesn't get an opportunity to find the right words to convince her otherwise before she's marching towards the entrance.

As soon as the big guy opens the door, Dóra tasers him in the neck. Rado's behind Dóra and doesn't see clearly. The slob shakes, then it's as if he recovers and grabs at her throat.

Rado pushes past Dóra and rams an elbow into the man's solar plexus, so that he instinctively releases Dóra. He'd never dare try any of the moves he uses on the slob against an opponent on the mat. He lands a kick to his shin. He breaks a few fingers and hammers his knee into the man's crotch so that he drops to his knees. Finally, he has him in a headlock and counts the seconds until the big man's out for the count without suffocating. After a few seconds his heavy body sinks to the floor with a bump, taking the lobby curtains with him.

Dóra and Rado make for the bar. The men who left when they arrived earlier are back where they had been. But there's nobody behind the bar. Gústav Karl's nowhere to be seen. Rado goes over to the men at their table.

'Where did he go?' Rado asks a man in a carpenter's blue waistcoat and overalls. The pupils of his eyes are huge. The man's clearly completely stoned.

'You can just ...' The man smirks at Rado and makes to get to his feet, but doesn't get to finish his sentence as Rado catches hold of his collar and wrenches him downwards so that his face smashes against the table. Rado grabs a handful of his hair and hauls him back upright. He gives his companions at the table a dazed look, and then looks at Rado, who shows no emotion. He hadn't meant to break the man's nose, but that was the adrenaline at work.

'He's round the back,' whispers a man in a creased shirt with a bootlace tie. The face is familiar, and Rado has the feeling he's a player in the business world.

Rado and Dóra exchange glances and make their way together towards the bar. Dóra raises the taser and looks behind the bar. Nobody there. Silently, Rado points to the door, signalling that he'll go first. She nods. Rado draws a deep breath, and then hurls himself with all his weight at the door. It's ripped off its hinges and he's thrown into the kitchen, flat on the floor. He sees Gústav Karl standing over him with a baseball bat. He's about to let fly with the bat when Dóra crashes into his side, and the blow, so powerful that the bat splinters, misses its target. Gústav Karl gives Dóra an open-handed smack and grabs the hand holding the taser, forces it against her chest and pulls the trigger. She judders and Rado sees that she's losing her footing. From below, he lets fly a kick at Gústav Karl's knee that sends him crashing on top of him.

Rado's survival instinct kicks in and he immediately tries to overpower Gústav Karl, who knows a few tricks of his own, plus he's much stronger. But it's not enough. Rado knows his kick smashed the man's knee, and it doesn't take long to work out what Jiu-Jitsu his opponent does and doesn't know. Finally, it's a guillotine choke hold that nails him down. Gústav Karl thrashes about like a novice to begin with, while he has some remaining energy. Rado wonders whether to finish this off properly. It's not as if anyone is going to mourn this psychopath. But then he catches sight of Dóra standing over them. Rado's semi-relieved. The last thing he needs is to make this bad day worse and cause someone's death. She reaches down and ties Gústav Karl's hands and Rado relaxes his hold, but Dóra puts a foot on the man's chest to keep him on the floor.

Rado drags himself to his feet and looks around the kitchen. There's just the three of them in there. His whole body hurts. He wonders if his left shoulder is partly out of joint. There's a pulsing pain through the left side of his body from his neck down to his hip. Gústav Karl appears completely calm on the floor. He's struggling to catch his breath, but there's a strange dignity about him. It's as if he's at one with having lost this round. He's like a footballer who's been substituted off the pitch just before the final whistle of a lost match.

'Where is he?' Dóra stands over Gústav Karl and leans hard on the foot against his chest.

'He's gone,' Gústav Karl replies.

'Where?' Rado grimaces and massages his left shoulder. But that's all Gústav Karl has to say. He's too wily, knows when to tell the police nothing.

'What now?' Dóra glances at Rado, who looks around the kitchen. He goes over to a closed door. He opens it to reveal a closet that's been soundproofed with thick sheets of ply. There's a chair in the middle. Rado switches on the light and sees that it's bolted to the floor. The floor around it resembles an abstract painting. There are bloodstains everywhere. Some are old, brown and dried up. Among these are deep red stains of fresh blood.

Rado beckons for Dóra to take her boot off Gústav Karl's chest and to take a look at the closet. She does as asked and stoops to examine the stains around the chair. Some are so fresh that the blood has barely congealed.

'Who was the last one in this chair?' Dóra glares at Gústav Karl, who looks back at her calmly. Dóra nods, picks up a buff hammer and lands a blow on his knee. The pain makes him jerk back. Rado's also taken by surprise. He's about to speak, but Dóra beats him to it.

'We can continue,' she says.

'You're insane, you fucking bitch!' Gústav Karl snarls. 'And you're OK with this?' he adds, his eyes on Rado. His disgust comes across as bizarrely convincing.

'Shall we talk about your cleaning closet?' Rado asks, and glances into the main hall where the men who were around the table are tiptoeing out. The big guy by the door rolls around, trying to snap the ties, but it's hopeless.

'Where's the computer?' Dóra asks, but Gústav Karl stays silent. He stares at Rado, trying to maintain his disdain for these unprofessional methods. 'Are you deaf?' Dóra asks, fishing a large steak knife from a block on the steel worktop.

'Hey!' Gústav Karl yelps as Dóra slips the blade between his legs and slides it up to the outline of his genitals that can be seen encased in his cycling shorts. 'Rado?'

Rado leaves the room, and goes across the hall to the slob, who's rolling around like a whale washed up on dry land.

'Where's the computer?' Rado says.

'You have to undo me,' he begs. 'I can't breathe. I think I'm having a panic attack.' He stops thrashing and continues to hyperventilate.

'Didn't you play basketball for Tíndastóll?' Rado bends down and examines the man's face. 'Aren't you Hannes Bjarki?'

'Yeah,' the big man replies and looks hopeful. He can see

a chance of being untied.

'Then you should have stuck to basketball,' Rado says and aims a kick at his chest.

'What are you doing to me?' the slob whines.

'Where's the computer?' Rado squats down and pokes a finger a few times at the man's eye, and he howls in pain.

'What the fuck is all this? You're cops! You're not allowed to do this!'

The big guy tries to hide his face, but he can't. He's exhausted. Rado places a hand over his nose and mouth. His eyes bulge in surprise and he tries to pull his head clear so he can catch his breath.

'I'm not going to ask you again,' Rado says, getting to his feet as he hears a howl from the kitchen. He doesn't care. Morgan's still a missing teenager, girl, boy or whatever.

The psychopath on the kitchen floor was happy to joke about his father-in-law's death. His colleagues have no respect for him. They no longer trust him, and God only knows how long the woman he loves has been lying to him.

He's tired of the whole miserable mess. Rooms like the cleaner's closet in there next to the kitchen suck all the life out of him. It feels to him as if the only way to get that and a little self-respect back is to let go the reins and run on pure instinct, just like his damaged partner, this alarmingly sick woman who's there in the kitchen, seems to do so effortlessly. He has no intention of interfering with whatever she wants to do to Gústav Karl. The man's earned everything he gets. He deserves it all.

The slob on the floor's no genius, but he's starting to understand that Rado doesn't care about anything, and that fills him with a fear that comes bursting out of him like steam under pressure.

'There's a false wall in there, in the ... closet,' the slob gasps. He's not sure what word to use for that space. 'And a door behind to another ... room. The computer's there.'

'Thank you,' Rado says and heads for the kitchen. He's half-way there when he turns and looks at the big guy. 'Why did you give up basketball?'

'I had anxiety issues because of Covid.'

'Did you catch Covid?' Rado asks.

'No. Just anxiety attacks because of Covid,' the slob admits, and turns his head aside in shame.

'OK,' Rado says and turns to go to the kitchen. He's tired of this idiotic conversation.

When Rado goes into the kitchen, he finds Dóra has cut Gústav Karl's trousers off him and he lies on the kitchen floor, naked from the waist down. His shrivelled prick lies across the knife blade like a snail or an oversized worm. Rado has never seen Gústav Karl in such a state. He's as white as a sheet. He's petrified. He tries manfully to pull himself together when Rado appears in the doorway. But the weird circumstances won't allow that. Rado can see that Dóra's pupils are dilated. She's under the influence of some drug. He hopes that this is holding her back to some extent. It's one thing to rough up a criminal in the process of an arrest, but it's another and altogether a more serious matter to remove their genitals. That's a conversation Rado really doesn't want to have with Elliði. Possibly because both Dóra and Gústav Karl are wearing stab vests, they seem to him to be varieties of the same species. It reminds him of travelling to Poland for a holiday when Ewa was pregnant with Jurek. Their flight home was via Berlin and they spent a few days there. One of the places they visited was the zoo in what had been East Berlin. That's where they got to see all kinds of cats from the old Eastern Bloc. Different varieties of the same dangerous animal.

'Everything all right?' Rado asks, looking at Dóra. She nods and withdraws the blade of the knife from under Gústav Karl's dick, which flops down onto his hairless balls. Rado peers for a moment, to make sure he's not bleeding. Then he holds out a hand and Dóra hands him the steak knife.

'Can I take a picture?' Dóra asks, nodding towards Gústav Karl.

'No.' Rado shakes his head.

'OK,' Dóra agrees. 'I counted the windows outside and in here. There's one missing. There has to be another room here.'

'I know,' Rado says and goes into the closet, where he taps the walls. It takes a while, but he finds a button, presses it, and one wall opens. Rado hesitates, and then steps inside without knowing what's waiting for him in there.

The secret room is some kind of control room with several screens displaying several (legal) sports websites, and a larger screen shows an Italian football match playing out, while a smaller screen in the corner relays feeds from the CCTV cameras on the landing below, in front of the hall and behind the bar. Rado sits down and shakes the cordless mouse in the hope of seeing a cursor on the screen so he can select a display and scroll back.

'What are you doing?' Dóra asks, standing behind him.

'Trying to get this thing to rewind.' Rado shakes the mouse, but there's no cursor to be seen on the screen.

'Just take the hard drive with us,' Dóra says, stooping to reach under the table the screen rests on, and unplugging a little black box.

'Don't you want to go through it here? Isn't that quicker?' Rado asks.

'No. I've found him.' Dóra drops the hard drive in her pocket.

'The dad? Where?' Rado stands up and glances around. Then he looks at Dóra, who grins and waves her phone in his face.

22

The past had come calling when Rado and Zeljko were teenagers, everything their parents hadn't told them. Rado always found this a weird tactic. They knew perfectly well that there had been a war and that was why they had fled to Iceland, but apart from that, their life before the move was practically never discussed.

Sometimes their mother would mention her own parents or other relatives in passing, in connection with completely everyday things; what to have for dinner or how to fold laundry or paint a wall. If the brothers used this as a springboard for more questions, she would instantly retreat into her shell. It was the same with their father. The past was a minefield and they learned not to venture into it. This wasn't because they were reluctant to trouble their parents, but because it was so clear that it was too much for them.

If they applied pressure, then days of oppressive silence would ensue. Their father wouldn't have the will to get out of bed and their mother wouldn't say a word. It's difficult for young lads to not be hurt. When Rado was fifteen and Zeljko was just seventeen, everything changed. This was when his mental problems began to show, with episodes of furious anger and depression. He had found a book by a British journalist about Srebrenica and he had bombarded their parents with painful questions. Rado was never certain if Zeljko had done this because of his illness, or if he was sheltering behind it. Their parents had been advised by the psychiatrist who was treating him to show their son patience and understanding, to do their best not to upset him without good reason. The medication he was taking was supposed to calm him, quieten his thoughts. But it didn't. His medication was constantly being adjusted to improve his responses to it. Some days he was like a ghost, hardly able to speak. On other days he was unstoppable. On the day he brought up the slaughter at Srebrenica, he had been buzzing after a fairly quiet week. It was as if he knew that their parents would be paralysed by any questions relating to that horrific event, and he had clearly prepared himself in advance. He began spouting facts about the mass murder that he had clearly learned off by heart.

After begging him to stop, and their father's ineffectual attempt to drag him into the room the brothers shared, their parents locked themselves away in their own bedroom. Zeljko sat solidly at the kitchen table, facing Rado, and reeling off the story of the killings, the events leading up to them and the aftermath, while Rado sat transfixed and listened to the narrative of how Bosnian troops had stormed Srebrenica and over ten days executed more than eight thousand Bosnian Muslims between the ages of sixteen and sixty. This was the worst mass killing – otherwise described as genocide – to take place in Europe since the Second World War. While Zeljko kept to the facts, Rado listened. But then Zeljko shifted into speculation, saying that their parents and family somehow shared the guilt of this atrocity. Their only way to reach heaven would be to repent, or to pay for their crimes with their lives. That evening, while Zeljko slept in the room the brothers shared, in the living room Rado and his parents discussed having him sectioned and put in an institution. Nothing came of this, because the following morning Zeljko disappeared for good.

Rado moved out a few years later, after his father's

death. His mother saw this as a betrayal. He felt that she was taking out Zeljko's disappearance on him – all that anger and all that sorrow. It was just too much.

His mother still lives in the flat in Árbær. Despite their difficult relationship, Rado still calls her every day. He always invites her if there's a family event. But she never comes. There's always some excuse. She behaves as if she's already dead or departed. Rado doesn't have the words to describe it. He makes sure to take Jurek to see her regularly.

But during these visits she shows limited interest in the boy, little warmth, and Rado is sure the boy senses this. At some point the boy will understand that she's in pain. He'll sense the sorrow in this little flat that contains nothing but what she has lost. Rado doesn't want to expose Jurek to that. He barely made it out alive himself.

23

Dóra had fitted a tiny security camera by the bins that stood next to the door of Hákon's flat in the Laugarnes district, and this sent an alert to her phone whenever it was triggered by movement.

She shows Rado a still image on her phone of Hákon sneaking in. The picture isn't all that clear, but Dóra is certain it's him.

Rado insisted on driving and pushed the unmarked patrol car as fast as he dares through the afternoon traffic up to Laugarnes. His whole left side has been left numb after the struggle at the hall that afternoon. They left Gústav Karl and the slob cable-tied on the floor, but Rado had no concerns that they wouldn't be able to free themselves.

He also knows that Gústav Karl isn't going to take treatment like this lying down. This visit has provided them with some dangerous enemies. Rado has done his best to convince Dóra that at some point, Gústav Karl will come looking for payback. But she doesn't seem too worried about it. Rado wonders if there's a physiological reason for her calmness. Perhaps she's aware that her condition is terminal, and is therefore completely unconcerned that a psychopath is lurking somewhere, plotting brutal revenge?

Rado brushes these thoughts aside. He needs to keep his edge. Time to stop the tumbling washing machine in his head and focus on what's next.

They decide to not drive right up to the house, but park further along the street and walk up to the flat so as not to startle Hákon. Dóra opens the boot and takes out another stab vest, handing it to Rado with a comment that they have no idea what they're walking into. He nods and pulls it on. He's not sure that he has the energy for another fight today.

They climb over the fence and jog through gardens that are deep in snow. They're both soaked to the knees by the time they reach the house, where they agree to split up and each approach from a different direction.

They reach the door to the basement flat and with silent gestures they figure out a plan of attack. Rado can hear Dóra's shallow breaths as they storm into the place.

Rado notices bloodstains on the floor. He goes into the living room and finds Hákon curled in a foetal position on the IKEA sofa. He doesn't even make an effort to get to his feet when he catches sight of Rado. The stale stench of booze blends with the smell of piss.

'No,' he croaks, burying his face in his hands. Rado turns, but Dóra is nowhere to be seen.

'I'm from the police,' Rado says, cautiously approaching Hákon to check if he has a weapon.

'She's not here,' he hears Dóra say behind him, before she marches past and over to Hákon, roughly hauling him upright.

'Where is she? Where've you been?' she demands. Rado says nothing. He's not sure he'd do anything different. Dóra relaxes her grip on Hákon, who's slumped in the middle of the sofa, staring at the floor. A trickle of drool mixed with blood runs down his swollen face. He has two black eyes and the swelling forms uneven, odd angles on his otherwise amiable face. His eyebrows stick out like those of a Klingon.

'What have you done?' Dóra repeats, almost gently, and Hákon looks at her in bemusement.

'Nothing,' Hákon says at last. But neither Rado nor Dóra believe him. Dóra's forming a theory.

'Did Gústav Karl take your daughter as payment? Where is she?'

'No,' Hákon says and shakes his head so that the dribble of spit parts and drops to the floor. 'It's not like that. It's all my own fuck-up. Nothing to do with Morgan. I just owed Gústav Karl.'

'You've been with him since yesterday?' Dóra sits on the coffee table facing Hákon, who nods.

'I went there with my pal and we were playing poker. I've had better luck. Gústav doesn't cut anyone any slack. I think he got a kick out of giving me a hiding,' Hákon says, and Rado and Dóra exchange glances.

'Surely you realise that your daughter is still missing?' Rado says, and Hákon looks back at him without understanding. 'Nobody knows what's become of her.'

'Exactly,' Hákon says, fishes a cigarette from his pocket and lights it. 'But she's done this before. Taken herself off somewhere. I told you that.' Hákon looks over at Dóra, takes a puff and the filter's stained red with blood.

'Are you that stupid, or just utterly useless?' Rado wants to shake Hákon. 'Her coat was found soaking wet by the Drowning Pool! Along with one shoe and her phone.'

'Do you have kids?' Hákon asks, catching Dóra's eye, and she shakes her head. 'See, they have meltdowns, these teenagers. She'll show up.'

'You want to make a formal statement about Gústav Karl?' Rado asks, but Hákon doesn't reply.

'What are we going to do with you?' Dóra asks. 'Where's your phone?'

Hákon rummages in his pocket for an old, scratched phone that looks as if it's from the early days of mobile technology.

'Is there a phone charger here?' Dóra asks and Hákon nods. 'Keep your phone switched on.'

'I'm going nowhere,' Hákon says, and leans back against the sofa.

'Because she might call. Or come here.' Rado looks around the room and then at Hákon. Although he doesn't know Morgan, he's certain that she wouldn't come back here unless she had no other option.

'Can you think of anyone she might be with? Any family members? Other friends we don't know about?'

There's a tone to Dóra's voice that chimes with Rado. It's the tone he uses with his three-year-old son when they're looking for some lost garment or toy.

Hákon shakes his head.

'There's nobody,' he says firmly.

They're standing in the living room when Rado's phone starts to buzz. He holds it up and checks the screen.

'It's Elliði,' he says to Dóra, and wonders if news of their visit to the meeting hall has reached Elliði. Dóra nods and Rado answers. Elliði's formal on the phone, informing him that they're to come to his office at the station. Before they leave, Rado asks Hákon if he wants him to call an ambulance. But Hákon shakes his head.

'I'll be all right,' he mumbles.

It barely registers as they leave the flat. As far as Dóra's concerned, that's in character for a man who doesn't seem concerned at the disappearance of his next of kin.

'What's it all about?' Dóra asks Rado as they drive back to the station. 'All this?'

'I don't think he's lying. I don't get that feeling,' Rado says. 'He knows nothing.'

'No,' Dóra sighs. 'Why's Elliði calling us back to the station?'

'Don't know.'

'You think she's still alive?' Dóra glances across at Rado. He says nothing and feels a stab of terror at the thought that the girl might be dead, that she could have been murdered. Maybe it's because he's exhausted and his entire body hurts, or because Morgan has nobody else. But the question hits him hard. He gasps to catch his breath. This girl neither of them have ever met is occupying a big part of both their hearts. Somehow, she's managed to worm her way in, past their stab vests.

24

They're squashed like sardines in the little office at the police station on Hverfisgata, and there's an eerie silence. Elliði sits behind his desk as Dóra and Rado make their appearance, and behind him stands Chief Superintendent Bjarki Freyr. He's well over sixty, tall, radiating authority.

They both try to read Elliði's expression, but there's nothing to be seen on the chief superintendent's face. He's just as stonily impassive as always. Dóra always feels like she's done something wrong when she's in his presence. If it's possible to be the human incarnation of a clenched fist, then that's him.

'Why the stab vests?' Elliði wants to know.

'We've come from the dad's place. Wanted to play it safe,' Dóra says.

'Is he ...' Elliði begins and stops speaking, uncertain what he's asking about.

'He's unpredictable,' Rado adds.

'The search for the girl hasn't produced any results.' Bjarki Freyr takes a step towards them and looks at them, one after the other. Neither of them looks great. A bruise is starting to swell under Rado's eye, and Dóra is as pale as death.

'I've brought in the city rescue squads to walk the beaches. The Coast Guard helicopter is scanning the area between Thingvellir and Mosfellssveit. Divers are checking nearby bodies of water. I have a team knocking at every summer cottage in the national park. The media will be carrying an appeal to the public for information. In case anyone knows what's become of her,' Bjarki Freyr says.

Dóra and Rado catch each other's eye, and glance at Elliði, who looks away. It's clear this investigation has been taken out of their hands.

'Well,' Elliði says. 'You've done ...'

'Gunnthór will pick this up and take this investigation to its conclusion.' Bjarki Freyr places a hand on Elliði's shoulder. 'The status you two have within the force is currently untenable.'

'Status? What status?' Dóra demands, taken by surprise.

'Wasn't your eye bleeding while you were at a crime scene?' There's a shadow of a condescending smile on Bjarki Freyr's lips. 'Isn't that something that needs to be assessed before taking further steps? Such as whether you're fit for duty? Like Elliði here, I have full confidence in you, but I don't want to see the force having to defend itself against legal proceedings stemming from ... your condition. In terms of health. That's aside from your own wellbeing and a duty of care for ... our people.'

'I ...' Dóra stares at Elliði.

There's a deafening silence in the little office.

'And what about me?' Rado asks at last.

'Good question. It goes without saying that all sorts of things have cropped up over the years. We live in a small country. Turning a blind eye to certain things is part of the old Iceland. Times have changed. As things stand, the force is seeking an independent legal opinion on your situation. In the meantime, you're on leave,' Bjarki Freyr says with a meaningful glance at Rado, who can't help admiring the chief superintendent's smooth delivery of a practised answer, as if he's just the messenger boy. Which he is – but he's so much more than that. He's such a wily beast. How can you be angry with an agency? Rado smirks and shakes his head.

'The child seat that's in the Tesla,' Bjarki Freyr says. 'I understand from forensics that you're free to take it. Your Toyota has Isofix attachment points, doesn't it? It's a 2008 model, isn't it?' The chief superintendent manages to drop a little concern into his voice. The content of his words serve to wipe the smile from Rado's lips. Are they going to take the flat as well? Is Jurek going to become homeless?

'2006,' Rado groans. As if the year of manufacture makes any difference. The barb has slipped past the stab vest.

'The authority will take full account of your contributions to and conduct in this investigation,' Bjarki Freyr says in conclusion, as he leaves the office. He's leaving Elliði to bear the brunt of the fallout from what he had to say. It's a tactical move of the best and cruellest kind. Bjarki Freyr has Dóra and Rado flat on the floor without even having to raise his voice, without putting a single crease in his starched-and-pressed uniform.

Without a word said, they decide to absolve Elliði of any blame. There's no point bearing a grudge. He's given them more support than anyone else has. He doesn't try to raise their spirits in any way. These people are adults, and he's also tired. He's working day and night to prepare cases against little Jurek's mother's family. That thought alone gives Rado an even clearer insight into the ridiculous situation he's in; all in a fresh, new and just as humiliating manner. Dóra's also unusually quiet. Rado wouldn't have been surprised if she'd had a meltdown in the chief superintendent's presence, or at least dropped a few fully inappropriate comments. But no. Not a word from her. She has no inclination to drag Elliði down with her. Or maybe she's just tired.

Their shift finished, at her request, in the same place it started, at Hlölli's stall. They sit and eat wordlessly in the jeep. The last thing Rado feels like doing is marching over to forensics and fetching Jurek's child seat. But he'll have to. He'll have to swallow his pride and do it.

'So that's that,' Rado says at last, putting aside a half-eaten sandwich for the second time that day. 'Will you promise to let it lie? I can see you're sick. I mean, physically. You're also a bit special and all that, and I'm concerned about your health.'

Dóra gazes out through the windscreen for a while before speaking. Then she turns to Rado.

'The doctors want to carry out another operation. They say the technology is so much better now. They reckon they can extract the fragments they didn't dare touch before,' she says, and belches.

'That's good,' Rado says. 'Isn't it?'

'My head started working differently afterwards. When I woke up in hospital after the ... being shot. But I didn't realise it myself. Just went on being me. People around me behaved differently, especially around me. Then I started to have these spells. Taking dives, up and down. By then I'd figured out how this was working.' Dóra puts her sandwich aside and looks over at Rado. 'How can we just stop searching for her? Can you tell me that? How the hell do they work out that Gunnthór's the right man to run this investigation?'

'Shouldn't we start by looking out for number one?'

Rado pulls away and drives out of the square.

'Could be,' Dóra says, as Rado heads for the police headquarters on Hverfisgata where the white Volvo's waiting for her.

Rado watches Dóra drive the Volvo out of the station yard, as if to convince himself that she'll keep away from the investigation. This is symbolic, at best. Dóra's not likely to allow herself to sit idle. Then Rado pulls himself together, gets out of the jeep and makes for the rear entrance to seek out Guðjón in the forensic department to reclaim his son's car seat. The forecast is for wet and windy weather, and an ongoing thaw. It's going to be hard work getting him to and from play school in the buggy.

He finds Guðjón in the forensic department and the child seat is there on the floor. The Tesla is nowhere to be seen. Rado seriously doubts that they've found anything incriminating in it. He suspects that it's now in the hands of the financial crime division. Rado casts an eye over some of the stuff the forensic team are dealing with. He shudders at the sight of half-charred children's toys and a teddy bear wrapped in plastic on one of the steel shelves. He knows that this is evidence in a house fire case a few weeks ago in which a Romanian family died.

Rado's reaching for the child seat when Agnar, one of the department's staff, bustles in. He gives Rado a nod. He knows Rado has permission to take the seat. Agnar is much the same age as him and they get on well.

'Did you find anything on her phone?' Rado asks as he snaps shut the seat's straps. It's the only way to pick it up with one hand.

'What phone?' Agnar asks, and it's obvious he has no idea what Rado is talking about.

'The girl who went missing,' Rado says, putting the seat down again.

'We have her shoe and a coat. Nothing to be found on either. Guðjón's doing the autopsy on ...' Agnar suddenly remembers the link between Jurek Senior and Rado, and flushes awkwardly. 'I mean ... There was no phone.'

'Could you check for me?' Rado asks. Agnar appears to think it over for a moment, and nods. He disappears into the forensic department's office for a moment, and then returns.

'Like I said, I didn't get any phone,' he says, hands in the air. 'I can ask Guðjón. It might be waiting to be registered, but I doubt it.'

'OK.' Rado nods, picks up the child seat and makes for the door. He's fumbling with its fastenings in the Toyota's back seat out in the car park when he's suddenly dragged clear of the car's open door and falls flat on the icy ground of the car park. He looks and sees Sævar leering down at him.

'Now, then,' Sævar says, and delivers a kick to Rado's midriff. He's wearing steel toecaps and Rado can feel ribs giving way, despite being cushioned by the stab vest.

Sævar comes closer and catches hold of the lapel of his bloodstained coat, swinging his right fist back ready to slam it into Rado's face. Rado closes his eyes, but the blow never lands. After a few seconds, he opens his eyes to see Bjarki Freyr standing behind Sævar, holding back his arm. Not that he needs to. The chief superintendent's presence is enough to make Sævar freeze.

'Enough,' Bjarki Freyr says, letting go of Sævar's arm. Rado scrambles to his feet. He's soaked, and makes a pretence of wiping away the worst of it with his hands. The whole left side of his body is on fire after the fight earlier in the day, plus the effects of Sævar's boot.

'Fuck off home to Serbia, you fucking foreigner,' Sævar snarls.

Bjarki Freyr shakes his head. Rado's speechless. He steals across to the jeep, bangs shut the back door, gets in and drives away.

Rado thinks over Sævar's words. Maybe that's an idea. To fuck off to the old country. It can hardly be worse than the misery of this lousy island.

Sævar and Bjarki Freyr stand there in the yard and watch him drive away. The Groke's watching as well. He's across the street. Now he has nothing to wait for.

25

Hector sits in a little van that's marked as owned by an electrician who doesn't exist. All the same, his name and phone number are on both sides of the van and across both rear windows. There's a small window in the side that's completely tinted. That means that nobody can see inside. But anyone inside can see out.

In the back of the van there's a small chemical toilet. There's a six-pack of Coke, all kinds of snacks and sweets, a mess of fast-food packaging and a few wraps of speed. It's like a madman's cosy night in. But there's also a camera on a tripod that Hector uses to snap pictures of everyone coming and going at the meat packing plant that he's supposed to be breaking into. This is a butterfly break-in. Hector once did time with an English guy who used that expression. It's breaking in without knowing what's there to be stolen. Hector could have pushed Nóri harder, asked him if there's a safe in there or some locked strongroom. If they need to get into anything like that, then Hector will need assistance. At least, he'll need more preparation. He suspects there's either a pile of dope in there, or else an amphetamine factory. If that's what it is, then no doubt Nóri will want to add it to his own empire.

All Hector has to do is wait for the meat packing plant to be empty, then get past the fence and inside the building through the ventilation shaft that he and Nóri had examined so carefully on the plans. Then he's to photograph everything inside and sneak out without being seen. He's not to leave any traces.

It's blindingly clear to Hector that there's something very crooked about the way the meat packing plant is run. Not that he bases this opinion on his own experience of the world of employment. This is far from the first time he's sat and watched unseen. Nobody turns up at the plant until midday. No raw material comes in and no production gets shipped out. Not a single van. Not even one cutlet. The only cars he's seen pass through the gate are a newish BMW jeep, a Merc that looks so expensive you wouldn't dare eat a hot dog inside it, and a black Jaguar I-Pace. He doesn't know the people who come and go, and yet he does. He recognises his own kind. There's something going on there, but he doesn't know what. All he knows is that he has a window of around ten hours, if nothing goes awry, to slip through the fence, neatly, so it can be patched up again, open the ventilation shaft with a key and crawl into the building with his camera.

Hector could no doubt have persuaded Nóri to have one of his own people sit there and take pictures. But some things are best done yourself. Preparation is the prelude to everything. Hector wants to be able to get to work at a moment's notice, as soon as the mood's on him. It's a process he can't describe. He just senses it when the time is right. But he'll have to be careful with the speed, take just enough to stay sharp and not so much he goes haywire. You have to hand it to the Sons of the Gods that their gear is the real thing. After that unfortunate misunderstanding over the protection money was resolved, they've accepted him. They don't take the piss or rough him up in any way. Nóri won't have that. Hanging out with them at their club house is like sitting around with a good crowd who are all cool and relaxed. Nobody rides in the middle of winter, so the guys allow themselves all the time they need to tinker with their bikes and chew the fat. Some of the guys have even asked if he's interested in becoming a member, plus they gave him back most of the stuff he'd stolen.

Hector feels it's not a bad idea to join. It all depends on how this break-in turns out. It's best to focus on that for the moment. Leave the future until it happens.

26

Rado's hardly able to stand on his own feet by the time he goes through his front door. He can hear that Jurek's watching children's TV in the living room. An aroma of food wafts from the kitchen. He takes off his coat and the stab vest, which he hides at the back of the closet in the hall.

He pauses in front of the mirror in the hall and checks his face. It doesn't look good. There's a swelling under one eye, scratches on his neck and a small cut on his left cheek. He uses the mirror to rehearse a nonchalant smile and does his best to maintain it as he goes into the living room to say hello to his son.

'You got a hurt,' Jurek says, leaning to one side so his father doesn't obscure his view of children's hour on TV.

'Dad's all right,' Rado says, but doesn't believe it himself as he hears his own words. Ewa appears from the kitchen and there's a look of concern on her face. Rado follows her into the kitchen and takes a drink of water straight from the tap.

'What happened to you?' she asks, placing a hand on his back as he's bent half double under the kitchen tap. He flinches and winces.

'It's been a long day,' he says, straightening up. 'And I'm afraid it might be the last one.'

'Who did this to you? Surely searching for some girl can't be that dangerous?' she says, hands on her hips.

You did this. He longs to blame her for everything, but isn't sure that'll hold water. *Not yet. Not quite.* There's so much he needs to get to the bottom of. It's like when your place is a mess and you need to clear up. If you don't know where to start, you end up doing nothing. At least, to begin with.

'I'm going to have to clean myself up,' he says, turning off the tap.

'Dinner can wait,' Ewa says, sounding like an exhausted housewife. Rado goes to the bathroom and turns on the water in the shower.

He pulls off his wet clothes and looks in the mirror. There's an ugly bruise down his left side from collarbone to groin. He steps into the flow of hot water, closes his eyes, and opens them to stare at the water in the shower tray, pink with blood.

Dóra's surprised that she made it all the way home. This time it wasn't the white Volvo's fault, but her own. She's struggling to keep her eyes open. Everything's misty and she's driving on instinct rather than eyesight. That's all right, as there's precious little traffic on the streets. Everyone's gone home. The carpentry workshop is in darkness as she parks the Volvo and gets out. She has a paper bag of medication and is looking forward to a hot bath and taking her pills. That's what's best. The hot water opens the arteries so nothing obstructs the chemical respite the medication brings. They gave her something at the hospital, and she hasn't taken anything since. That's a whole day. *Deaden the desire.* That's what she's heard some of the skulls say. This is such a weird waltz. Who looks forward to medication? What kind of anticipation is that? Does that make someone a junkie?

Dóra fishes out her bunch of workshop keys and wrestles the heavy door open, sliding it aside. There's sand and ice in the groove in the floor, so she's not able to open it all the way. She has to squeeze sideways through the opening. Then she closes the door again. She stretches for the switch for the upstairs lights.

But nothing happens. Dóra stands perfectly still. She sees nothing. All she can smell is wood and lacquer, blended with an underlying scent of burnt timber from the big saw. She's not even sure of that. She just reckons that scent has to be there. But there's someone in there, sharing the darkness with her. She senses it so strongly. She tries to draw breath as quietly as possible. Finally she can't stand it.

'Morgan, is that you?' she says firmly, out loud.

The Groke moves in the darkness. Wearing the night vision headset, he takes silent steps towards her. He's standing practically beside her. He inspects her face in the green glow. There's no sign of fear on her face. All the same, she has to be aware something's wrong. The Groke raises his weighted cosh and is ready to strike. He chooses carefully where it should land. He's going to stage a fire, an electrical fault. It's almost too easy. The fuse board is old, and there's varnish, wood and kindling everywhere. The firemen will find the woman's body on the floor by the stairs. Head injuries will be attributed to her falling after losing consciousness. His blow isn't meant to kill. She'll have to keep breathing to get smoke into her lungs. That's the way the customer wants it. He wants to be in the clear, just in case the fire service manage to save her and the old man over the other side who's knocked out by the tranquilliser that won't show up in a blood test.

The Groke strikes Dóra's head and for a second she stands still, before collapsing to the workshop floor. The Groke takes off the night vision gear and switches on a small torch that was there on the workbench. He bends over and grips Dóra under the arms, dragging her to the stairs. That's when he hears movement by the door and looks up. He sees his brother standing in the opening and looking at him.

'Is she dead?' Rado asks. 'Did you kill her, Zeljko?'

The Groke is taken by surprise. It's been a long time since he heard anyone use his real name. It's even longer since he last heard his brother's voice.

'You shouldn't be here,' Zeljko says.

'Neither should you,' Rado says. 'I've searched for you. Over the years. Colleagues in the police. In other countries. One was sure you'd enlisted in the Norwegian army. But he couldn't find anything about you. Thought you might be dead.'

'No,' Zeljko says, and glances into the workshop where the big saw is. 'What now?'

'Now I cuff you,' Rado says, taking a step towards where Dóra's lying on the floor. There's bleeding from her head, but he can see she's breathing. 'I guess someone paid you to ... execute her. I want to know who that is.'

'Aren't you going to hug me until I calm down?' Zeljko smiles and Rado shivers.

'Zeljko, you're sick,' Rado says with all the conviction he can muster.

'There's a curse on us, our people. Our parents and me. And you. Considering how everything's working out for you right now.' Zeljko has an odd accent that Rado can't place. His Icelandic is rusty. Suddenly Rado smells something burning in the workshop. 'You have a few moments before this place turns into an inferno. So it's your choice. You go for me, or you save her.' Zeljko jerks his head towards where Dóra lies on the floor. He takes a few steps to the left so that Rado can reach her. Something crackles in the workshop and Rado sees tongues of flame licking at the windows. 'There's an old man in the office. He's her uncle,' Zeljko says, pointing to Dóra. 'He'll need help as well.'

A few seconds pass as the brothers stare at each other. Then Rado makes a move, takes Dóra in his arms and lifts her. By the time he's upright, Zeljko is gone.

Rado bundles Dóra out through the narrow entrance and carefully lays her down in the snow outside. Then he takes a deep breath and goes inside to fetch Rúrik. He finds him lying on the office floor. The old man's surprisingly light. By the time Rado manages to ease him out through the door, the flames are reaching into the main workshop.

Rado peers towards the workshop. Can he take his brother's word for it? Is that safe? He curses under his breath and squeezes back through the narrow opening. He looks around him and sees the steps leading to the upper floor. He runs over and rushes up them. He throws himself against a locked door at the top. He takes a run-up, kicks the door down and goes into a space that must be Dóra's flat. That's where he was heading. He'd meant to tell her there was something suspicious about the missing person inquiry, that Morgan's phone had disappeared – or been made to disappear.

Rado searches the flat until he's sure, and then scrambles back down the steps. He staggers when he's half-way across the workshop. He can't draw breath. The fire's consuming all the oxygen in the place. He uses the last energy he can muster to crawl to the door and haul himself out.

Lying in the snow, Rado finds his phone and calls the emergency line as he struggles to draw oxygen into his scorched lungs. Then he leans over Dóra and checks the injury to her head, without touching it. Her breathing is shallow.

He doesn't know what to do. Wake her up? Leave her be? He takes off his coat and spreads it over her.

He opens the jeep and places the old man on the back seat.

It's only as he scans around him that the shock hits him at last, of seeing Zeljko after all these years – that he's still alive. He's not exactly surprised at the way his life's worked out. Rado has heard stories of former soldiers taking on this kind of assignment, travelling from place to place so their movements can't be tracked. The specialisation of modern society also reached deep into the underworld.

The ambulance is there ahead of the fire engine. Dóra's lifted gently onto a stretcher and her head secured.

Rado notices that the old man in the Toyota has come to and is struggling to get out. That's not going well, as there are child locks on the back doors. A patrol car hurtles up and halts behind the jeep. Rado recognises the two officers who hurry across.

'What happened here?' one asks.

'Anyone inside?' the other asks, and Rado shakes his head.

'The place caught fire. I found two people and dragged them out. The building's empty.' The tension drops as the officers take this on board and realise who he is. Rado doesn't say a word about his brother. It's as if he was never there. That's maybe no lie. The man who fled the scene had his face and body. But it was as if he had borrowed both.

27

It's four in the morning when Hector calls Nóri to let him know he's going in. He can hear the murmur of voices and music in the background.

'Remember, just take pictures and then get the hell out. Call me when you're on the outside,' Nóri says and hangs up.

Hector looks down at his last line of speed on the mirror balanced on his knees in the back of the little van. He snorts it and pulls the balaclava down over his face. He's wearing black Nike gear he stole during his crime spree. He's put black tape over the logos. Otherwise he would have had to rip them off, and that would have been painful. It was a complete stroke of luck to come across a tracksuit like this in extra small.

He quietly shuts the van's back door and marches briskly to the point he's chosen to snip through the wire. He's repeatedly checks to see if it's electrified. It isn't. But it's a high fence, topped with barbed wire. That indicates poor thinking. Nobody other than a rookie would try to go over it.

There's a little dip in the street where he's able to lie flat. He's pretty sure he's out of sight from the meat packing plant. The winter darkness helps.

He takes out the sharp cutters and starts snipping his way in. The cut is dead straight, neat. He's already cut a section of wire ready to close the gap behind him. He feels for it in the zipped pocket in the back of his trousers.

Certain that it's there and ready, he pulls open the slit in the wire and slides himself through the opening.

The sound of a car gives him a jolt of adrenaline. He lies still for a while. The sports gear he's wearing is supposed to be waterproof, but he can feel it becoming soaked through. He hears the car pass the meat packing plant, and the sound of its engine disappears into the distance. Hector counts silently up to a hundred. Then he gets to his feet and jogs to the wall where the ventilation shaft starts about two metres above ground level. Hector has something for that. He has some collapsible steps in a little backpack, with powerful glue made to his own formula. It's strong enough to carry his modest weight, but not so strong that he won't be able to remove the steps on the way out, leaving no traces.

He presses the first set of steps to the wall and ascends. Then again and again, until he reaches the hatch. He has a special spanner to open it. The bolts are stubborn and if it hadn't been for the line he snorted in the van, he's not sure he would have been able to free them to open the hatch. The wind catches it, and it booms like a deep-toned drum. Hector can't close it behind him, but he has a solution for that. He wraps a length of twine around the door and pulls it to so that it doesn't move. It's only then that he switches on his head torch and looks around the ventilation shaft.

He pauses and listens. He tries to breathe soundlessly. He's fully balanced, he's what he's destined to be. As weird as it sounds, this is his natural environment.

He crawls with short, deliberate movements. It's something he's done countless times before. Being as lithe as he is gives him the advantage of not touching the sides of the shaft at any point. Anyone else would be given away by the sound of their movements. He counts each movement and mentally compares it to the map he has in his mind. His reckoning is that he's close to the production hall. There's supposed to be a grille that can be opened by simply lifting it from its frame. Then he just needs to poke out his head and one arm to take pictures of the space. And then the next, and the next. There are grilles in every room in the place. But there are no fans. He's already made sure of that. That supports the theory that there's no meat production in there. At least, not in any official manner. That would mean inspecting the premises, and fans are the most expensive element of any ventilation system. The rest is just metalwork.

The shaft he crawls along is dusty and Hector struggles to not cough. There are beads of light that seep in, indicating that the lights are on. That's good, as it makes photography easier, even though his specially selected camera can produce images in almost complete darkness.

Hector stops by the grille, which isn't even straight in its frame. The important thing is to not drop it to the floor. He firmly takes hold, pulls it cautiously towards him and light floods into the shaft. On his elbows, he pushes it under his chest. Then he wriggles closer and pops his head neatly out, the camera in his hand, and starts taking pictures. The autofocus means all he has to do is point and click systematically to cover everything. That's what he does. He's already snapped off a few pictures when he realises that the space isn't deserted. He withdraws his hand and disappears back into the shaft as silently as he can. He hadn't known what to expect in there, but what he's seen down in the meat plant fills him with fear.

28

Rado gazes out at the illuminated city in the winter darkness from a corridor at the City Hospital. Dóra's fighting for her life a few metres away. He feels that a veil has been torn away from his life and he's now facing stark reality. But that's always been the case. He just chose to not see it that way.

Dóra's uncle Rúrik is elsewhere in the same hospital. He has suffered a touch of smoke inhalation, but otherwise there's nothing wrong with him that's unusual in a man of his age. All the same, the doctors want to keep him in overnight.

The surgeon who spoke to Rado before the operation isn't optimistic. On the plus side, this is the same doctor who examined her when her eye started to bleed. She's received a heavy blow to the head and her brain has swollen. He has no option but to perform an operation immediately, one that would usually need to be prepared in advance.

Every time Rado hears movement, he expects to see this same doctor bringing him bad news. He feels that this whole institution has nothing better to do than maintain the same lie. The place is full to bursting and run by an insufficient number of staff, long burned-out. Rado knows he must pull himself together and out of this mood. There's nothing he can do. If he hadn't turned up at Rúrik's workshop, there'd be no operation in progress right now.

The fire teams managed to overcome the blaze before it spread to nearby buildings. Rado doesn't know what he's going to say when he has to make a statement. He should have reported his brother's presence, alerted border control at the airport. But something holds him back. The last time he tried to have his brother locked up, he disappeared from their family's lives. It's not hard to tell that he's still wracked with guilt over this. He can't face the thought of making his brother's hopeless situation even more hopeless. However pathetic it may sound, he harbours a hope deep down that he can straighten things out, that he can return to serving as a police officer. The truth is that this part of his life has ended.

For the thousandth time, Rado hears movement and glances along the corridor. His heart lurches as he sees Elliði approaching. He sees Rado and comes storming over to him.

'Where is she?' he demands.

'In theatre,' Rado replies.

'Her parents and older brother are arriving tomorrow on the morning flight from out west.' Elliði lets himself drop into a chair. 'I don't understand what happened. Was she attacked? And was Rúrik as well?'

'I found them both unconscious in there, and then the place went up in flames,' Rado says.

'What the fuck's going on here?' Who would want to harm her?' Elliði fidgets in his chair.

'Forensics don't have her phone,' Rado blurts out.

'What phone? What are you talking about?' Elliði asks, glaring at him.

'Dóra found Morgan's phone at Thingvellir. But forensics don't have it. They have their shoe and coat, but not the phone. That's why I went to talk to Dóra. To ask her about that. She says she handed it in.'

'You think this is about the girl who disappeared? I mean, the way you describe this, they're in there unconscious and the place is on fire. Rado, that's attempted murder.' Elliði jumps to his feet.

'If it's not connected to her disappearance, then what?'

'That's what we'll have to ask her when she comes round,' Elliði replies.

'I think ... I spoke to the doctor before she went into theatre. Going by what he said, we shouldn't expect too much. What I'm saying is that ... There's no certainty she'll come round.' Rado places his hands on Elliði's shoulders and looks into his eyes. 'This isn't smoke inhalation,' he says. 'She received a heavy blow to the head. Nobody can withstand that. Least of all her.'

'She's still in danger?' Elliði's eyes flash along the hospital corridor. 'Should I have her guarded?'

'We had a bit of a ruck with Gústav Karl today,' Rado says. 'But I have the feeling this is something else.'

'How about I have him picked up?' Elliði reaches for his phone, but Rado stops him.

'I don't imagine Gústav Karl could have organised something like this with practically zero notice. This is something that has to go deeper. Someone sees her as a threat. Or there's something she knows. Someone's ready to go to great lengths to make sure it doesn't get out.'

Elliði impassively watches Rado as he digests his words.

'Then there's the phone,' Elliði says abruptly. 'How does a vital piece of evidence in a missing person investigation go missing?'

'I know you make use of her, putting finishing touches to all sorts of cases. Was she working on anything that could possibly have put her in danger?' Rado stares at Elliði, who looks down at his hands.

'No,' he says after a long pause. 'Nothing.'

Part Two

Four months later

29

Today it's Rado driving Dóra up to the rehabilitation clinic at Reykjalundur. Jafet usually takes her, but he can't make it. There's a relationship between Jafet and Dóra that Rado can't quite understand. It's not easily defined. But it's to Jafet's credit that he does everything he can to support her. Whether this is still a loving relationship isn't something Rado can be sure of. He knows that Jafet has changed her diapers, washed and fed her. Isn't that love?

She moved in with him after the fire. Or rather, Jafet moved her into his place, his little city centre flat. It's round the back of a nightspot that stays open to three in the morning, with all the boozing and noise that comes with it. These aren't ideal conditions for a sick person. But they make it work. It was never an option for Dóra to move back to her parents' farm up in the west. All the services Dóra needs are here in the city.

To begin with, she couldn't even hold a spoon. Couldn't speak. She was like a newborn, but with more of a temper. Rado's given to understand this is a side effect of the brain damage. She can string together simple sentences and somewhere inside that scarred head of hers, that she demands be kept cropped close, is the person with whom he investigated the missing teen, and who changed both their lives. Dóra didn't recognise Rado when he came to visit her once she had regained consciousness. By then she'd been kept in a coma for a month.

'She's a miracle on two legs,' said the doctor who performed the first operation on the night his brother had tried to kill her. That was the first operation of many. There are so many now that Rado has lost count. But he sat and waited outside during every one. He watched over her at her bedside, because he didn't dare pray.

He's wracked with guilt. At some point he'll tell her about his brother and what happened that night at the workshop. But that won't be for a while. The nerve damage team at Reykjalundur say that her recovery is unparalleled. She has an iron will and works like a horse. She's a tough customer. But there are also days when she's overwhelmed. Those are the days she doesn't want to get out of bed or has a meltdown. That's when Rado can deal with her more easily than the even-tempered, laid-back Jafet. Sometimes he calls and asks Rado to come downtown, when he can't cope and a peacemaker is needed. And he does it − always. Even if it means waking up little Jurek and taking him as well. Then Jafet sits outside in the Land Cruiser with the little boy while Rado tries to calm Dóra. Sometimes that calls for physical strength. One time she stabbed her own hand with a knife. It wasn't deep, but enough to be worrying. Sometimes she calls him herself, somehow managing to select his number with her trembling fingers. She still speaks slowly. Those who don't know her reply just as slowly. They think she's mentally impaired. When she calls, she wants to talk about Morgan, about the investigation. The way she talks, you'd think a mere few days had passed, not four months. The search for Morgan is ongoing, the case is still open. Rado suspects it's not high on the list of priorities. But he can't be sure, as he's still on extended leave. The force has yet to reach its conclusions, whatever that's supposed to mean.

Dóra asks about progress combing the beaches, whether they should bring in dogs to search the national park. Then her thoughts wander and she forgets what they were talking about. She can't keep track. Rado doesn't have the heart to correct her. He gives her the same report every time she calls. He tells her more manpower has been brought in, that as they speak, bloodhounds are ranging through the national park.

Rado helps her out of the jeep. She can walk if she holds his arm, which is what she does. On the way up there in the car she had started the same spiel as he sometimes hears over the phone. His thoughts elsewhere, Rado reeled off the same answers as usual, that everyone's taking part in the search, that there's even a helicopter that has been called out. The doctors told him to play along, to not try to put her right. He's not to tell her that there's been no sign of Morgan for months, that there's zero likelihood that she's alive. The truth could cause her anxiety, even a nervous breakdown.

He's helping her through the doors at Reykjalundur when she stops suddenly – or as suddenly as someone who moves so slowly can do it – looks at him and comes out with something he hasn't heard before. It's time forensics took a look at Morgan's phone.

Rado feels a surge of anger deep inside.

What the hell happened to the phone?

'I'll ask,' he says and realises that he means it. He'll help her into the clinic and Reykjalundur, and then he'll go straight to Elliði.

30

Rado tracks Elliði down in a gym in the Vatnsmýri district of the city. They decided this was a better place to meet than the station on Hverfisgata with too many curious eyes and ears.

Elliði's leaving a group session when Rado catches sight of him through the gate where people scan their irises for access. Elliði goes through the gate and nods to him. Then he glances around, as if checking they're not being watched.

He doesn't look good. His bony frame has a paunch and his face is grey. The sweat's running off him.

'What do you want?' Elliði says.

Rado has already run into him a few times at Jafet's place. But they haven't discussed work or anything that's happened. That's likely because it's not easy to find the right words. It's too closely linked to what happened to Dóra.

'Her phone. It's bugging me,' Rado says, looking into Elliði's eyes.

'The girl? Yeah,' Elliði says. 'I don't know what I can tell you. It never did turn up.'

'Dóra said she found it. She's hardly going to lie, is she?' Rado's voice rises. The lad at the reception desk looks up.

'She's not lying. Why would she do that?' Elliði says in a low voice. 'But it's not on record at forensics. Neither Agnar nor Guðjón recall having taken delivery of it. Maybe she didn't hand it in right away? Could it have been destroyed in the fire? Have you checked her Volvo?'

'Yes,' Rado nods. 'It's not there.'

'Why are you asking about the phone now?' Elliði wipes the sweat from his forehead.

'Because she was asking about it. This morning. She hasn't mentioned it since she came to after the first operation.'

'You reckon her memory's coming back? Has she said anything about the fire?'

Elliði's suddenly tense.

'No, nothing. I don't know. I was going to ask if you could do me a favour? Is there a chance you could get me a copy of the case file? I want to show it to her. See if that sparks anything.'

Rado eyes Elliði.

'The girl's school has been in touch. They're holding a memorial event for her soon.' Elliði sighs. 'You're not the only one who wants some answers.'

Elliði gets to his feet.

*

Rado transfers the case files relating to the disappearance of Guðbjörg Hákonardóttir, which Elliði passed on to him, from a memory stick to the iPad Jafet bought for Dóra. Her own iPad was destroyed in the fire, along with everything else she had. She was left with nothing but the clothes she was wearing when he dragged her from the workshop, and the white Volvo that the firemen pushed away from the burning building.

The access code for the iPad is the first six numbers of the Fibonacci sequence, minus the zero, and that was Dóra's choice. She told both Rado and Jafet, in case she were to forget the code, plus they also got a mini lecture about the origins of the sequence. It had something to do with the rate at which rabbits breed. Rado decides to give Dóra a few days to dig into the case files before sitting down with her. Or it might be weeks. It depends on what works for her. Jafet had his doubts, but Rado promised to tread carefully and to apply no pressure. Rado had taken a look through the files himself, to see if there'd been any progress. The only addition is a collection of pictures from the phones of Morgan's classmates, taken that morning at Thingvellir. But Rado couldn't see that this shed any further light on her disappearance. The key to this is hidden somewhere in Dóra's head – in something she alone knows, or knew. It could well be lost, along with everything else she's forgotten.

Rado feels that since being put on gardening leave, he's increasingly shut away inside his own thoughts. The funeral of Jurek Senior took place in Gdansk, which emptied his and Ewa's savings account. At Ewa's request, Rado wasn't present for the funeral. They're separating. She calls it a break, but that's not the feeling he gets. They each have their own part in how things played out. Rado's still living in the flat in Urriðaholt. Ewa's at her mother's place. He offered to move out, but this is the way she wants it right now. No doubt it'll end up with the place being sold, and each of them buying a place of their own to live. Rado would like to buy her out, so that little Jurek can stay in the same district and go to the same nursery. The little boy is mostly with him and goes to his mother at weekends. However things are going to work out, he's too young to understand what's happening right now. Nothing seems to take him by surprise.

As far as Rado knows, the prosecutor still hasn't issued a formal prosecution against Ewa's father's associates, or against Ewa herself. She's cautiously asked him what this is likely to mean, but he has no idea. He no longer has friends among his colleagues on the force – apart from Elliði, and he doesn't want to trouble him.

He's developed a routine of getting up and taking the little boy to nursery. If there's anything he can do to make life easier for Jafet in looking after Dóra, then that's what he does. Otherwise, he stays at home and lets his imagination roam. He thinks back over his life and how it has played out, his marriage, his brother. All the things he no longer has.

He and Ewa have slept together a few times since the start of their break and her move to her mother's place. To begin with, this was a way of bridging some gap. But they both sense that the gap is too wide. He has asked her several times to put her cards on the table, to tell him the extent of her father's influence and what she had been aware of. How on earth could she – as she maintains – have been able to keep herself at a distance from it all?

It's something he could certainly discover for himself, but he feels it's important to hear it from her. He feels he has a right to this. But she doesn't seem to see things that way. Any pressure he applies is met with a wall of silence. Every time he pushes, he eats away at the foundations of their relationship.

Revisiting Morgan's disappearance takes him out of his shell. It gives him something to think about. He has made a thorough record of every possible detail he recalls from the short time that he and Dóra worked on the investigation. She picked up Morgan's coat and shoe that morning at Thingvellir when the teachers reported the disappearance. She handed both over to forensics, and both were properly recorded and checked. That evening she found the phone, near the Drowning Pool. Rado remembers asking Dóra about the phone when they were on the way to the Hagi School. He recalls finding Hákon, the girl's father, on the sofa at his place, after the visit to Gústav Karl. Rado doesn't remember if the phone was mentioned then. He thinks the whole thing over from every possible angle.

Early on Tuesday morning, after dropping Jurek off at nursery, Rado drives up there. Time for a look at the place where it all started, by the Drowning Pool. Most of the snow has melted and spring is about to break. Rado's not sure what exactly he's doing there. But it seems important to start with something tangible, and the Drowning Pool certainly is. He looks around. In this place it would be a hell of a challenge to snatch a teenager without anyone noticing. So the implication is that they must have gone willingly, at least to begin with. Rado tries to visualise the sequence of events around the disappearance. Maybe Morgan could have had a fall, and that's why their coat and one shoe were soaked? They could have dropped the phone from a pocket on the way? It could be that they left the group to seek shelter in the reception centre. Or in the coach? What about the driver? Did Dóra check on him? Did she speak to him? These are questions that demand answers. There's nothing in the case files he got from Elliði for Dóra to read through. The driver could possibly have overpowered them in the coach, tied the teenager up and put them in the luggage space. All the same ... Only a madman would do something along those lines. But Rado can't be certain. The driver theory is weak. That would mean one person was at work.

Rado looks around the Drowning Pool. It's cold, and it's raining. The promise of spring in the air isn't convincing. That's to say if it manages to penetrate the gloom which seems to have enveloped every aspect of his existence.

31

She opens her eyes and doesn't know where she is. It's hard to find words to describe it. *Removed from the world?* Further removed than in a dream. She wakes with a sob in her throat, without knowing why. *Can you sob over nothing?* It doesn't help that the bedroom where she wakes up is strange to her. She's at Jafet's place, in his apartment. He's back in her life. To her it feels like this has happened without her noticing, without her having had anything to do with it. But here she is. Otherwise, she'd no doubt be in some institution. She has to go there as well, but only during the daytime. She's in therapy all day long. But this is where she is at weekends and in the evenings. It's the place where Jafet preferred to be rather than with her above the workshop. He says he loves her. She's not sure what feelings she has for him. The relationship figures in her thoughts. There's a connection there. That's all there is, if she's totally honest about it. If someone had told her when she woke up after the first operation that he was her brother, she'd have just nodded and gone along with it.

It takes a long time to get up. Her consciousness struggles with a daze that takes a while to shake off. It demands precious energy. In her condition the energy that gives her life is valuable, the most valuable.

Can you try throwing this ball? Can you write your name? Just the first letter? Do you remember? What's your name? Can you tell me what the tool in the picture is called? What's it used

*for? These exercises are burning up energy at a great rate. Let's
go back to the start.*

She has another energy source, but she doesn't dare use
that. It's the rage that churns inside her, and she makes
efforts to keep that at bay. It doesn't always work. That's
when the healthy energy tank runs dry. Then she provokes
everyone, testing the limits of their patience. Jafet's
mostly on the receiving end of this as he spends the most
time with her. It's as if she's checking that his feelings for
her are genuine. She feels she needs to make certain.
Conversely, she doesn't know what feelings she has for
him.

Her situation is like being in a dream in which you can't
speak. The mouth opens, nothing comes out. The only
difference is that she knows she's not going to wake up.
She's as wide awake as it's possible to be. Each day is like
every other. It feels like crawling up a slope through loose
gravel. Every inch gained is a struggle.

She finally realises that it's Saturday morning. Up to now
Jafet's had some guy come in to open the record shop,
which is open from eleven to three on Saturdays. Last night
she told him she would be fine. She'd call if anything were
to come up. He's not more than ten minutes away from
home. He had her call him a few times last night as they sat
on the sofa in the little living room in front of the TV. That
was to make sure she could. The most challenging part of
this drama wasn't finding his number on her phone, but
swallowing back the anger that rose up to her throat. But
that's just the way it is. This is what's on offer.

People around her don't understand that it's one thing
to confuse a hammer and a screwdriver. But that's nothing
to do with the hammer and the screwdriver. She's well
aware of the differences between these two tools. The
problem is putting it into words. Losing the ability to
express herself is more complex than just the words one
remembers, or doesn't remember. One of the hardest

languages to learn, Icelandic is sometimes a mystery to her.

Lying on her back in the fresh morning light, she reaches for the iPad and her fingerprint lets her open it. She taps the folder on the screen and it opens. She doesn't have the energy to read the case files, but she can check the pictures.

The advantage of her condition – if she's feeling particularly positive, which doesn't happen often – is that she finds she's in some kind of no man's land. This flat, the people around her, and if she's honest, the missing person investigation, are all things she knows nothing about. She'll have to examine the whole thing from scratch, the same as all the cases she's put to bed for her colleagues over the years. She has nothing to prove, and has no emotional investment in this. She has no connection with this girl, Guðbjörg Hákonardóttir, who wanted (or wants) to be called Morgan. The obsession that had troubled her in so many ways also seems to have disappeared.

Morgan's disappearance is like a crossword, or a chess problem, or a riddle a traveller must guess to be able to continue. Maybe that's the closest to it. She feels she's the traveller, right here in this flat, in this city, and even in her own consciousness.

After an hour of inspecting the pictures, she gets up and makes for the bathroom. She checks her face in the mirror. She's pale. Her skin is white and the scar that runs from her right eyebrow and upwards, over to the back of her head, is even whiter. It looks like wax, and she knows what wax is.

She picks up the pill box with its compartments for each day of the week, conscientiously loaded by Jafet, and swallows down the Saturday dose. He told her off a few days ago when he found her chewing the pills, told her she shouldn't do that. Swallow them down instead. Dóra, who is usually willing to relearn everything she had forgotten, found herself wondering for the first time if he was telling her the truth. It seems so much more sensible to chew them. But that's not what we're supposed to do. She asked one of the doctors on the trauma team. He confirmed that Jafet was right.

She sits on the toilet and pees. There are snow squalls outside the half-open bathroom window. Then Dóra feels her way back to the bedroom, picks up her phone that lies on the bed and selects Rado's number. They only worked together for a short time, but she feels she's known him all her life.

*

An hour later Dóra hears movement. It's Rado and he calls out to her. She gets to her feet and goes into the living room where Rado stands in the doorway with a little boy at his side. Dóra doesn't remember his name.

'Are you a cat princess?' the boy asks, his eyes on Dóra.

'What's that?' she asks.

'A cat that's a princess.' The boy watches her with serious eyes.

'What's a cat?'

'Just a cat,' Jurek replies.

'And what's a princess?' Dóra asks.

'You a cat princess,' the little boy tells her.

'So,' Rado says, crouching in front of the lad and brushing snow from his coat with his palms. 'Shall we take your coat off?' Little Jurek nods. Rado looks around the compact living room and finally plants the boy in an armchair, then he takes a puzzle book from his backpack and hands it to him.

'You called?' he says, turning to Dóra.

'Yes,' she says after a long pause. 'I lied to you. Or rather, I'm lying to you.'

'And?' Rado's not sure where this is going.

'When I call and ask about the case, then I'm lying. I only ask about things I reckon are ...' Dóra's having trouble keeping track.

'I know,' Rado says. 'It's all right.'

'This iPad.' Dóra holds it out to him in one shaky hand. 'I looked through the pictures because I don't trust myself to ... can't read the report. I don't understand what you want from me. Sometimes I pretend to understand. You ... the doctors, Jafet, people expect certain things of me.' It takes Dóra a long time to get these words out. 'Like you. It's as if you often feel guilty about something and I have no idea what. Maybe I'd like to know.'

Tears trickle down her cheeks. Rado's tense.

'It was just to see if ... an idea. To see if it would trigger any memories.'

Rado's eyes go to the boy. He'd had to bring him as well. There was no choice. Now he's not sure if overhearing this conversation is healthy for him. 'I have no expectations.'

'Wow. Thanks.'

'I didn't mean it like that,' Rado sighs. 'Like I said, it's just an experiment. A few days ago I took you up to Reykjalundur and you mentioned Morgan's phone. You asked when forensics were going to be finished checking it.'

'Phone?' Dóra places the palm of one hand on the scar above her eyebrow and strokes it gently.

'Yes. You found it at Thingvellir, but forensics have no record of it.' Rado holds his breath.

'No,' Dóra says. 'I don't remember finding it.'

'All right,' Rado says, taking care to conceal any disappointment.

Dóra strokes the scar and grimaces.

'Does the scar hurt?' he asks without thinking.

'No, I'm not Harry fucking Potter,' she snarls, and Jurek looks up from his puzzle book.

'But you know who that is?' Rado asks.

'Yeah. I'm not brain dead!'

32

Rado's been invited to a birthday celebration. He's more than a little surprised to have been asked and wonders for a long time whether or not to accept. He finally decides that he has no choice. A few weeks have passed since the day he and little Jurek braved the driving snow to visit Dóra. He's met her a few times since then, but the missing person case is right off the agenda. She doesn't mention it, and neither does he. Every time he meets her, he can see an improvement in her condition. Sometimes it feels that he could even try to forget what happened at the workshop, that this never needs to be mentioned again. Of course, this is just a daydream.

Now the city smells of spring and barbecued meat. Going by what Ewa told him a few days ago, their lawyer doesn't expect either her or her brother to be prosecuted. A few of their father's gang have been convicted of minor offences, but there's nothing serious. The storm in the teacup has blown itself out. All it did was wreck their marriage.

Rado hasn't heard from Elliði, but there has to be a conclusion to his case before long. His CID colleague Katrín is celebrating her fiftieth birthday. Although he's worked with her in the department for some years, he doesn't exactly know her well. But he feels it bodes well that she invited him. He hopes it means he's no longer out in the cold. It's better to meet his colleagues in such an informal situation before he goes back to work.

BROKEN

Katrín lives with her husband and two daughters, who Rado recalls are both at college, in a townhouse in Fossvogur. He doesn't recall what the husband does, but believes he's heard he works at the Statistics Directorate.

Rado's at Katrín's door on the dot of six o'clock, with a bouquet of flowers and a bottle of wine. It's a bright summer day. No doubt their colleagues have all chipped in for a birthday gift for her, as usual when there's a big birthday at the department, but as he's been on leave these past few months, he's been left out of that loop. Katrín opens the door for him. She's dressed in a sleeveless dress with a flower pattern. He almost fails to recognise her. She asks him in, he congratulates her on passing such a milestone, hands her the flowers and the wine, and she offers him a glass of sparkling wine from the tray in the hall. This is a bright, airy house, with three floors. There's a low murmur of jazz from the living room on the next floor up.

'We're upstairs, on the balcony,' Katrín says, steering him by the elbow up the stairs. Then the bell rings again, and she's gone, back to the front door. Rado takes a deep breath, and then a gulp of the ice-cold sparkling wine, which instantly goes to his head.

Most of his CID colleagues are on the balcony, standing in a semi-circle around Magnús, Katrín's husband. He's wearing an apron with an Independence Party logo, beside a large barbecue loaded with meat of all kinds.

'Hi,' Rado says to the group as a whole, and raises his glass. There's a long moment, before his colleagues return his greeting. Some raise their glasses. Magnús, the centre of the gathering, is in the middle of some anecdote, and continues as if nothing had happened. Rado doubts somehow that Katrín has told him about the turmoil within the department. Most of them habitually refrain from discussing their work with their partners or anyone else close to them. It's not to keep their work secret, but it's more a mechanism to keep the two worlds separated. It's the only way.

As the evening passes, Rado's colleagues chat to him, one at a time. They ask how Dóra is doing and Rado does his best to tell them. They're more cautious asking about his circumstances. Nobody fails to notice that he's there on his own.

Magnús and Katrín see to it that nobody's glass runs dry. The department has clubbed together to buy her a painting by an up-and-coming artist called Arnar Ásgeirsson – Katrín and Magnús have a strong interest in art – and it falls to Elliði to make a little speech as he gives her everyone's best wishes on her birthday, and the artwork is unveiled. Katrín is overjoyed. Rado thinks it's impressive. It's some kind of drawing in ink, with symbols that are reminiscent of Nordic runes. Looking at them, he loses himself in it. There's some hidden magic in there. It's almost hypnotic. Elliði chats to Rado for a while, but doesn't let anything slip about his standing in the department. This evening he's on the other side of the line. No cop dramas. He's at his friend's birthday party, with a new boyfriend who Rado can see is a good bit younger than Elliði.

Guðjón and Agnar from forensics are there as well. Agnar's girlfriend is with him, a well-known TV chef. Magnús and Katrín ask her repeatedly what she thinks of the food, and she assures them that everything they've done is first class.

Guðjón comes across to where Rado's listening to the host's conversation with the TV chef. He's feeling no pain and is dodging his wife, who is trying to make sure he doesn't pass out while the party's in progress.

'Y'see this chick?' he whispers – far too loudly – to Rado. 'I mean, she has a cookery show on TV. But she's so bland that when she comes in, it's like someone's left the room!' Guðjón laughs out loud, and pats Rado's shoulder. Rado notices Steinunn, Guðjón's wife, with a pleading look in her eyes. This isn't the first time Guðjón's been dead drunk at a work gathering.

Rado nods to her and leads Guðjón up a short flight of steps and out onto the balcony, which is deserted. Everyone's in the living room, where Magnús is playing Beatles songs on the piano and conducting a sing-song.

Out on the balcony Guðjón lights a cigarette and Rado takes the glass from his hand. It's half-full of whisky.

'Give me the glass,' Guðjón says. He's struggling to stay upright.

'That's enough, Guðjón,' Rado says and puts the glass aside on one of the balcony tables. Guðjón stares at him and he relents. 'Let's keep it clean this evening, for Steinunn's sake.'

Guðjón glances through the living-room window where Steinunn sits alone. The others are all around the piano, giving 'Hey Jude' their all.

'OK.' Guðjón puffs his cigarette and looks out over the neatly kept garden. 'Where's your wife?' he asks, turning to Rado.

'We aren't ... don't live ...' Rado sighs.

'Didn't the old man know he had a heart condition?' Guðjón asks suddenly. Rado says nothing, stares back at him. 'Your father-in-law. I performed the autopsy. Did the blood tests. A man in his condition. Such a bad heart. Wasn't he on any medication? The blood tests didn't show anything. If he'd needed medication he could have had a doctor come to his cell.'

'Not now.' Rado tries to not let any feelings show.

'Sorry,' Guðjón mutters. 'Just haven't run into you for a while. All that's been bothering me.' He stubs out the cigarette and goes into the living room.

Rado watches him appear by the piano, demanding that Magnús play something by the Rolling Stones. Somehow he's contrived to have a bottle of beer in his hand, and

Steinunn's looking at her hands in the living room.

As he's leaving, Rado thanks Katrín for inviting him. She's a little tipsy, like everyone there, and hugs him. Her mascara's smudged and her voice is hoarse after having sneaked a cigarette. It's something she only does when she's had a drink. Magnús loathes smoking.

'I wasn't sure if I should have invited Dóra. I ... I mean, I ... she's so ... Isn't she at Reykjalundur, like Elliði says?' Rado nods and thanks her again for the invitation. Then he leaves quietly. In the jeep he wonders about what Guðjón said about Jurek Senior. Why wouldn't he have taken the medication? Did something happen in the cell after Rado left? He turns it all over in his mind as he drives home. Going over that day all over again.

Returning to an empty flat, he's overcome by darkness. This is at odds with the spring that's about to burst into life. But this winter has been almost too much for him, however positive he tries to be. He needs to sit on his hands. Do nothing, and life can continue. Let this chapter pass by. But instead he picks up the phone and selects the number of a man he'd never expected to speak to again.

*

It takes Rado all of Saturday to track down Unnar, who isn't answering his phone. Checking bransi.is, he notices that the latest updates were a couple of weeks ago, and the same goes for his social media activity.

It takes a while, but doesn't turn out to be a serious challenge to find him. Unnar's keeping his head down, but his friends aren't. Rado finds two of them on Facebook and doesn't have to apply much pressure before he has the address of a basement flat of an apartment block in Grafarvogur. Rado knocks, and it's not long before Unnar answers the door. He's wearing shorts, sandals and a Calvin Klein tee-shirt, with the arms snipped off.

'What do you want?' he asks from the doorway.

'To come in.' Rado pushes at the door and Unnar backs away.

There's a hesitant look on Unnar's face as he hovers next to Rado, who stands in the living room and looks around. There's a leather corner sofa, the one Costco sells, facing a monster of a flat-screen with a computer game playing out on it. Its flickering light is the only illumination in the room. Rado takes a look at Unnar and sees that his eyes are both bloodshot and dazed. There's no smell of dope, but it's obvious he's been smoking, which doesn't necessarily mean much.

'Lived here long?' Rado asks.

'Yeah ... no,' Unnar groans.

'Are you keeping yourself out of circulation?' Unnar doesn't reply. He blinks rapidly. 'We had a deal not that long ago,' Rado says, sitting on the corner sofa.

'Yeah,' Unnar says. 'Absolutely. I ... you never got in touch and I've ... Been doing other stuff. And aren't you suspended?'

'Yes,' Rado says. 'Sit down.' Unnar flinches and sits on a chair facing the sofa. Next to him there's a pile of dirty laundry. 'You remember what the agreement was about?'

'Sharing information,' Unnar says, rubbing his hands together and licking his lips. He's a little out of sync, slightly too slow. Rado's convinced he's on something.

'Precisely. And that's why I'm here.' Rado picks up the remote control from the table and switches off the huge TV. 'What do you have on my father-in-law and his associates?'

'What would I know? I don't suppose there's anything you don't know already. Can I get myself a Monster?' Unnar looks round-eyed at Rado.

'You live here. Do what you like.'

Rado gets to his feet. Unnar does the same and slips around him and into the compact kitchen. There's packaging from frozen pizzas and tubs of protein powder and food additives. Rado also spies packaging from some psychiatric medication on the kitchen table. That could explain Unnar's state.

Unnar opens the fridge and takes out a can of Monster Energy. He pops the lid, takes a long drink and immediately looks better.

'This agreement of ours ... Yeah? That's all good. I don't want to ...' Unnar looks down at his hands.

'Did something happen to you?' Rado sees that Unnar's freckled hands tremble slightly.

'Well ... no ...' Unnar whispers. 'I just ...'

'Has someone threatened you? I can ...'

'Aren't you out of the police?' Unnar asks.

'I'm on leave. Not for much longer,' Rado says firmly. 'If there's someone who's ... Hey, talk to me.'

'I can't. My ex lives in Sandgerði ... My kids. They could ...' Unnar shivers.

'If Jurek's gang has done anything to you, I can talk to them. Or anyone else who's not happy with you. Clear the air,' Rado says with determination. He sees a spark of hope in Unnar's eyes.

'What do you want to know?' Unnar asks, after a long pause.

'Jurek's gang. What were they up to? Dope? Burglaries? Something else?' Rado leans against the door frame.

'A bit of everything.' Unnar takes another gulp from the can. 'Why are you asking me? Your wife must ... I get it. So you don't know anything? Fuck!'

'Fuck, what?' Rado growls. 'Explain.' His eyes stay calm.

'They're into everything. Just everything. But mostly dope. It's not a gang as such. It's more a circle around Artur.' Unnar takes out a vape and puffs. The artificial smell of chewing gum and berries fills the kitchen.

'They're into everything? You mean they were?' Rado peers at Unnar.

'No.' Unnar takes another puff of the vape. 'Jesus, man. Where have you been?'

'And Artur's the big man now?'

'Yep.' Unnar nods.

'But he's completely ...'

'Completely what?' Unnar stands still and stares at Rado.

'I mean he's not someone who could manage that kind of outfit.' Rado shakes his head. 'He's a clown.'

'Until he takes off the false nose,' Unnar says and lifts his shirt to show a smiley face that extends from just below his nipples to his navel. Rado squints at the image and sees it's composed of the burn marks of innumerable cigarettes.

'Who did this to you?' Unnar pulls his shirt down again.

'Who do you think?' There are tears in Unnar's eyes.

'You should report this,' Rado says, placing his hands on Unnar's shoulders.

'Yeah. Sure. Two guys wearing ski masks turn up in the middle of the night and hold me down.' Unnar shakes his head and grins. 'Good luck finding them.'

'Why do you think Artur did this to you?' Rado asks.

'I was working on material concerning his gang. I'd been asking around. He got wind of it. Someone told him. I've had threats before, but I've always tried to be fair. Earned myself a bit of respect.' Unnar reaches for a cigarette from a packet and lights one. Rado watches him standing there with a cigarette in one hand and the vape in the other, like he's been hypnotised. 'Artur has been running this gang for a few years. Those I've spoken to say the old man hadn't been involved in anything for a long time. Nothing happens ... I mean, they don't do anything without his say-so.'

'You're sure of this?' Rado asks in surprise.

'You tell me? They're your family!' Unnar shrugs, takes a puff of the cigarette, and then another of the vape. His arms are both tattooed all the way up with a cacophony of symbolism. There are skulls and the figure with the scythe. Nordic gods with hammers and spears. There's a samurai wielding a sword. But the man himself comes across as tired and soft, as if he's just a canvas for all these images of darkness and power.

33

After calling on Unnar in his basement flat in Grafarvogur, Rado sits for a long time in his Land Cruiser before driving off. He digests what Unnar has told him. Could he have so seriously underestimated Artur? Or allowed his love for Ewa to blind him? No, it's more complex than that. If he's honest with himself, it's a blend of shame and prejudice. He's ashamed of his wife's family. He looked down on his petty criminal father-in-law, who went about in cheap jogging trousers he bought in sales and who stank of copious amounts of cheap aftershave and tobacco. The same went for Artur. This is something he has to face. But what does this information mean in relation to Artur, if this is all true, and what weight does it carry in connection with that momentous day? He knows only that this is a trail he'll have to follow all the way to the end. That might shed some light on everything that happened.

Rado parks in front of the house in Seltjarnarnes. A few youngsters are taking basketball shots at a hoop on a garage across the street. This gives Rado a pang as he thinks back to simpler times. Him and his brother, before he became sick. They both did football training at the Reykjavík club. They were both promising. But their parents couldn't afford studded boots for both of them. So they took training sessions in turn. Played matches in turn. The coach even called one day and offered to buy another pair of boots, but their father wouldn't have it. He banged the phone down on him. Rado increasingly let his brother use the football boots. He felt that he was the one who needed the training more. Maybe he was already starting to suspect that his brother wasn't quite right in the head. That was until he went for a lad in the team they were playing and gave him a beating. After that they both stopped training.

Rado takes off his overcoat, folds it and places it on the jeep's front seat. There's something in him that makes him want to cross the street and join in the game. Instead he goes to the front door and rings the bell. After a while Steinunn opens the door, still wearing a dressing gown, even though it's well into the afternoon. She can't hide her surprise at the sight of Rado.

'I'm sorry to call so unexpectedly,' Rado says. 'But I really need to speak to Guðjón.'

'That's all right,' Steinunn says with resignation. Her face is drawn and Rado can smell the booze. He knows that some women whose husbands are heavy drinkers end up drawn to the bottle as well. It's no doubt because their husbands' drinking has made their lives miserable. Maybe it's a way to understand for themselves, to find a way into the closed world that the booze keeps them locked up in.

'He's in the garage,' Steinunn says and steps back, leaving the front door wide open. Rado hesitates for a moment, and then steps inside, closing the door behind him. He's been to their house a few times before and goes straight to the kitchen, and the door that opens into the garage. He can hear muted music playing in there. It's a double garage and Guðjón has fitted out the rear part of it with a desk, sofa, a bar and a sound system. He's lounging on the sofa when Rado appears in the garage. Nick Cave's coming through the speakers. There's a strong smell of alcohol.

'I shouldn't have said anything yesterday,' Guðjón says

in a hoarse voice as he catches sight of Rado. The ashtray on the table in front of him is overflowing. Guðjón fishes a half-smoked cigarette from it and puts it in his mouth. 'I was drunk yesterday.'

Rado says nothing. Guðjón's had a drink, and he's not beating about the bush. He knows this isn't a social call.

'I was the last one to see him alive. Did you know that?' Rado stands over Guðjón.

'No,' Guðjón says in surprise. 'You went into his cell?'

'Yes. You know what for?'

'No?'

'To bring him his cardiac medication.' Rado takes a seat in an armchair next to the sofa.

'You want something?' Guðjón asks.

'Yes,' Rado says. 'The raid. You were part of it. Earlier in the day.'

'I meant a drink,' Guðjón says.

'Why no prosecutions? You don't have anything?' Rado asks.

'What does this have to do with the raid?' Guðjón stubs out the cigarette. 'And I'm not sure I'm at liberty to tell you.'

'If there are no prosecutions, then there are no secrets that need to be kept,' Rado says calmly. 'I need to know what happened.'

'Yeah, all right.' Guðjón runs his fingers through his hair. 'There are no prosecutions because we didn't find anything. Or, y'know, we found trivial stuff. Nothing like what we were sure of finding.'

'Which was what?'

'Just ... A much bigger shipment. The drug squad had it all mapped out. We just didn't find it.' Guðjón sips from his glass. 'The financial crimes division found some stuff ... but I mean ... there are building contractors with just as crap accounts. That's not a crime. Not enough to justify a raid. The tax office might give them a fine. And that's after all the work that went into it. It's just bullshit. Tangled up in our own feet. It's like they knew we were coming. You're not under any suspicion. I understand the drug squad kept you busy elsewhere.'

'Yes,' Rado says. 'The whole gang's arrested, and old Jurek, but not Artur? Why wasn't he arrested?'

'He was nowhere to be found,' Guðjón says. 'That morning his phone's switched off and he just vanishes. I know the drug squad had his flat staked out, but in all the commotion he managed to slip away. He didn't come back to the flat.'

'He came to my place, after the SWAT team had been there,' Rado says.

'I don't know anything about that. They would definitely have brought him in if they'd found him there.' Guðjón gets up from the sofa. He's unsteady on his feet. 'All I can tell you is that it was a total farce. Nothing was found and the prosecutor doesn't have anything to prosecute. I've heard it mentioned that it's time to bring you back in. So just be satisfied that this is all over.' Guðjón knocks back what's left in his glass. 'Why do you think he didn't take his medication, the old man? He must have known that without it he was dead meat?'

This is the question, exactly as Guðjón posed it, that echoes through Rado's head as he drives away from Seltjarnarnes. Ewa had pressed him hard for an answer to the same question. But he has no answer to it.

BROKEN

34

Rado stands in the lobby of the apartment block in Reykjavík's upmarket Shadow District where Artur either has his lair, or his home. He extracted the address from a drug squad colleague who had a fit of guilt for having had him spend weeks staking out the shady lawyer so that he wouldn't get wind of the raid. Artur's wearing a white singlet and grey cotton jogging bottoms. He has reading glasses on a chain around his neck. He comes across as sober and coherent.

'Come in,' he says calmly, opening the door wide.

Rado follows him in. The apartment is bright and neat. There are books of all kinds on the shelves hung on the wall facing the big window that provides a view of the sound and the slopes of Mount Esja. Rado peers at the volumes. They're mostly finance and economics tomes. There are biographies of world-class high achievers, artists and scientists. Candles flicker on the glass table in the living room. The place is stylishly austere and tidy. Artur stands in the living room and watches Rado.

'OK,' Rado says, as he makes efforts to keep the churning rage within him in check. 'How did your father die?'

'He suffered a heart attack,' Artur says, and Rado kicks a small glass table that stands next to the white sofa. Artur doesn't even blink.

'I'll ask again. How ...?

'We're going to do this now, are we? OK, the

medication...' Artur's jaw juts forward. 'I have a guy, a chemist, who fixed it.'

'What did you make me do?' Rado whispers.

'It had to happen this way,' Artur says.

'Had to happen? What's that supposed to mean?' Rado's hands tremble.

'He was no longer trustworthy,' Artur says with firmness. 'I was sitting on two hundred kilos of speed and couldn't be sure that ... He ... My father would keep quiet about it.'

'So you ...?'

'He had at most a few weeks of life left.'

'It's still murder.'

'He suffered a heart attack,' Artur says placidly. His words shout practice. Like a mantra.

'But how ... who helped you?' Rado asks.

'Helped me? Nobody,' Artur replies, unperturbed.

'Don't try that with me.' Rado's index finger points at Artur.

'You helped me. I mean, you went into his cell.'

'Stop it!'

'What is it you want?' Artur asks without the slightest trace of agitation. Rado draws a deep breath, tries to regain his equilibrium.

'So you think it's just fine for your father to die in a police cell for the sake of two hundred kilos of speed?' Rado glared at Artur.

'Of course it's not fine. But you don't understand. Everything was at stake. Everything we've built up.'

'Who helped you? On the inside?' Rado asks.

'From the cops, you mean?'

'Yes.'

'That's not important,' Artur replies, still perfectly calm.

'Not important? Have you any idea of the shit that's going to rain down on you?' Rado snarls. 'I'm going straight to the station to the drug squad. If you think that last raid was bad, then that was child's play compared to ...'

'Enough,' Artur says, determined. There's a half-smile on his face. 'Shall we have a word with your brother?' Artur waves his phone in front of Rado. 'Are you going to arrest him as well? Or does he get away with it, like last time?'

Rado stares, unable to speak.

'Strange what a small world it is sometimes,' Artur continues. 'He's worked for me a few times, your brother. For me. I remember when I met him first. I could hardly believe it. What are the chances? A Serb who speaks Icelandic and is so like my brother-in-law? Not to mention little Jurek. It's the chin, the cleft. They both have it, but you don't. Naturally, I wasn't certain. Not until he let you get out of that workshop alive. After that I was completely sure.'

'Where is he?' Rado gasps.

'Shall we call a halt here, Rado? You've nothing. Just go home.'

'Does Ewa know? Does she know what you did, Artur?' Rado takes a step towards him. He feels he catches sight of a slight tic over one eye. Rado goes over to the shelves and catches sight of the biographies of Steve Jobs, Elon Musk and all manner of self-help books, with the focus on business. 'So this is what the clown looks like when he takes off the false nose,' Rado says at last.

'It comes and goes,' Artur says, cold eyes fixed on him.

*

Rado's sitting on the sofa with a glass of whisky in his hands at home on Urriðaholt when the doorbell rings. He gets to his feet and fetches the little lead-weighted cosh from the drawer by the door before he opens it. It could be a visit from Artur, who is clearly more to be reckoned with than he had imagined. But it's not him or his goons, but Dóra.

She's been taking whole leaps forward recently, at least physically, which the doctors say is normal for those recovering from head injuries. The mental side of things, the sensory aspect, develops more slowly. Rado sees that her movements are all quicker. She's more like the person he remembers. The little he remembers of her is all based on that single eventful day.

'Come in,' Rado says. 'On your own?'

'Yes,' she replies.

'How did you get here?'

'Took a cab.' Rado shuts the door and ushers her into the flat. She glances around and notices the whisky bottle on the living-room table. 'Making a weekend of it?' She winks. It's hard work, but she manages it.

'Sit down,' he says.

'Where's your son?'

'He's with me from tomorrow morning,' Rado says. 'I have him every other week.'

Rado watches Dóra sit down with difficulty. It's as if her sense of balance hasn't fully returned. He wonders whether or not to tell her everything. That could bring her recovery tumbling down like a house of cards.

'I need to tell you something. I don't know if ... I mean, what effect it's going to have on you ...' Rado sighs.

'OK,' Dóra says.

This is the toughest evening Rado has experienced since his brother disappeared from his life the first time. Dóra has trouble understanding everything Rado tells her, and a few times he has to repeat himself so she keeps track. Then she repeats the whole story he's told her, from encountering Zeljko at the workshop to the visit to Artur in his Shadow District apartment. She asks Rado to fetch another glass and he pours her a little whisky. With an unsteady hand, she lifts it to her lips and sips.

'So you believe Artur is responsible for the death of his own father and that he has someone on the inside? One of us?' Dóra's brow furrows.

'We're talking about two hundred kilos of speed that weren't found. Those raids turned up nothing,' Rado says. 'That's goods worth millions on the street. Jurek Senior was pulled in during the raid. I'm asked to take his heart pills to him in his cell. The ones that, y'know, don't work.'

'You think he did this so the old man wouldn't spill the beans?' Dóra asks, sipping her drink.

'I think he simply saw an opportunity to get rid of Jurek Senior,' Rado sighs.

'Why do you call him Jurek Senior?'

'My son's name is also Jurek,' Rado says in surprise – even though he's told her this more than once before.

'I didn't know,' Dóra says. 'And what about me? You suspect that Artur's responsible for your brother trying to burn me alive? Why? I had nothing to do with the raid. Why would Artur send him after me?'

'Maybe he or his friend in the force thought you might know something. You have a knack of sniffing things out,' Rado says, putting down his glass. He's starting to feel it going to his head.

'Let's put that aside and try to take a look at the big picture.' Dóra knocks back the rest of her whisky. 'The question is, what gets us to run errands on a drug dealer's behalf and gloss over something as serious as killing a prisoner in a cell? This is someone with nerves of steel.' There's a drop of whisky on her chin, but she makes no move to wipe it away. 'Is there any way to prove that Artur is behind Jurek Senior's death?' Dóra says, looking up at Rado.

'I don't know,' Rado says. 'Guðjón's in a bad way these days. He's drinking far too much. He told me at Katrín's party that the autopsy showed Jurek's heart condition was serious. I had no idea. But that alone proves nothing.'

'And the fake medication you took him? What happened to that? Was it just one pill?'

'No, it was a bag of packs of tablets. I've no idea what became of it,' Rado says.

'Katrín had a birthday party?' Dóra asks suddenly.

'Yes,' Rado replies guardedly.

'I wasn't invited,' Dóra says with a shrug.

'Katrín wasn't sure you were ... well enough.'

'I can assure you that I'm very well,' Dóra says after a moment's silence.

Rado sees that the dribble of whisky is dripping from her chin, and he thinks of the fluid of a different colour that trickled from her eye a few months before. That was outside the basement flat in the Laugarnes district. He allows himself a half-smile. Dóra is starting to remind him of the woman she was back then.

35

Elliði sits for a long time and says nothing. It's as if time and the silence somehow cancel out what Rado and Dóra have told him. But of course, that doesn't happen. The reality is that they're sitting in his living room in the Kórar district of the city. It's as well that his latest boyfriend, Indriði, isn't at home. He's out of the country, working. It would have been a hell of a challenge to explain this visit to him. They tell each other everything. Or, as far as that goes in Elliði's case. There are limits to what he can share with Indriði, although he tells him what he's able to. That's even when he doesn't want to. Indriði feels this is a more wholesome way to live.

Elliði switches on the coffee maker. It's a cartridge machine that Indriði bought. Elliði went along with it, but always feels that the coffee it produces comes with a flavour of disappointment. It takes the machine just a few moments to warm up, before he puts in his cup and presses a button.

'Isn't it more likely that this is just ... coincidence? That this doesn't connect to anything?' Elliði says as he sips coffee. He knows ... no, he senses that there's something crooked about this. But for the moment he has to try to puncture the balloon that's little by little filling his tastefully decorated living room.

'Yes,' Rado says. 'But. All the same.'

'Rado ... This man ... the one you ran into at the

workshop? Who is he?'

'He was sent to finish me off,' Dóra says quickly.

'All right,' Elliði says. The balloon's getting bigger and bigger there in the living room. 'There's a hole in the logic. Let's assume this is correct. That Artur sent you into the cell with fake medication. Who gets rid of the packaging? And what's the connection with what happened to you, Dóra?'

'We're going to have to tell him,' Rado says with a glance at Dóra.

'Tell me what?' Elliði says with a sigh. He's not sure he wants to hear any more of this.

'I know the man who was at the workshop. He's my brother.'

Elliði drops the Versace cup, which smashes on the floor.

'Your brother? Just how fucked up is this?'

'It's a long story,' Rado mutters.

'Indriði isn't going to like this,' Elliði mumbles, picking up the largest shards from the floor. 'Shouldn't we be trying to track him down?'

'I haven't seen him since we were in our teens. You know that outsiders are sometimes called in to do particular bits of underworld dirty work? I suspect that's what he does for a living,' Rado says. 'It's not just anyone who has the ability to call in people like that. It seems most likely that Artur and his mole in the force saw Dóra as a threat. There's something she knows relating to the raids. There's been no other recent operation on that scale.'

'You're talking about a major conspiracy here. Fine. Let's look at that.' Dóra and Rado catch each other's eye. 'The Minister of Justice wants a campaign against organised crime. The focus is on stopping foreign gangs that are operating here. Whether this is an election promise is neither here nor there. Around the same time, the drug squad gets a tip-off that Jurek's sitting on two hundred kilos of speed that's been smuggled into the country. The top ranks decide to run co-ordinated raids against Jurek's gang. This peaks with an operation that involves most departments of the force. The thing is, no dope is found. Jurek is murdered while in custody and a contract killer is put on your trail,' Elliði says, glancing at Dóra.

'That's pretty much what it looks like to me,' Dóra nods.

'Your brother, Rado. You reckon there's no way to find him?'

'There has to be a way, but I doubt it could be done without word getting around. If he is found, I doubt he'd say a word.'

'But what is it that you've seen or sniffed out that kicked this off?' Elliði asks Dóra.

'I've no idea.' Dóra shakes her head. 'I've been trying to think back to those days I was on the missing person case. I remember a lot of it. But there are still a few gaps. But I don't recall having had anything to do with the raids.'

'Either they think you don't remember anything, or this person hears gossip about you at the station,' Elliði says.

'They gossip about me at the station?' Dóra barks.

'No ... I mean ...' Elliði flushes.

'I'm just messing with you,' Dóra smirks.

'It's as well you've kept hold of your sense of humour,' Elliði says.

'Or they've managed to cover their tracks while you were ... away,' Rado says.

'There's another connection,' Dóra says.

'What connection's that?' Rado turns to her.

'You said you had no idea that it was Artur who was really running Jurek's gang. How on earth would anyone on the force have known that? We're missing someone here. That's whoever brought them together. It's someone who knows the real Artur,' Dóra says, eyes on Rado. 'It's someone in some position of confidence. Artur's lawyer, for instance?'

'Doesn't have to be,' Elliði says. 'It could be someone in

the drug squad. Someone with underworld links.'

'Are you going to pursue this?' Rado asks Elliði, who raises his hands in the air.

'No question. This is top-level corruption. But you're going to have to tread carefully and not speak to anyone about this. I'm not calling you back to the department right away, Rado. Don't speak about this over the phone. Just use Telegram. You know how it works. If you need to reach me, then come here. Nobody gets away with trying to kill my friends without me taking action,' Elliði says with grim determination, and Rado gets a glimpse of the motherly side of his boss that's carefully hidden at work, but which he feels suits him and makes this somehow more convincing. 'Do you think you're in any danger?'

'I don't know,' Dóra replies.

'We won't take any chances,' Rado says, knocking back the last of the bland machine coffee.

It's well into the night by the time Rado helps Dóra to her feet and they say goodbye to Elliði. Rado can see him standing in the living-room window, watching as they get into the jeep and drive away. Rado can see that Dóra is exhausted. So is he. But there's a restlessness to him. One thing they didn't discuss with Elliði, and which he also hasn't talked over with Dóra, is his son. He knows he can't tell Ewa anything. He asks himself if going after Artur is putting the boy in harm's way. Isn't a man who murders his own father in cold blood capable of anything? But he's too tired to think straight. That'll have to wait until later. Things are complicated enough already. He feels his head's on fire. It's positively crackling.

36

Rado's at Dóra's and Jafet's place at ten the next morning. Jafet's about to leave to get the shop ready for opening, but stays to offer Rado a coffee in the kitchen, since Dóra's in the shower. The flat's so small that it's as if she's practically there in the kitchen.

'Jafet!' Dóra calls from the bathroom, and he's up there to help her. He supports her, wrapped in a dressing gown and hair in a towel. 'Good morning,' she says, before disappearing into the bedroom with Jafet to get dressed. Rado can hear them talking in muted tones. He knows Dóra needs help getting dressed. Sisyphus is here in 101 Reykjavík as well. Rado feels he can sense a note of vexation between them. It's in the rise and fall of their voices, even though they're whispering.

Jafet leaves the bedroom before Dóra. The look on his face says everything. He tries to carry himself bravely.

'There's more coffee over there. I have to be going,' he says, and is gone. A few moments later Dóra appears from the bedroom and sits at the kitchen table. She seems relaxed, maybe a little tired. It's not easy for Rado to read her thoughts. She reaches for the coffee pot and picks up a mug. The kitchen is so small that she can do this without having to get to her feet.

'What's the matter with you? Who died?' she asks, and sips coffee.

'Drank too much yesterday. I finished the bottle when I

got home. Haven't done that since ... I don't know when,' Rado says with a sigh.

'What's going on?' Dóra narrows her eyes as she looks at him. 'How are you feeling?'

'I'm just hungover.'

'And there's something on your mind,' Dóra says.

'There's something strange about that? It's not as if ...'

'I'm going to stop you right there,' Dóra warns. 'Every single day. No, every single movement, every thought, demands a huge amount of energy. I'm struggling here. How about you? Are you struggling?' she says, and Rado looks away. 'Now he wants us to have sex.'

'What?' Rado stares at Dóra in astonishment.

'My boyfriend,' Dóra says. 'It doesn't matter how hard I try, I'm as dry as dust, understand? Maybe it's him. Maybe it's my head. I'm just saying that your wife might not have known what was going on. I mean, do you love her?'

'Yes,' Rado groans.

'Then why aren't you fighting her corner?'

Rado freezes. Then he nods and it's as if the sob reflex in his throat is cleared. He feels tears forming in his eyes and brushes them away. Dóra reaches for his hand and squeezes it, remarkably tightly. Her grasp is so hard that Rado feels a little more hope and fondness in his heart, and a brief whimper escapes his lips.

'What's his name?' she asks suddenly.

'Who?'

'My boyfriend.'

'Jafet,' Rado says and looks at her searchingly. 'His name's Jafet.'

'Of course it is,' Dóra says, and winks.

The day passes in the little flat. They've decided to concentrate on Morgan's disappearance, as if to see if this jogs Dóra's memory. They go through the copy of the case files. They've printed out all the pictures from the report and hung them in the living room, which is far too small. But this is where they feel it's most sensible to work. They can't be at Rado's place on Urriðaholt. Ewa could appear there and start to ask questions. There's also a chance that Artur has them under surveillance.

Morgan's face stares down at them from the walls. It's impossible to see this person other than in a symbolic and almost holy way. Each and every picture becomes the icon of a martyr with a clear and dazzling brightness. It's like a filter in an app. Rado says stop, and points this out to Dóra.

'You're oversensitive,' she says accusingly. Although she's not serious, she agrees to take down all but one of the pictures of Morgan. That gives them breathing space again, because she feels the same as before. They both feel they've failed Morgan. They examine drawings and pictures Morgan put on social media. In this little flat there's just one lie that won't go away. That's referring to the missing person in the present tense, as if Morgan still breathes and laughs.

This wears off by the afternoon and they abandon the lie. Morgan can no longer be living. They have gone. They've lost track of them. They are dead. They allow this change of reference to take place. Then they put their sorrow and anger aside, concentrating on puzzling together the days they spent together investigating Morgan's disappearance. There's nothing new to be found in all the material they have.

Dóra floats the idea of again speaking to the teachers who were present on the school outing, but Rado's dubious. The word mustn't be allowed to get around at the station that they are working on the case. They're both on extended leave from duty. Rado suggests asking around about Hákon, Morgan's father. Neither of them have any real idea of how that would take things further. They just want to know how he is.

The memorial service for Morgan will take place in a few

days. There's no hope that anything there will help them, but they've decided to take the risk and attend.

It's four o'clock when Rado gets to his feet. It's time to fetch little Jurek from nursery. He can see that Dóra is exhausted. They agree to meet again and continue tomorrow. Rado asks when Jafet is expected home. After speaking to Elliði about the attempt on Dóra's life, he feels her life could be in danger. She says Jafet will be home soon, and that calms his concerns, even though there's not much that Jafet would be able to do if Artur were to make a move against her.

As Rado arrives at the nursery, the manager is there in the cloakroom. She's called Linda, and is around fifty, plump and with short grey hair. Rado has never seen her without a smile on her face. She always wears slightly hippie-style clothes in drab earth colours. She often wears a scarf on her head. The children at the nursery adore her, as does Jurek.

This time she looks serious and asks him to come to her office, where Ewa is already waiting, for a few words, and Rado follows.

'Has something happened to Jurek?' Rado asks.

'Not at all,' Linda assures him. 'I just thought we ought to have a chat about how he's getting on.' Rado takes the empty seat facing the desk, beside Ewa. 'He's a delightful boy,' Linda says, propping herself against the corner of her desk. 'But there are some changes taking place for him. Are you separating, or separated?'

'Yes,' Ewa says firmly, and blinks.

'There have been clashes with the other children,' Linda says. 'Ups and downs. There's been a bit of drama. What's he like at home?'

Rado catches Linda's eye.

'Just ... As he usually is,' Rado replied. Ewa nods agreement.

'That's the way it is sometimes. Children feel they can hold on to the way things were if only they keep to the habits they're used to. It all comes out here instead. Maybe to shield you,' Linda says, and there's no other way to take this than as an accusation. That's despite the smile.

'What do you advise we do?' Rado asks, before Ewa has an opportunity to speak.

'Make time to speak to him. Make sure he takes part in both your lives. He needs to feel he's part of it,' Linda says, and Rado instinctively grasps Ewa's hand. He knows there's a chance she'll lose it.

'We'll take care to do that,' Ewa says, teeth clenched.

The phone on Linda's desk starts to ring. She says regretfully that she'll have to take the call, and with a wave of her hand, she leaves the office. Rado and Ewa are left sitting there.

'I know things are fucked up ... But this little boy we have together ...' Ewa says quietly.

'I miss you, too,' Rado says, looking over at her. Then he stands up, goes out to the play area and takes little Jurek in his arms. He checks the cleft in the boy's chin, and his obsidian-black eyes.

Ewa is in the cloakroom when they come in. Rado feels a change in the little boy as soon as he sees his mother. All three of them in the same space. That hasn't happened for a while. He becomes suddenly tense. It's as if it's all down to him, as if he has any influence on how their futures could work out.

He takes hold of his mother's hand, still holding on tight to his father's. Rado feels a surge of sympathy for him. This was a tactic he used as well, when he was young – holding on tight to those he loved. He had the same childish belief that it could be done.

Little Jurek extracts a promise from them that they'll go to the petting zoo, all three of them. He's not letting go, and they agree. But not today. Rado's not even sure if the place is open on Mondays. He doesn't ask Ewa about any future plans. Something tells him to keep a distance for the moment. He's trying to protect her, but it's also his own cowardice. He has no idea what her reactions could be if he accuses her brother of murdering their father. He feels there needs to be some distance. Rado has no control over what Artur could tell Ewa about their father's death. That's not within his power.

37

Dóra stands facing the white Volvo. Neither Jafet nor Rado have any clue what she's up to. Jafet thinks she's taking a harmless walk around the city centre. Dóra's rationale for wanting to see if she can drive is simple. She's used to sitting behind this car's wheel, with a sandwich or a coffee, and on the phone. If she concentrates fully on driving and goes carefully, she should be able to drive it. She naturally has no idea of the extent of the damage to the parietal and occipital lobes of her brain, and how capable she is of sensing spatial relationships and other key functions that these parts of the brain control. But sometimes you just have to jump in at the deep end.

There's the rush of a familiar feeling as she sits behind the wheel. The pale leather seats are cold to the touch and she senses a faint aroma of oil. The Volvo judders into life as she turns the key, and she gives it some gas.

So far, so good.

For the last few months the car has stood outside the music school on Lindargata. Jafet has a friend there who let him leave the car in its parking lot. Dóra turns out of the car park and onto Sæbraut. She flicks on the radio and the car's filled with chugging techno. She quickly turns it off. Indistinct images flicker through her mind.

She drags open the workshop door. Someone's in there. The lights don't work. She stands in the darkness.

Dóra draws a deep breath. The iPad is on the passenger

seat at her side. Without meaning to, she drives to Morgan's home in the Laugarnes district. She pulls up outside and kills the engine. She recalls coming to this place early one morning with two police officers. That was the time her eye started to bleed. She tries to relive this experience from what Rado has told her about that day. It's practically impossible. She gets out of the Volvo and walks up the drive to the house. She's gripped by an emotion that's difficult to define. It's most like floundering for something she's forgotten. But no, she hasn't forgotten anything.

'So you're back,' a voice behind her says. She turns to see a freckled, flabby woman with green eyes and a sharp nose, standing in the doorway of the house next door.

'Have we met before?' Dóra asks, crossing the drive towards the woman.

'Aren't you from the cops?'

'Yes.' Dóra adjusts the cap she borrowed from Jafet. Her head itches beneath it. 'When was that?'

'A few months ago,' the woman says haltingly. 'About the time Morgan disappeared.'

'Sure,' Dóra says, and takes off the cap. The scar on her head doesn't escape the woman's gaze, and her eyes widen. 'Have you seen anything of her dad?'

'He's in long-term rehab, somewhere out of town,' the woman says. 'Everything went wrong for him after Morgan disappeared, the poor man. Or got worse, let's say. Pretty much everything was going wrong for him before. He lost his job and everything.'

'Where was he working?' Dóra asks and the question results in an odd look on the woman's face. 'I'm sorry I have to ask. I had an accident. My memory isn't as good as it was.'

The woman relaxes a little.

'Well, yes. He was working on that new skyscraper uptown. Elysium.'

Dóra thanks the woman for her help and goes to the

basement flat's window. The curtains are drawn. She knows what the place is like. There are pictures on the iPad of the flat. She remembers some things, such as Morgan's room. She remembers her drawings, and the sketchbook she's sure was missing from the drawer. Dóra looks around but can't see the neighbour anywhere.

Getting inside is no problem. The door's not even locked. Dóra stands still for a moment. It's perfectly silent in there. She goes into the living room. It's deserted, but cardboard boxes are stacked up on the floor. Dóra reaches for a switch, but nothing happens. No doubt the power's been cut off. It's more than likely Hákon's going to lose the flat. She checks the kitchen. The cupboard doors hang open and there's a milk carton on the table. A few plates have been wrapped in sheets of newspaper. It's as if Hákon has walked away from an unfinished task, simply run out of steam and gone into rehab.

Morgan's room is exactly as Dóra saw it last. It's as she remembers it. She sits at the desk and opens the drawers where she found the teen's sketchbooks that time before. They're still there. She pauses at a coloured drawing of the tower. She hesitates, and then, as carefully as she can, she tears the drawing from the book.

Dóra's back behind the Volvo's wheel when her phone starts to vibrate. It's Jafet calling. It's only half an hour since she went out. She picks up, tells him she's still walking and is fine, that she'll soon be home. The problem with the trauma she's suffered is that it doesn't just hurt the victim. It batters everyone around her as well. It varies in degrees, but recently she feels Jafet is stifling her. It doesn't help that they live in just a few square metres. She'll have to do something. It's time to move out and recover her independence.

'Where's the lube?' There's accusation in Jafet's voice. Dóra's struggling not to laugh. 'Where have you been?'

He folds his arms as they face each other, standing in the living room. She looks back at him and tilts her head to one side.

Why's he so angry?

There's a hell of a lot she's forgotten, but somehow she clearly recalls the frequent arguments with this long-haired, fair-haired man she lives or stays with.

'What are you thinking?' she asks at last.

'You're ill. You have to watch your step. People who suffer brain injuries need to be careful. They're more prone to infections.'

'No need to google me, OK? You're not my dad. And you're not my boyfriend either. You've been totally brilliant. I don't know what I would have done if I hadn't been able to stay with you. But if I recall correctly, you moved out. We split up. Many times. Wasn't there a reason for that?'

Dóra places her hands on her hips.

'It was ... I ...' Jafet stammers.

'You can't be worthy and annoyed at the same time. I might have brain damage, but I can see it's not working between us,' Dóra says.

'But you ... but you ...' Jafet blinks relentlessly.

'It's true, isn't it? Nobody's asking you to be a saint. I need to find another place to live. It's not the end of the world.'

Dóra looks around and picks up her backpack.

'Hold on! Are you leaving? What about your medication ...? You're in no state to ...' Jafet holds up his hands.

'I'm discharging myself. From this relationship, or whatever it is.' Dóra stuffs her belongings into her backpack. In the bathroom she clears the cabinet of all her medication, leaving it practically empty. 'Could I hold on to the iPad for a few more days?' she asks Jafet as she emerges from the bathroom. His thoughts elsewhere, he nods.

'It looks so ... crazy. That you're splitting up with me. I ... People ...'

'They can fuck themselves. Thanks for everything. See you,' she says, shuts the door behind her and stumbles down the cramped stairway, out onto where Laugavegur is alive with people. Spring is finally here.

38

The Groke stands in the meat packing plant and checks out the team. He's in black from top to toe. These are all men he's picked himself. He's worked with some of them before, while those he doesn't know come highly recommended. Word gets around.

The Groke pulls a chair over to the table where the laptop is running a live stream from the gang's headquarters, and sits down. There's just one entrance to the industrial unit where the gang has its base. That makes everything so much simpler. He reckons there are around twenty of them there. As far as they know, there are no firearms on the site. But there are no doubt knives, tasers and blunt instruments. There could be a shotgun.

He raises his eyes from the screen and gazes at the team. Their energy is kept in check. They're saving themselves. Some of them stretch, getting their heads geared up. They're akin to athletes. They'll all be gone tomorrow, taking morning flights to Europe. Travelling alone, no two in the same plane. There's nothing to connect them. They'll all be dressed like tourists who have been hiking in the mountains. Anyway, that's not far removed from reality. None of them has a criminal record. None of them will ring any alarm bells at border checks.

He had brooded for a long time over whether or not to take the risk of a return to Iceland. He eventually decided to go for it. That trip hadn't worked out exactly as he had planned. He should never have taken the job at the carpenter's workshop. According to Artur, there's no chance of him being picked up by border control. That's already been fixed. They have a free hand as long as they don't rock the boat. Europol's not looking for him. This should all work out fine.

The target this time is a biker gang that stole two hundred kilos of speed from Artur and his people a few months ago. Now it's payback, and time to collect whatever's left of the gear, plus make sure what's missing is paid for. Artur's too canny to use his own people for an operation like this. That's likely to get too messy. The Groke and his guys are much more skilled. They won't depart from the plan, which is to beat, break and disable. But no killing. That gets too complicated. It creates too much noise. Iceland's too small for that kind of stuff.

All the same, they went pretty close to the line when they interrogated the man who betrayed Artur. This was the one who thought he could take over from old Jurek. He did a deal with the top biker to tell them where the speed was, against a payment. His plan was to get rid of Artur and take over. After applying all the right pressure, the Groke and his people know everything they need about the bikers and their clubhouse. He checks the time, and signals to his men. They nod and make their way smartly to the exits. There are two jeeps with darkened windows outside. They get in and set off. They take care not to go too fast. The Groke drives the first one. The city's streets are still familiar from his younger years. His thoughts go to Rado and his little son.

He hadn't thought about him for years. He buried him and his parents at the back of his mind when he fled Iceland. Since their encounter at the workshop, memories have been returning. Not that he wants them to. They don't worry him, don't cut deep. These are just images, fragments of a former life. He doesn't do anything with them, but just lets them pass on by like the fleeting memories they are. He doesn't try to analyse or digest them. He stands apart from them. It's as if there's a plate-glass wall between him and the person he once was.

It's a twenty-minute drive to the industrial district where the Sons of the Gods have their lair. The Groke has already checked out the surroundings. There are only companies there. It's more than likely there are some security cameras. But they'll all be masked on the way in and the way out – and long gone by the time there are any repercussions. There are no children at the location, but there could be women. Since the bikers got hold of the gear, their entourage has grown. He notices a van parked across the street, opposite the clubhouse. That's some of Artur's people. Their job is to take the stuff and any valuables once the Groke and his team have finished their work. The jeeps turn into the street, without increasing their speed.

As they pull up outside the industrial unit, they get out silently. Loud rock music blares from inside. One of the team takes out a battery-powered saw and slices through the lock in a shower of sparks. Then they storm in. The Groke is in the lead. It's a simple plan. It's to push up the stairs to the upper level. One man is stationed at the outside door with a gun that fires forty-millimetre rubber bullets, the same as the cops use on demonstrators. These aren't lethal, but not far off. It depends how you handle it. His task is to make sure nobody leaves. The rest of the Groke's team are tasked with overpowering the gang members. They're armed with clubs, claw hammers and roughly one-metre-long whips of steel wire. The Groke has brass knuckles. To begin with, the bikers don't realise what's happening. They've been on the alert now for weeks, and nothing's happened. Artur has made no attempt to retrieve the gear. The concluded finally that he either didn't dare, or else he didn't have the manpower for it, that the police raids had left him completely out of the game. A third possibility never occurred to them, that it was part of the game plan to leave them alone to become forgetful and feel secure. The moment the Groke smashes in the face the first one to try to stop him, bending his brass knuckles as he does so, is when they realise just how mistaken they've been. There's a gradual realisation among the biker gang that this is a systematic assault. They do their best to resist but it's hopeless. The Groke's men overpower them, one after another, and slam them to the floor where they're tied hand and foot like pigs ready for slaughter. They've done this many times before, first in the service of sovereign states and military forces, and now as contractors on the open market. At first the long-haired, leather-clad men believe this is a police SWAT team. Then they realise it isn't. Not one of the men in black has said a single word, let alone informed them that they're under arrest. This is something very different.

The Groke pauses on the stairs and reviews the scene in front of him. His men have this completely under control. They're quick, and very precise, at any rate for an operation like this. There are more skilled operators available, but that would be overdoing it. The Groke rushes up the steps and faces Nóri in the doorway. He's brandishing a sword. It's not a handy weapon for a tight space, with no room to swing. The Groke uses his bodyweight to slam him against the wall that separates the offices on the upper floor. He knocks him out with a right hook to the temple. The large, leather-and-denim clad body collapses at his feet. The Groke takes hold of the scruff of his neck and checks the back of the denim waistcoat, emblazoned with the word *President*. He hauls him to the steps and pushes the unconscious figure so he tumbles down them. His head hits the floor with a loud crack. Someone switches off the music. The Groke has never understood biker gangs. Why advertise that you're a criminal? He goes back to the offices to check that there's nobody there. They're deserted. The last of the air has been let out of a balloon that's been stuffed with pure amphetamine these last few months.

The Groke goes slowly down the steps and takes out a pair of wire cutters. The hog-tied men strewn like driftwood across the floor watch in horror as the Groke drops to his haunches and cuts off Nóri's fingers. Nóri surfaces briefly as the first one comes off, and then he passes out again. It's as if his body senses the pain that's to come and has decided to keep him unconscious.

One of the Groke's men goes among the tied men and tapes their mouths shut. Another comes into the room with a wheelbarrow that's full of hammers. The Groke nods, his men pick up the hammers and they set about systematically beating the biker gang's members. They break bones and damage internal organs. Some of the hammers have rubber heads, the blows from which turn innards into jelly.

One of Artur's men appears in the doorway and steps cautiously inside. He looks at the battleground and takes out a phone. He says a few words in Polish and two other men appear and begin a systematic search for the drugs. It's not more than five minutes since the door was broken open.

Not a word is said. This is the Groke's order. There's no space here for words, no room for language. It just complicates matters. It leaves space for orders, threats, pleas for mercy. It slows things down. This is work to be done mindfully and in silence. That makes for clarity and flow.

One of Artur's men nods to the Groke. The stuff has been found. The Groke gives his men a signal and they drop the hammers that clatter to the white-painted concrete floor.

Red on white. Job done.

39

Dóra splashes out and takes a room at Hotel Holt. It's only a single room, but it's not as if she needs much space. There's an old-fashioned charm to this place. She checks in, drops her backpack in the room, and goes down to the cognac lounge to recline on the leather sofa and order herself a drink.

She examines the drawing of the tower she tore from Morgan's sketchbook. She wakes the iPad and looks through the case files. But the words begin to dance before her eyes so she puts it aside. All the same, she has a vague intuition that this tower and its construction have something to do with Morgan's disappearance. It's just a hunch. She picks up the iPad again, and searches online for everything she can find about Elysium.

She finds a slew of articles about the plans for the tower, the ecological thinking behind it and more of the same. But there's also negative comment. Some of those behind these articles are environmentalists who claim that the tower's builders are giving the public greenwash, that it's not about the recyclable building materials but the effect the building will have on the natural world around it. Several well-known commentators are scathing about the prices of suites in the tower and the fact that the area around it is both closed off to unauthorised access and guarded in a way that's reminiscent of a Hollywood movie in which the rich and the poor are kept carefully separate.

But to Dóra's way of thinking, they're missing the point. Elysium is simply the peak of what has long been happening in this stratified society where the lower classes are largely migrant foreign labour. These are the people who mop floors and wipe arses, and their skin is mostly darker than that of the arses they keep clean. She shuts down the iPad, knocks back what's left of her drink and gets to her feet. Her eyelids are getting heavy.

She goes to the lift and the doors slide open. She selects the third floor. For some reason she finds herself humming a song on the way up. *You're not Alone.* She has no idea what song this is, or how she comes to know it.

*

Dóra has breakfast at Hotel Holt among the tourists chattering in a muttered babel of languages. She understands fragments here and there, but not everything. The language receptors in her head are too damaged. That's all right, she thinks. Not understanding gives the brain a chance to rest.

She spies Rado in the doorway and waves to him. He comes across and sits at her table, facing her.

'You could have crashed at my place,' he says, pouring himself a cup of coffee.

'I'll be here for the moment. Then we'll see.'

Dóra tries to spread a piece of bread with butter and jam. Her movements are like those of a child.

'Did something come up between you?'

'We had an argument about lube.'

'As happens,' Rado says with a sigh.

'Would you butter this for me?' Dóra pushes the plate across to Rado.

'Jafet said you went somewhere yesterday. In the car?' he says.

'Did he call you?'

'He's worried about you,' Rado says, as he slides the plate back to her and watches as Dóra tries to pick up the slice of bread. He can see that she's exhausted. That makes the small things so much harder. 'Can I ask where you went?'

'To Morgan's home.'

'What for?'

'I don't know. Maybe just to see if I could jog my own memory.'

'And?' Rado waits. He knows from experience that she might not manage eating and speaking at the same time. Finally, she swallows.

'Look at this.' She hands Rado Morgan's drawing of the tower.

'What's this?' Rado sips his coffee.

'Found it in Morgan's sketchbook,' Dóra says, glancing around as a group of Chinese tourists storms into the dining room.

'What is this?' Rado inspects the drawing of the tower. 'I mean, I can see it's a sketch of Elysium, but what's significant about it?'

'The first time I went to that basement flat and checked their room, I had the feeling they were ready to leave. Whether they were planning to run away, or do something dramatic, such as suicide, I couldn't say. But they left behind these old sketchbooks. This drawing was in one of them. Take a close look,' she says, pointing with a finger that trembles.

Rado peers at it again.

'It's a picture that she ... they drew of the tower,' Rado says and shrugs. 'So what?'

'I've checked everything I can find online about Elysium, all the outlines of how it's supposed to look. You know these computer-generated images are never quite how a building turns out to be. But this drawing is exactly like the tower. For example, this was changed.' She points to a neon yellow girder that spans the lobby. 'That's not on any of the plans that I've seen. And look at these.' Dóra points at the glass balconies that encircle the middle of the tower.

'And what does this mean?' Rado asks.

'We need to speak to Hákon, Morgan's father. There has to be a connection between Morgan and the tower.'

*

They track Hákon down to the Vík rehab centre. It's in Kjalarnes, half an hour from the city, so it's not as if he had gone far in his quest to get his life back on track. After a short conversation with the rehab manager, a woman of around thirty, they're given an office where they can talk to Hákon. They wait for him in the corridor. When he appears, accompanied by the rehab manager who looks as if she bears sole responsibility for rescuing Hákon from his demons, he's barely recognisable. He's put on some weight and there's some colour to his cheeks. He looks awkwardly at Dóra and Rado, grasping the rehab manager's hand for support.

'This is just a chat, isn't it?' the woman asks. 'You haven't ... y'know ... found anything, or ...?'

'No. We haven't found them,' Dóra says. 'We just have a few questions.'

'You're up to this?' the rehab manager asks and Hákon nods. He's suddenly as pale as a ghost.

They sit in the office and Hákon takes a good look at the long scar on Dóra's head, without saying anything. The rehab manager waits outside.

'Did they go with you up to Elysium?' Dóra asks.

'Yes. Sometimes,' Hákon says. 'She thought it was exciting, the tower.'

'And this was acceptable? I mean, this is an area with security all round. It's not as if just anyone could march in there,' Rado says.

'It wasn't a problem. She just sat in the site office and

drew and stuff. Sometimes she went up with me, when I was working in the top-floor suites. Where you met me,' Hákon says, glancing at Dóra.

'Where I met you?' Dóra asks in surprise.

'The day she disappeared,' Hákon says.

'Yes, of course. How often did they go up there with you?' Dóra asks, taking out the iPad.

'This thing with *they*. Sorry. And this Morgan stuff. Her name's Guðbjörg and she's a girl,' Hákon says in irritation.

'Of course,' Rado says. 'How often did she go with you up there?'

'Just a few times. I don't know. Maybe five, six times. What's this about, exactly?' Hákon asks, looking at them in turn. 'Is she dead? Have you found her?'

'No,' Dóra replies and shows Hákon the iPad screen. 'Is there anyone you can think of she could have got to know there?'

'No. I didn't notice anyone,' Hákon says calmly and shakes his head. 'Do you suspect anyone?'

'No,' Dóra says. 'But we're doing everything we can to solve this case.'

'What case?' Hákon asks suddenly.

'What do you mean?' Rado asks, looking at him intently.

'Is this a missing person or a murder case? There has to be a difference, right?' Rado and Dóra say nothing. 'She's dead, isn't she?'

'I think we can assume that,' Rado says quietly.

'They say you can't get through this twelve steps thing they have here without a little bit of hope. Of something ... better. That it's within reach.' Hákon coughs, tears in his eyes. 'Find her for me so I can say a proper goodbye. I'll stay clean until then.'

He gets to his feet, opens the door and slips away.

'We need a word with Elliði,' Rado says in the jeep outside the rehab clinic.

'What for?' Dóra asks.

'We need a list of everyone who's worked on that tower. That could throw us a lead.' Rado's brows knit in thought.

'And we can't forget the employment agencies. Half of the workforce on this came from Eastern Europe. Romania and Albania.'

Dóra sighs.

'Do you really not remember going up into Elysium?' Rado asks, glancing at Dóra.

'I thought I'd dreamed it.'

'Fuck,' Rado whispers as he pulls the jeep away from the rehab clinic.

*

It's Indriði, Elliði's boyfriend, who opens the door for Rado and Dóra at the house in the Kórar district. He's dressed in a suit and white trainers, which is the uniform of the budget airline for which he works as a flight attendant.

Indriði's on his way out, and Elliði has just got out of the bath. Indriði excuses himself and asks them to wait in the living room, as he's going to be late for work. They both sense that beneath the courteous exterior, there's something bothering Indriði. A few moments later Elliði makes an appearance, wearing pyjama trousers and a dressing gown.

'What's his problem?' Dóra jerks her head in the direction of the front door, and then catches Elliði's eye.

'He thinks we should adopt ... a child,' Elliði says, rolling his eyes.

He wears white trainers to work. He's a child himself, Dóra catches herself thinking.

'We've only been together five minutes,' Elliði continues, going over to a desk under the window and switching on a laptop. 'Can I get you anything?' he asks, sitting down at the computer.

Dóra and Rado shake their heads, and then explain their presence.

'Well, I have a pal who was in the financial crimes division,' Elliði says. 'I had him check out Elysium for me. It's a holding company called Elysian that had the tower built. It brought in KM, which is the main contractor, and then there are all the subcontractors, electrics, plumbing, and all sorts. That's hundreds of people. Isn't this on the shaky side? I mean, a drawing in a sketch book?'

'We must be able to narrow things down,' Dóra says. 'We can focus on those who were directly involved with the construction site. Check them out against the records.'

'In any case, we'll have to slim the names down before I run them through the LÖKE database. We'll see if any of them have convictions for sexual offences,' Elliði says. 'What about the drawing? Where could she have seen that? From the site manager or the architect?'

'She could have seen a picture of the final version of the tower in one of the site offices, and copied it,' Rado says. 'The question is whether you can contact KM and get a list of all those who were at the site?'

'Let's start there,' Elliði says, standing up. 'Are we any closer? Anything coming back to you related to the raids?' he asks, looking at Dóra, who shakes her head cautiously.

'Not a thing.'

40

Rado picks Elliði up at Hlemmur the next morning. He woke him up with a phone call, stressing that they needed to let Dóra sleep.

As he pulls up outside this former bus station that for so long had been almost an extension of the police station nearby, where colourful characters hung out when they weren't in the cells across the street, he can't help but be astonished at the change that's taken place. It would never have occurred to him that this place could become a gourmet's paradise. He finds it absolutely bizarre. But this is the new Iceland. There's designer coffee and sweet pulled meat on sourdough bread on offer everywhere. Rado has a loathing of sourdough. Ewa drove him crazy with it during lockdown. She nurtured the culture and baked remorselessly. It was practically abuse by carbohydrate. The freezer in the basement is still stuffed with it.

Rado notices a man in a dun-colour suit sitting alone at a table. His hands cover his face. It's Indriði. Rado acts as if nothing's out of the ordinary as Elliði gets into the jeep. Elliði has a high turnover rate when it comes to boyfriends and partners.

'Where are we going?' Rado asks. Elliði rolls down the window and lights a cigarette.

'Down to Hafnarfjörður,' he says. 'That's where this character lives.'

He holds out his phone for Rado to see the screen.

'Who's this?'

'Guðbergur Smári. He did time for deprivation of liberty and rape. He was inside from 2009 to 2012. I checked on him. We had him lined up for a few other things as well, but the prosecutor didn't think we had enough to pin him down. He's a total sleazebag,' Elliði says, rubbing his eyes.

'You all right?' Rado asks.

'You mean Indriði?' Elliði glares.

'No, no,' Rado says. 'Or, yes.'

'I finished it. It's complicated, but thanks for asking.'

'Isn't it brutal dumping someone this early in the morning?'

'He has a flight to catch,' Elliði says, dropping the cigarette out of the window and rolling it shut.

Guðbergur Smári's registered address is one of a terrace of houses in the new district outside Hafnarfjörður. According to the KM personnel manager, the man's on leave after a minor accident at the tower construction site. Elliði's fairly sure he'll be at home. The plan is to take the temperature and see how it feels. If they feel it's worth it, they can take him to the station in Hafnarfjörður to take his statement.

It's almost nine by the time Rado turns into the cul-de-sac where Guðbergur Smári lives. There's a drizzle of rain and nobody's about. He parks the jeep and they both get out.

'I'll take the lead,' Elliði says and Rado nods as they go up the paved path to the front door. There's a little white van marked with the KM logo in the drive. Rado and Elliði both take a long look at it. Elliði stretches his neck before he rings the bell. A moment later the door swings open and a tall man of around fifty faces them. He has a crooked nose and bright blue eyes, and his face is covered with tiny deep scars from forehead to chin. He's wearing a chequered dressing gown that hangs open, over a *Ready to roll my rock* tee-shirt.

'Are you Jehovah's Witnesses?' he asks at last.

'No. We're the police,' Elliði replies. 'Guðbergur Smári?'

'Yes,' he says, pushing the door wide open with a broad hand. 'Come on in.'

Rado and Elliði follow him inside.

'Wife's not home,' he says, as if that's the reason he decided to let them in. He ushers them to the living room. 'What do you want?' he asks, arms folded. Rado tries to get a feel for the man, but he's not easily gauged. It's also hard to look him in the face. The scars are so disfiguring that the instinct is to look away.

'We just wanted a chat,' Elliði says, and Rado can tell from his tone of voice that he's been taken by surprise.

'Sit down.' Guðbergur Smári gestures to the living-room table. 'There's coffee in the pot.' Before Rado and Elliði can say anything, he's disappeared into the kitchen. A moment later he's back with a coffee pot, milk, a sugar bowl and three cups lined up on a tray. He places everything on the table and then takes a seat. Elliði and Rado feel forced to sit down as well. Guðbergur Smári pours coffee for them and pushes the tray towards them so they can help themselves to milk and sugar. Rado looks around the living room. On the wall hangs a large framed painting of Jesus with two children standing on a bridge that looks to be somewhere in the Alps – however that could have come about. An old Yamaha keyboard occupies a space opposite the sofa that looks like it came from the home of someone who died, or from a charity shop. The living room looks like it's been furnished entirely from there, when the staff take it into their heads to showcase a living-room vibe from the thirties or forties. The present day makes its presence felt as a Huawei modem's lights flicker on the telephone table by the window.

'What happened to you?' Elliði asks, sipping his coffee.

'Got a faceful of steel splinters. I got cut up all over. I was working in a machine shop,' Guðbergur Smári says.

'No, I mean why are you at home now?' Elliði places his cup on the table. 'An accident at work?'

'Yeah, this time,' Guðbergur Smári says, lighting a cigarette. 'I caught Covid. I've been getting migraine attacks ever since. They just ... knock me right out.'

'How long have you been working for KM Contractors?' Elliði asks.

'What has that to do with anything?' Guðbergur Smári asks placidly, sipping his coffee. Rado almost expects it to start dripping from the deep scars on his cheeks, as if they're gills. 'Probably about five years altogether.'

'So you were working at Elysium?' Elliði says and Rado is sure that he's decided there's no point trying to weigh up Guðbergur Smári. He's not picking anything up, no flickers of expression. According to what Elliði told him on the way, it was discussed at the time whether or not Guðbergur Smári had any conscience, as the psychologist failed to get him to accept any responsibility for his actions. In his case, this was the brutal kidnap and rape of a teenage girl. This called for a more intensive kind of interrogation in a more confined space than this suburban living room.

'I'm still working there,' Guðbergur Smári says, holding Elliði's gaze fixedly, as he has done since he brought in the tray of coffee. It's another symptom of an empathy shortfall.

'Isn't the construction finished?' Rado puts in, and Guðbergur Smári turns his head to look at him.

'Finished and not finished,' he says, leaning back in his seat. 'I can tell you I saw a programme on Discovery the other day about a church, or a temple rather, in Japan. Every twenty years, this church, temple, whatever, is demolished and rebuilt as it was before. They reckon this has been going on for almost two thousand years. They say it's done at the architect's request. The Japanese, I mean. There's nothing wrong to be seen there, I mean it never weathers. Some people say it's symbolic, that this circle of demolition and rebuilding is some kind of concept of eternity. The point with a building like Elysium is that work never comes to an end. There's constant maintenance going on.'

'And you're part of that?'

'Yes, but not just me. There's quite a few of us. What's this about, anyway? What do you want from me?' he asks, sounding barely interested.

'Did you ever see this girl at Elysium?' Elliði hands him a printout of the photo of Morgan. Guðbergur Smári takes it and peers at it.

'No, can't say that I have,' he says at last, folds the picture in two and tosses it back across the table.

If their plan was to take the temperature before going any further, then it's clearly close to freezing in this living room.

Elliði's silent to start with on the way back downtown. Then it's as if a turbine in his head has kicked into gear.

'We need to check the CCTV at Thingvellir. At the hospitality centre. All the pictures in the report. See if he's on any of them. Or that van. Rado, you're going to have to shadow him.'

Elliði fishes out a cigarette and lights up.

'Dóra and I are both formally still on leave,' Rado says.

'Still getting a paycheque, aren't you?' Elliði asks.

'Yes,' Rado agrees with a nod.

'Then won't you follow this up?'

'You think that if he took her, she's still alive?' Rado asks after a moment's silence.

'We ... Well. I don't know,' he says at last, puffing out smoke. 'I'll get confirmation of whether he was at work or off sick on the day Morgan disappeared.'

Rado feels a pang as Elliði speaks her name. Then his phone starts to buzz. Dóra's calling. He has an intuition that today he'll have to ask Ewa to fetch the lad from nursery. It's going to be a long day.

Dóra's in the breakfast room when Rado gets to Hotel Holt, having dropped Elliði off at the station on Hverfisgata. She looks rested and doesn't appear to be having any trouble buttering her toast. There's a scattering of tourists in the room. Rado has to wait a moment before he can squeeze past the crowd at the buffet. He casts an eye over the paintings that adorn the walls, admiring a landscape of an expanse of lava, berry-rich tundra and distant peaks. The picture is reminiscent of Thingvellir, even though he's not sure if it is there or not. He gets the feeling he's looking at a photo of a crime scene, that Morgan's rotting corpse is lying there beneath the surface.

Dóra nods to him as he sits opposite her and recounts the trip to Hafnarfjörður. Even though there's hardly a chance anyone there will understand them, he keeps almost to a whisper, all the same.

'What do we do now?' Dóra asks.

'We need to check all the imagery from Thingvellir. See if we can catch a sight of him. Or his car. He has a KM Contractors van. No windows in the back. I noted down the number.'

His voice quivers slightly.

Dóra's clearly made friends among the staff of the hotel and gets them into the cognac lounge that's normally not open until late in the afternoon, so they can speak undisturbed.

'Why didn't you call me?' she asks when they're sitting in the deep leather armchairs in one corner of the lounge.

'We wanted to let you sleep,' Rado says.

'I'd have wanted to go with you,' Dóra says shortly.

'I suspect that's not the last time we'll be speaking to this man. There's something crooked about him.

Something dark.' Rado takes his laptop from his backpack, calls up a photo of Guðbergur Smári and shows Dóra. 'Do you remember seeing him? He's been working at Elysium since construction started. He's still working there.'

'No,' Dóra says, and hands the computer back to Rado. 'I reckon that's a face I'd remember.'

They sit for a while and go through images from the report. Dóra used the iPad and Rado the computer. He fast-forwards through the CCTV footage from the hospitality centre, but Guðbergur Smári is nowhere to be seen. He must have taken care to keep out of sight.

Dóra's the one who catches a glimpse of the white van, in the car park outside the hospitality centre, in the background of one the pictures taken by Morgan's classmates. The KM Contractors logo on the side is clearly visible.

'That's him,' Dóra says, handing him the iPad. He examines the image and tries to zoom in on the van, but the phone image isn't in high resolution and the registration plate isn't in the picture. Rado scans through other pictures taken by Morgan's class, but this is the only one that shows the van.

'We have to be certain. KM Contractors is a big company. We have to make sure they weren't working up there in the national park,' Rado says, handing the iPad back to Dóra, reaching for his phone and calling Elliði, who tells him he's been trying to reach the personnel manager at KM Contractors but the man's on a flight to Copenhagen. He's expecting a call when his flight lands so they can check if Guðbergur Smári was at work or at home on the day of Morgan's disappearance.

'I'll go out to Thingvellir and see if any of the staff remember seeing him. I know it's a long shot, but it's worth a try,' Rado says, slipping the laptop into his backpack.

'A long shot? The guy looks like Freddy Kruger. Nobody's going to forget that face,' Dóra says.

'Did Morgan have an iPad or a computer?'

'No. The class had laptops for homework. But these had all been handed in a month before the trip to Thingvellir. There was nothing to be found on the computer they had. What are you thinking?'

'In the cases he went down for, he groomed his victims online. If he abducted Morgan, then he must have used the same method. Set up a meeting, and so on. The shoe and coat indicate that she didn't go willingly.' Rado gets to his feet. 'Did Morgan have a debit card? Isn't giving gifts part of grooming? Wouldn't it have been easiest to put money into her account?'

'I'll check the statements. I don't recall there were many transactions on there. Her father sometimes paid in small amounts for her, and she earned some money from youth work last summer.'

Her last summer, Dóra thinks.

'OK,' Rado says. 'I'll be in touch.'

The hospitality centre's packed when Rado arrives at Thingvellir. He parks the jeep and gets out. He has a photo of Guðbergur Smári on his phone and takes a close look at it. It's almost a cliché. The guy looks like the axe murderer in a bad movie. He's not sure he'd believe that the cops were looking for someone like this. Most people would think he's joking. But the staff are painfully aware of Morgan's disappearance. People have drowned in the lake or lost their lives in accidents, but the possible abduction of a teenager is something different. Rado knows that there were prayers for them recently in the church at Thingvellir, and there was a newspaper article about the disappearance. As always, there were veiled accusations of racism within the force and the general lack of concern for Icelanders of foreign origin, immigrants, foreigners and asylum seekers. There was not a word about him being of foreign ancestry, or that his colleague had almost lost her life in the search for Morgan.

*

Dóra hesitates for a moment, and then takes the right turn onto Sæbraut, the direction leading out to the city's edge and to Elysium. She feels compelled to go out there. Maybe that'll help bring back something more. There's no mention of her visit to Hákon in the case files. No doubt she hadn't had time to update the system before she was assaulted. She recalls just fragments of that call. She sees herself watching Hákon on his knees, laying tiles in the vast bathroom. She remembers counting the tiles. That was when she informed the parent that his child was missing. So that was to distract herself. Or it was because she's sick in the head.

She wonders whether or not to call Rado but decides against it. He wouldn't be overjoyed to know she's driving. But it's not just that. It's because she isn't properly able to put into words what's taking her up there.

There's traffic at the Elysium gate. The last part of the way leading up there is a private road and Dóra watches the luxury SUVs and sports cars coming and going as the drivers flash a card against a reader by the gate. Dóra waits patiently in the queue behind an electric BMW that looks like it's been plucked from a Batman movie.

There are two security guards on duty in a little hut by the gate. Maybe *hut* isn't the right word for this guardhouse that's built in the same style as the tower. It's a mixture of grey Siberian wood, concrete and neon-coloured girders. It's the same style but not on the same scale. The guardhouse is like a miniature version of the distant tower. Dóra fishes her ID paperwork from the glove compartment and winds down the window of the Volvo, which looks seriously out of place among all the other vehicles.

'Who are you?' the security guy asks.

Dóra holds her identification up for him to see. He squints at it, then nods and the gate lifts open. She puts her foot down and drives along the winding road that passes through the lava fields up to the tower. It's not far. To the left is a sign indicating the residents' car park, and another for guests. Dóra notices a gaggle of smartly-dressed people making their way from the car park to the main doors. Judging by their appearance, she's sure these aren't residents but visitors. There must be some big event taking place.

She gets out of the Volvo, leaving it parked in a visitor space. She's stiff after being behind the wheel, and her hips hurt. It's not just her car that looks out of place. She's dressed as if she's heading up into the mountains, in a waterproof coat, thick sweater, walking trousers and trainers. Women with brain damage avoid heels. Dóra wonders why intelligent women don't do the same.

She catches sight of a group of people in their best clothes heading for the main entrance. She stays behind, almost in the lee of them. She follows them into the tower. The entrance resembles the lobby of a luxury hotel, or a modern art gallery. A cocktail party is taking place. There's finger food and champagne. A jazz band is playing on a dais in one corner.

Dóra recognises faces in the crowd. There are people here from the worlds of business, politics and the arts. The band suddenly falls silent and a spotlight somewhere in the room picks out the smiling face of a man in a black suit and a white shirt.

'Good evening and welcome,' he says, and then repeats himself in English as he makes a short speech about the tower, how it came to be, and announces that this evening there will be apartments open for viewing on every floor, including the penthouse and the roof garden, from where the firework display scheduled for dusk can be seen. It's clear that he knows the majority of those present, since he doesn't bother introducing himself by name. Dóra's sure she's seen pictures of this man in the news and assumes he's the architect who designed the tower. All the same, she's not completely sure. She catches sight of the Minister of Justice, the Parliamentary President and Chief Superintendent Bjarki Freyr in person among the guests. She sidles towards the lifts, which stand open and are watched by a group of black-clad security guards.

Dóra steps past them and into one of the lifts that quickly fills with people before the door shuts. Someone presses a button and the lift shoots upwards. It stops at the fourth floor, where a group gets out. The button's pressed again, and the doors hiss shut. This time it's going all the way – to the rooftop apartment. Dóra listens to people speaking in the lift. According to them, the buyer of one of the penthouses is an American influencer who got rich by letting people watch him play computer games online. Dóra doesn't catch his name. Not that she would recognise him if she were to bump into him. The names of the owners of the other three penthouses are mentioned in the lift, which stops a minute later and the doors open.

She leaves the lift and looks around. She has a recollection of having been here before. But that was different. She just doesn't remember. The passage looked quite different then. It had been a shell. Dóra is certain this has to be some kind of service entrance. In the brochure she picked up down in the lobby there was something about the penthouses having their own lifts that opened directly into the apartments.

An Asian woman with a floor-polishing machine almost sneaks past her, avoiding eye contact. The door of one penthouse stands open and Dóra goes inside. The place looks familiar, although it's a far cry from the space she visited before. She wanders through the empty apartment and admires the fabulous view. In the middle of the apartment she comes across a spiral staircase she recalls seeing before. She goes up the steps and is now more sure of herself. She's been here before. This was where she met Hákon. She goes along the passage to the bathroom, which she's certain is behind a door, and opens it. Standing in the doorway she has a vision of Hákon, crouched on his knees, laying tiles. The bathroom is large, and tastefully outfitted. But there's something about it that's not the way she remembered. Dóra can't work out what it is. She stands still for a while, trying to recall.

'Like the look of it?' a voice behind her asks. Dóra turns and sees the suited man who just now was in the spotlight, addressing guests.

'Looks good,' Dóra says, with an appreciative nod. The man smiles amiably, but Dóra senses a tension. There's a strange electricity about him.

'I'm told you're from the police,' the man says.

'Yes.'

'Was something reported, or ...'

'No, nothing like that. What was your name again?' Dóra asks.

'Huginn. I designed the tower.'

'Of course. Now it's coming back to me,' Dóra says. 'Why did you choose that name? Elysium? Were all the names from Norse mythology already spoken for?'

'I suppose so. But I didn't think up the name. We have people who do that stuff. It comes from Greek mythology. It means heaven,' Huginn says.

'That's maybe more appropriate,' Dóra says, adjusting the cap on her head. 'If I recall correctly, heaven was just for the selected few. Gods and their friends.'

'It's just a name,' Huginn shrugs. 'A name for a building. You should take a look at the roof garden.'

His phone begins to ring and Dóra watches as he takes it from his pocket, answers and marches along the passage and down the spiral stairs. He's a good-looking man, and looks fit. But oddly broad across the hips.

41

Dóra stands for a long time gazing at the tower before going into the parking garage. She has a memory of a lift that clung to the outside of the building. She remembers suddenly how frightened she was going up in it. Fleeting fragments of the trip in it come back to her and she feels faint. She remembers the lift juddering and in her recollection it's like a cage.

A couple come walking towards her. It's a man and a woman of around forty. They're vaping, and clearly drunk.

'Are you going to climb the tower?' the woman slurs and laughs. 'Just saying. Because of the mountain boots and all that.'

The man pulls her along with him, giving Dóra a look that's both drunk and apologetic. At the same moment, Dóra's phone starts to vibrate. Rado's calling and she answers.

'I talked to Elliði. Where are you?' he asks.

'What did he say?'

'Guðbergur Smári wasn't working on the day Morgan disappeared,' Rado says.

'Elliði needs to get forensics to check his van. Get the man to the station to make a statement.'

Dóra opens the Volvo's door and gets in.

'It's not him,' Rado says.

'What do you mean?'

'He was out of the country. He was at a football match in Liverpool.'

'Shit.' Dóra slaps the Volvo's wheel.

'See you at the hotel,' Rado says, and hangs up.

Dóra's in the cognac lounge when Rado shows up. It's been opened up and in one corner there's a group of British men of around sixty, talking quietly. They're dressed as if for fly fishing. Rado drops into an armchair beside her and sighs.

'Don't you need to fetch Jurek?' Dóra asks, checking the time on her phone.

'I spoke to Ewa. She'll do it. Where were you when I called?'

'Up at Elysium.'

'What were you doing there?'

'I wanted to see if I could jog my memory by going there.'

'And?'

'I don't know. I just remember fragments. Did Elliði say anything about the staff agencies?'

'He's looking into it. He has a whole department to run, apart from being on this with us.'

'I know. So we wait for that?'

'Yes. I reckon that's best. Shouldn't we call it a day?' Rado says, getting to his feet. 'I think we could both do with a rest.'

'Speak tomorrow,' Dóra says, just as a waiter appears with her drink. 'Unless you'd like one, to take the edge off the day?'

'No, thanks.' Rado nods and leaves the cognac lounge.

*

When Dóra marches out of Hotel Holt, backpack on her back, after saying goodbye to Rado, she doesn't notice him. She goes from the hotel over to the car park where the white Volvo waits. Rado's sitting in the jeep, a little further along Bergstaðastræti, with a view of the hotel entrance.

He watches her start the Volvo and drive towards Laugavegur. He follows, keeping a distance, even though he's not certain she'll recognise the jeep. She crosses over Skólavörðustígur, Laugavegur and onto Hverfisgata. He watches her turn into the yard behind the police station, but doesn't risk following. Instead, he carries on and parks further along on Snorrabraut.

Dóra's getting into a black van behind the station when Rado comes walking over to her.

'What are you up to?' he asks placidly.

'Are you spying on me?' she snaps back.

'No. I'm taking care of you.'

'You see anyone else about?' Dóra makes a play of looking around.

'I repeat. What are you up to?'

'I'm not going to get you mixed up in this. It's something I have to do. I've a certain hunch,' she says in a low voice. 'Go home, Rado.'

'What are you planning on doing?' Rado holds the driver's door open.

He sees two uniformed officers taking a smoke break by the back entrance nearby.

'You don't want to know.'

'I have to know.' He's not giving up.

'Do you trust me, or do you think I'm crazy? Honest answer.'

'Yes. And yes.' Rado's face cracks into a smile.

'Meaning what?'

'Yes to both questions. More or less. I trust you, but you're not all right. But I don't think you're nuts. No more so than most of us.'

'Thank you. I'm endlessly grateful to hear you say that. I need to do something I'd prefer not to involve you in. I'll never be whole again. I'll never go back into this building here and do my job. In the position I'm in, I see one possible move I can make. But it has to be mine.'

'My brother,' Rado says after a moment's hesitation. 'When we were teenagers, he became mentally ill. He became dangerous. One evening I asked my parents to have him locked up in a psychiatric ward. The next morning he was gone. I've no idea if he heard us talking. But he left and didn't come back. I had no faith that he could be cured. He was difficult and I was ashamed of him. I thought life would be easier without him. It wasn't. It was more empty. I still feel that what he did was my fault to some extent.'

'It isn't.' Dóra places a hand on Rado's cheek. 'If you want to come along, then I'm not stopping you. But I don't need saving.'

'I know,' Rado says, clasping Dóra's hand that's still against his cheek. 'What I'm trying to say is that I have faith in you. Do what you need to do. I'm with you. All the way.'

Rado's behind the wheel of the black van as they leave the yard behind the station on Hverfisgata. Dóra scrounged the keys to the black van, which had been used at some point for surveillance before being left unused, from Ragnar, the duty inspector. He didn't even ask if she was on leave or still on the force. He just said that the clutch could be sticky at times.

Rado and Dóra go to the Húsasmiðjan DIY place on Skútuvogur where they rent an industrial vacuum cleaner, and buy a cleaner's trolley and two black overalls, which they pull on over their clothes there in the car park. All Dóra has told Rado is that she aims to smuggle herself into Elysium because she's not certain her ID is going to get her past security at the gate again. She's found out that there's a service contractor with its own gate not far from the main entrance. The plan is to pretend to be from a contract cleaning company to get in. She wants to take a closer look at the tower. Dóra's not saying exactly what it is she wants to look at. That doesn't matter to Rado. His feeling is that they're not going to get much further with this case. Or these cases, for that matter.

They drive past the main gate and continue to the semi-subterranean service gate further along.

'I can do this on my own,' Dóra says to Rado before he turns in there.

'You can't even butter a slice of bread,' he replies.

There's a van with a bakery logo on its side coming the other way at the security point. There's a young man on duty there. He waves to Rado, signalling for him to stop.

'Good afternoon,' he says with as much authority as he can muster as Rado winds down the window. 'What's your business here?'

'We ... is come for clean,' Rado says. 'You know. Carpet.'

'Who sent you?'

The young man picks up a small tablet computer.

'GH Clean,' Rado says. Dóra had found that this was one of a myriad of companies with service contracts at Elysium.

'GH Contract Cleaning,' the young man says, correcting him. 'I can't see that anything's been booked.' He inspects the list on his tablet, and then looks over at Dóra, who has pulled the cap down to hide her scar, and then into the back of the van where he can see the industrial vacuum cleaner and the trolley.

'Is toilet,' Rado says. 'Kaput.'

'Ah, got you. An emergency.'

The young man nods his head and signals to his colleague to open the gate. He fishes two visitor passes from his pockets and hands them to Rado with instructions that they must wear these at all times while they are on the premises, and to hand them back as they leave. Rado nods his agreement, puts the van into gear and they drive through the gate.

'Well played, my man,' Dóra grins.

'It comes easy enough,' Rado says. 'That's how my dad talked.'

He doesn't mention the shame he used to feel every time his father opened his mouth in public. These days he's just ashamed of having been ashamed of him.

The van disappears into the tunnel leading to the underground garage. This leads to a brightly-lit, concrete-walled space for the service companies' vehicles. There are several there, marked with a variety of names, everything from electrical contractors to florists and laundry services. There's plenty of traffic. There are tradespeople, delivery drivers and a woman shepherding at least ten little dogs on leads. She opens a door leading to a patch of grass outside and leads the whole pack out.

Rado finds a space and parks the van. He glances at Dóra, who nods and picks up her backpack from the space between the seats. Rado opens the back doors and takes out the trolley and the vacuum cleaner. Dóra pushes the trolley ahead of her while Rado struggles with the vacuum cleaner in his arms, as one wheel is jammed, making it impossible to roll it along the floor.

Two security guards step out of the lift as the doors open, and they nod to them as they get in. These are huge men.

'Any idea what the security is like on the upper floors?' Rado whispers as the doors slide shut.

'No, none. But I don't suppose there are trolls like those two wandering around on every floor, do you?' Dóra says.

'We'll find out.' Rado presses the top button and the lift jerks as it sets off in its upward rush. Dóra had read somewhere that the lifts in the tower travel at eighteen metres per second. At the end of its journey, which is as short as might be expected at that speed, the lift comes to a halt with a muted bump on the floor where the penthouses are to be found.

They hesitate for a moment, and then step side by side

from the lift, Dóra pushing the trolley and Rado with the vacuum cleaner in his arms. They're in the service corridor that lies behind the apartments. This extends the full width of this floor. There are doors that open into the kitchens and laundry rooms of the apartments.

'You can still take the lift back down,' Dóra whispers. She's as white as a sheet. 'It's not too late.'

'Do what you need to do. Or come back down with me. I'm not going anywhere,' Rado retorts.

Dóra takes off her backpack and opens it. She removes a pack of emergency flares and glances at Rado, who fails to understand what she's doing, and is too nonplussed to stop her.

At the end of the corridor, she lights a flare and places it on the floor. She runs back towards Rado and past him, lights another flare and hurls it to the far end of the corridor. The flares burn and the smoke quickly fills the corridor. Then she goes to one of the service doors, opens it, and gestures for Rado to follow her. He does as she asks, still in a state of semi-shock.

'I want to be certain the fire alarm system works,' she whispers, as if to explain what she's doing. They go into a laundry room adjacent to the large kitchen. Dóra lights another flare and places it on the marble floor.

They tiptoe into the kitchen. The apartment appears to be deserted. A sudden ringing breaks the silence. It sounds familiar to Dóra. It summons a childhood memory of the bell at school. Then it stops, just as suddenly, and the lighting in the apartment changes. This has to be an emergency lighting circuit that's triggered automatically. A rhythmic robotic chime replaces the alarm bell. It's like the wail of a car alarm. They've managed to set off the fire alarm system. They hear voices out in the corridor, as people follow the instructions that the loudspeaker blares out to them, ordering them to leave the building. Dóra and Rado wait silently in the kitchen. Finally, Dóra's patience is running out.

'Come on. Let's go up,' she says, and makes for the central spiral staircase. Rado follows uncertainly, while glancing around the apartment. At the top, Dóra rushes towards the bathroom. The door is half-open. There's someone there, back to Dóra. Rado follows her in. Huginn is standing there, the tower's architect. He's bare-chested, wearing jogging bottoms and slippers. He's clearly taken aback at the sight of Dóra and Rado.

'How did you get in?' he demands, his eyes shining with fury.

'Where is she?' Dóra says.

'Who? What are you talking about?' he retorts sarcastically.

'Don't bullshit me.' Dóra steps past Huginn, goes to the bathroom wall and starts tapping at it.

'What are you up to?' Huginn turns quickly and snatches at Dóra's shoulder. Rado gives him a heavy punch in the kidneys and he releases his grip. His hands go to his side and he drops to one knee. Then Rado understands what Dóra is doing, when he sees her feeling along the wall behind Huginn, tapping it again. On all fours, she examines the skirting board. Then she sits with her back to the wall and mutters something.

'Two thousand, three hundred and fifty-eight,' she says at last, getting to her feet.

'What the hell do you mean?' Huginn hisses, getting to his feet. He glares at Rado and then at Dóra. 'You shouldn't be here!' he snaps.

'Two thousand, three hundred and fifty-eight,' Dóra repeats, scratches her scar and catches Rado's eye. 'When I was here before, her father was tiling this room. I counted the tiles. He was half-way done with the floor. I calculated that he had eight hundred and seventy-four tiles to go. That means he had already laid fourteen hundred and eighty-four. There are only twelve hundred and sixty tiles on this floor. This room should be larger. There's something behind that wall.' Dóra kicks the wall and calls out. 'Open it! Let her out!'

'Are you a cop as well?' Huginn asks Rado. 'Do something! She's crazy! There's nothing ... nobody behind that wall. My lawyer will ...' He doesn't finish his sentence, but growls in frustration at the injustice that's being perpetrated against him.

Rado feels his phone buzz and extracts it from his pocket. Elliði's calling. He hesitates, not sure that picking up is a great idea.

'You went up with me in the lift,' Dóra says suddenly to Huginn. 'You said your name was Eiríkur. You lied to me. Did you still have Morgan in your van then?'

Rado sees the man blink rapidly. There's meaning behind that. There's something to what Dóra's saying. Huginn could easily have taken a KM Contractors van and driven it out to Thingvellir. Nobody would have noticed.

'Answer her!' Rado yells, punching Huginn hard in the belly. A look of surprised astonishment appears on his face as he sinks back to his knees.

The tower's sprinkler system suddenly goes into action and water rains down on them. In a moment, they're drenched. Huginn looks at them in turn as he gets to his feet. Dóra can see the cogs ticking over in his mind, behind his hair, skin and skull. He puts her in mind of a snared animal.

It seems to Dóra that they stand there for a painfully long time. She wipes water from her eyes and hears distant sirens. She has a splitting headache and she's far too hot. Rado says something, but she doesn't hear what. It's like he's calling to her from beneath the sea.

Then they see it. They both see it. The wall behind Huginn begins to inch to one side, and something, someone can be made out. There's a person behind the wall. Huginn buries his face in his hands.

BROKEN

It's not just the water that obscures Dóra's sight, but she has to squint to see clearly. The figure takes slow steps towards them. It's Morgan. They've changed. They have stubble and cropped hair. There's a distant expression on their face. It's as if they don't know who they are.

But it's Morgan. They have been found.

Rado watches Dóra and sees her sway, putting her hands to her head. He just manages to catch her before she falls to the floor with its two thousand, three hundred and fifty-eight tiles.

42

Rado sits in the waiting room at the city hospital. The clothes he's wearing are either Elliði's, or else belong to his former partner Indriði. His own clothes are wet from the tower's sprinklers.

Elliði's seated next to him, weeping unrestrainedly. It's as well there aren't many people around. Witnessing this, Rado's impressed. He's seen a lot during his career, but never anything like this. He makes no attempt to comfort Elliði, or to stop his tears. There's something inside the man that needs to come out, some burden he needs to shed.

Dóra's in theatre, an emergency brain operation. Her condition is dangerous, could go either way. Rado and Elliði are cops, so nobody feels any need to sugar-coat anything for them. It's as if the doctors, despite their intimate knowledge of the human body, believe they're made of sterner stuff than normal people.

For the second time in a few months, Dóra's parents are travelling south to Reykjavík to see their daughter in hospital. Jafet's coming as well. Rado felt he needed to know.

Finally, after what seems to Rado an interminably long time, Elliði stops crying.

'I have him in a cell down at Hverfisgata,' he says, wiping away tears and snot with his sleeve. 'I want you with me when we question him. His lawyer will be along soon enough.'

'Where's Morgan?'

'I had them admitted to the youth wing of the hospital. They're doped up on something. Forensics found ketamine and testosterone, and something they think is a hallucinogenic. They'll run a complete medical check.'

Elliði runs his fingers through his hair.

'You let Morgan's father know?'

'Yes,' Elliði replies. 'I spoke to one of the staff at the clinic. He'll get day release tomorrow to meet Morgan.'

'Are you in any condition to question Huginn?' Rado asks.

'There's nothing we can do here. Unless you'd prefer to wait?'

'Not at all,' Rado says. 'He'll have to be pretty sly if he thinks he can talk his way out of this. We have him nailed down. I mean, he built a prison cell in that penthouse.'

'Yeah. I just want to get an idea of what we're dealing with here. Get some insight into the man,' Elliði says.

'Dóra said something interesting when we found Morgan. She had been there to inform Hákon that his daughter was missing, and she met Huginn, but he gave her wrong information. Said his name was Eiríkur. She had forgotten that, but it came back to her when she went to the tower again,' Rado says.

'Come on. I want a crack at him before he gets a chance to think too much.'

Elliði gets to his feet.

*

Huginn Emilsson sits behind a table, facing Rado and Elliði, and says nothing, although the recording has already begun. There's a look of something resembling sadness on his face. At his side is his lawyer, Thormóður Óli, in his Gucci suit and with an expensive watch on his wrist. The vibe he exudes is a combination of brash assertion and ignorance. That's perfect for him and Elliði. No other lawyer would have suited them better. Elliði's somehow managed to put on a tough face and if Rado hadn't known better, it wouldn't have occurred to him that his close friend – their close friend – was right now fighting for her life in the operating theatre.

'My client wants to see a doctor. He has been physically abused. I'm concerned he might have internal bleeding,' Thormóður Óli says when he feels the silence has become unbearable. By speaking first, the lawyer has lost the first round.

'He hit me,' Huginn groans, looking at Rado.

'Is that true, Radovan?' Thormóður Óli asks.

'My name's Radomir.' Rado pauses and speaks. 'He appeared to be choking.'

'So you admit ...'

'Let's come back down to earth, shall we?' Elliði interrupts, stretching to sit straight at the table. 'Your client is suspected of deprivation of liberty, administering narcotics ...'

'That's a big word. Difficult to prove. As you well know,' Thormóður Óli says.

'And what about Article 202 of criminal law? Grooming and deprivation of liberty? How does that sound?' Rado asks. 'Or Article 220. These are crimes of violence we're talking about here.'

'I never did them any harm,' Huginn whispers, looking down at his hands.

'Let me ...' Thormóður Óli places a hand on Huginn's shoulder.

'I feel you need to know that,' he says, looking into their eyes. Rado and Elliði nod. This is what they want, for him to talk, and not Thormóður Óli.

'What happened? Can you tell us that?' Elliði asks, in a voice filled with as much sympathy as he can muster.

'Huginn ...' Thormóður Óli makes another attempt to

hold back his client.

'We met at the construction site. They were there with their dad. We just became ... friends.'

Huginn's hands bunch into fists on the table.

'What sort of friends?' Rado asks.

'I wanted to help,' Huginn says. 'They weren't happy in their own body. I could understand that.'

'Are you trans?' Elliði asks.

'I underwent a certain procedure but pulled out of taking it further. That doesn't matter. What I'm saying is that I understood what they were going through.'

'What happened at Thingvellir? You were there, weren't you?' Elliði asks, sounding almost amiable.

Huginn looks up sharply.

'I ...' Huginn gasps.

'This is where we call a halt,' Thormóður Óli breaks in. 'My client is highly distressed. He has suffered a significant loss due to the water damage to his home, which can be attributed to the break-in by police officers. That's a case that's a long way from being concluded, and a prosecution will be made, in cooperation with other residents at Elysium.'

Rado catches Elliði's eye, making sure that he considers the session is ended.

'Let's do that, for the moment,' Elliði says and gets to his feet.

Rado sits with Elliði in his office in the CID department, which is deserted. It's long past midnight. Huginn is back in his cell.

'Do you think he had any accomplices? Anyone who helped him kidnap Morgan?' Rado asks.

'I don't know. But we'll start with an application for custody and find out when we can speak to Morgan. Let's see what they have to say. This thing is so mad. He was holding them in that tiny space behind the bathroom.'

Elliði shakes his head.

'I'm not convinced he kept them prisoner there. He wasn't the one who opened the wall. That was Morgan,' Rado sighs. 'I think it's more a case of ... of him hiding Morgan.'

'Which means he brainwashed the kid?'

'We have a youngster at a difficult age, who is going through doubts about their sexual identity,' Rado says.

'And suffering from gender dysphoria,' Elliði adds.

'Huginn decided to "help" Morgan escape from her father. Morgan's dad was opposed to them being treated by the transition team at the youth medical wing. Huginn stages Morgan's disappearance at Thingvellir. Leaves behind a shoe and a coat. That's supposed to make it look like they died of exposure. Aren't we talking about some level of grooming here? Huginn grooms Morgan with promises of helping them through the transition process. I mean, we found testosterone in that apartment. We've seen this before. Maybe not exactly like this. But this is the process these abusers use. Find the victim's weaknesses. It's difficult to talk about this without coming across as weighed down by prejudice about trans people. What I'm trying to say is that I understand completely that the kid's gender dysphoria calls for the appropriate handling. But what Huginn's done ... I don't know ...'

'All we can pin on Huginn is deprivation of liberty,' Elliði says at last. 'He has a clean record. Thormóður Óli's going to set this up to look like Huginn rescued Morgan from a difficult home life, and from a father who's in rehab yet again. We live in weird times. You need to go home and get some rest. I'm going to sleep on all this. I'll call you as soon as I hear anything from the hospital.'

'You want me here in the morning?' Rado asks as he stands up.

'No. This place is going to be a madhouse. Let me talk to the guys at the top and we'll see how things look.'

43

When Rado gets home to the flat on Urriðaholt he's exhausted, but too wired to sleep. He takes a shower, then pulls on a clean tee-shirt and cotton jogging bottoms. Sitting on the sofa, he really wants a drink to calm the horrors in his head. Then he remembers that he and Dóra already finished off the only booze in the place. He had thought that solving the missing person case would be a relief. He hadn't dared hope that Morgan might still be alive. In truth, he's still struggling to believe it. Instead of celebrating a successful outcome with Dóra, things look darker than ever. He's struggling to keep his eyes open. There's a logic shortfall that's bugging him. For some reason, he's certain that the moment he shuts his eyes and falls asleep, that'll be the end of Dóra. That only one of them will have a chance to wake up alive.

A few hours later he wakes from a dreamless sleep. He gets to his feet and stumbles to the toilet. He looks in the mirror and inspects his own face. His eyes are bloodshot. He goes to the kitchen and makes coffee. He checks his phone while he waits for the coffee. Elliði hasn't called. There's no certainty that Dóra's operation is over. There's a feeling of trepidation in him. He changes his clothes. He's bathed in sweat after sleeping on the sofa. In the bedroom he opens the wardrobe and finds jeans, a sweater and socks. Ewa still has plenty of clothes in there. He withstands the temptation to inhale the aroma of them and shuts the wardrobe door.

In the living room he comes to a sharp halt, eyes on the coffee table. There's a little brown shoebox on the table. He doesn't recall it being there when he dozed off on the sofa. Rado goes closer and cautiously opens it. The box contains a pair of football boots, the same brand as he and Zeljko had when they were kids.

Rado looks around the flat to reassure himself that his brother isn't there anywhere. He's suddenly wide awake and his thinking is clear and direct. He replaces the shoebox on the table and goes back to the kitchen to get himself some coffee. His brother clearly sneaked in while he slept, placing the shoes on the table. But without doing him any harm. Something prompted his sick mind to do this. He doesn't know what fault is in his brother's head that makes him travel the world committing one atrocity after another. But it's no longer his business. He no longer bears any responsibility for him. Not that he ever did, beyond the point that was in his own mind.

It's clear to Rado that he has to rethink his own life. Right now it doesn't feel like he'll ever go back down to the station and sit at his desk at CID, let alone try to breathe new life into his dying marriage. He can't face sitting here and waiting to hear from Elliði. There's an invisible hand around his throat and it's tightening its grip. The reality of it is that it's been there a long time, since before Morgan's disappearance and the raid, and he's certain that to be released from its grip he needs to solve this case in its entirety. He needs to get to the bottom of who helped Artur clean up after Jurek Senior's death in his cell, and then sent his brother to shut Dóra up.

It's almost midday when Rado gets into the jeep and heads off. He's heard nothing from Elliði. There's nothing about the missing person case in the media. At least, there's nothing online, other than a report that the fire alarm system at Elysium had been triggered the previous evening for unknown reasons. The suits are no doubt figuring out how to best present the case to the public.

Rado has spent the morning going afresh over everything relating to Jurek Senior's death. The only person who could conceivably shed any light on his father-in-law's last hours would be Teddi, the warder who was on duty that night. Rado finds him at the Kempa boxing club, an industrial unit that's been turned into a gym. There's a boxing ring and a wall of mirrors beyond it. A few guys are training, while two men of around thirty are sparring in the ring.

Teddi's shadow-boxing on his own. He's pretty good. Soft movements with precision, light on his toes. Rado watches him warm up and then move over to the punch bag. Each round of punches is heavier than the last. Rado goes over and waits for him to take a break.

It's as if the whole place relaxes as the training clock pings, and some pull off their gloves while others jog on the spot to maintain their focus. Teddi just lets his arms drop to his sides, and notices Rado behind him.

'What are you doing here?' he grates.

'We need to talk,' Rado says.

'I've nothing to say to you. So it won't be a long conversation.' Teddi jogs on the spot, jerking one shoulder at a time forward. 'My lawyer ...'

Teddi doesn't get to say anything more. Rado hits him with an open palm slap. Then he picks up a pair of six-ounce gloves from a box on the floor and pulls them on.

'Wouldn't do that if I were you,' Teddi says with a smirk.

'OK,' Rado says, without taking his eyes off him. Everyone's attention is on the two of them. But nobody does or says anything. 'What happened to the tablets I left in Jurek's cell?'

'Don't know what you're talking about.' Teddi takes a

step towards Rado, who already knows where his punch is going to land. He does nothing, just lets it swing, and dodges. It's a heavy hook that doesn't connect properly because Rado shifted slightly, putting Teddi off balance. It's not much, but enough for Rado to land an uppercut with the glove that's so heavy it leaves Teddi unsteady on his feet. Rado punches Teddi again, in the chest this time, and he drops to his knees.

'Rado. Enough,' a man says behind him in a dark, hoarse voice, placing a hand on his shoulder. He turns, hesitating when he sees who it is. 'I need this guy for a tournament next week. I'm sure something can be worked out if you need to speak to him,' the man says calmly.

'I've nothing to say to him,' Teddi hisses from between gritted teeth.

'Teddi, cut the crap and talk to him,' the old man says and turns on his heel, just as the clock pings and everyone training at the gym clicks back into action.

A few minutes later Rado and Teddi are sitting in the office of Sigurjón, who runs the boxing club. Rado trained with him when he was in the Special Unit.

'I reckon I'll leave you to talk in peace,' Sigurjón says, stepping out of the office.

'The night Jurek died. What happened?' Rado asks.

'Am I allowed to talk to you? Is that clear? I mean, legally?'

Teddi tries to sound authoritative, but that doesn't work on Rado.

'What happened?' Rado glares.

'Nothing. Well, you know ... He had a heart attack.'

Teddi starts unwrapping the binding from his hands.

'When?'

'Getting on for morning,' Teddi says. 'I was in the corridor and heard a thud from in there, in the cell. I found the old man on the floor and he wasn't breathing.'

'Did you speak to him after I left? Earlier in the day, or in the evening?'

Rado's eyes are unwaveringly on Teddi.

'He asked for a glass of water just after you left. That's all.'

'And he got it?'

'Of course? What do you think?'

'Did you see him take anything? Any medication?'

'Yes,' Teddi says. 'I saw him knock back two tablets.'

'The bag. What happened to that?'

'What bag?'

'The bag the medication came in, Teddi. What happened to it? Were you paid to make it disappear? Was it Artur?' Rado growls.

'I don't see what you're driving at. Who's this Artur? Why should he pay me for that? I don't understand what this is about,' he says with a shrug.

'Well, OK. Fuck.' Rado pauses for a moment and gets to his feet. He's inclined to believe Teddi.

'I had to make a statement about the incident,' Teddi says suddenly. 'According to that, you were the last one to go into the cell with him.'

'And?' Rado's heart skips a beat.

'It's just that ... you weren't.' Teddi fiddles with the bindings. He starts to roll them up. 'But the statement says you were.'

'So who was it?'

'When I found him, I started doing CPR and Gorbi ... I mean, the chief superintendent, came in. He was in the corridor and he sent me to get help.'

Rado stands for a long time in the yard outside the boxing club, considering the next step. He calls Elliði, using Telegram, and he answers after one ring. That's not like him.

'Any news from the hospital?' he asks nervously.

'Not yet.'

'What's the name of your financial expert?'

'Runólfur,' Elliði replies.

'Where do I find him?' Rado can hear a mutter of voices behind Elliði. CID has to be on overdrive after everything that's happened in the last few days.

'I'll send you his number,' Elliði whispers and Rado hangs up. A moment later his phone buzzes with a message. Rado calls the number immediately and Runólfur picks up. He's at his desk at home in Breiðholt, gives Rado the address and tells him he's welcome to come right away. Rado gets into the jeep and pulls away.

Runólfur lives in a black, two-storey timber house in the Selja district. Rado feels the house has a Norwegian look to it. He parks in the street and as he gets out of the jeep, catches sight of a stocky man of around seventy standing by the open garage beside the house. He notices Rado and nods to him. This is Runólfur. He's wearing a bright red Adidas tracksuit and colourful Nike shoes of the type Rado wouldn't have thought an accountant approaching retirement would see as suitable.

'Rado?' he asks. His voice is rough and deep. It's also a little stiff.

'That's me.' Rado extends a hand and they shake. He notices that Runólfur holds his neck twisted slightly to one side. It's as if he has a disability.

'The door's broken. But there's a man on the way to fix it,' Runólfur says and makes for the house from the open garage.

'You're leaving it open?' Rado asks, looking inside the garage at the two mountain bikes, skis and all sorts of outdoor equipment.

'He'll be here soon. And I don't give a shit if someone steals all that stuff. It's not as if I'm going to be riding a bike anytime soon. Or going skiing,' Runólfur says, and a sliver of a bitter smile appears on his lips. He's no doubt had a stroke or some such debilitating illness. There's a cold humour to the man that Rado likes. It reminds him of Dóra.

Runólfur opens the door with a struggle and ushers Rado inside.

The house is tastefully decorated in a rustic Nordic style that somehow clashes dramatically with the way Runólfur is dressed.

'Elliði told me you found the girl. Safe and well. Hadn't expected that,' he says. 'Well done. What can I do for you?'

'It's probably best to come straight out with it. I have a strong suspicion that the chief superintendent is caught up in a certain matter.'

Rado's been rehearsing this speech all the way up to Breiðholt.

'A bent cop, you mean,' Runólfur says after a moment's pause, and gestures for Rado to follow him to a small office adjoining the kitchen. There are four computer screens displaying graphs and tables that mean nothing to Rado, and a couple of filing cabinets. There are two Eames office chairs. Runólfur sits in one and he offers the other to Rado.

'Got these from a bankruptcy auction. Never been used,' he says, rocking slightly in his seat. 'Can you tell me more?' Runólfur glances at the screens. 'Just playing with a bit of crypto.'

Rado watches as Runólfur taps at the keyboard, the graphs and tables vanish and the screens go dark.

'There,' Runólfur says. 'That's better. I suggest I take a little look at his finances. That's the simplest place to make a start.'

'How's that done?'

'I have ways and means.' Runólfur winks. 'But he's no doubt too smart to let any bribe money find its way into a personal account. Considering it's the chief superintendent who's in the picture.' He taps a keyboard and opens a browser on one of the screens. 'This will take a while. I have your number.'

44

Rado meets Elliði at Hlemmur, where he's sitting alone at a table, picking at some ribs.

'Any news?' Rado asks.

'Nothing so far. I spoke to Dóra's father. Her family's there. One of us ... or both of us need to show our faces.' Elliði gives up on the ribs and pushes the plate away. 'You know what happened to us on that shout?'

'You mean when she was shot?'

'Yes. It's hard to explain, but it often feels to me that I'm her killer. Because when she came around, she was a different person. Her parents have talked about this with me a few times. She looks exactly the same as their daughter, but that person is gone. In their eyes she's a stranger. She used to go and see them, out in the country. But it was too much for them. She has no memory of being brought up on the farm there. Didn't remember her own relatives. Nothing at all.' There are tears in Elliði's eyes. 'She didn't tell the truth in her statement. It states that she went into that office before me. That's not true. But she said it all the same. I often wonder about the person who gave me another chance. Was it the old Dóra, the one I knew before that happened, or the new Dóra, the one I didn't know?' Elliði brushes away tears.

'Come on,' Rado says. 'I'll drive you home and then go up to the hospital. You need to get some sleep.'

Rado stands up and almost leads Elliði out of the food

hall at Hlemmur. It's as if someone has flicked a time-travel switch back thirty years. That's back to the time when a cop escorting someone who had fallen on hard times out of Hlemmur was an everyday occurrence.

Rado's driving after escorting Elliði to his own front door when Runólfur calls, asking him to stop by. Rado turns off Reykjanesbraut and into the Selja district. As he's on the way, Ewa calls and asks if he can fetch Jurek from nursery. Rado says he can. He wants to tell her that Morgan has been found, but he's not sure it's a great idea. The press conference can't be far off. Then the whole country will know.

He's looking forward to seeing his little boy. Neither of them says anything about the promised visit to the petting zoo.

There's a man working on the garage doors at Runólfur's house as Rado turns up. He gets out of the jeep and nods to the man. As far as he can make out, the mountain bikes and the skis are still where they were. Rado knocks lightly on the front door. He hears Runólfur telling him to come in.

Runólfur sits at the living-room table with an iPad and some printouts that he's placing in piles. It's as if he's playing patience with one of those huge packs of playing cards that Tiger sells. He has reading glasses on the end of his nose and the cap of a highlighter pen held between his lips.

'Icelandic money is a strange beast. Take a look at this. This is the man's wife. She's a quota heiress. Well-connected enough to not lose the lot in the financial crash.' Runólfur hands Rado a printout of a newspaper page. He scans it. A recent news item referring to Bjarki Freyr's wife has been circled in yellow highlighter. According to this, she has just sold her majority shareholding in the Blámi investment company for a large amount. It's worth billions.

'So Bjarki Freyr isn't skint. That means this isn't about money,' Rado says and places the printout on the table. 'Blámi Investments is the largest shareholder in Elysium. It bankrolled most of the construction.'

Runólfur takes the cap of the highlighter pen from his mouth.

'Here's everything I could find about the sale,' he says, handing Rado a wad of paperwork.

*

In his living room Bjarki Freyr's watching a cookery show that's playing on the big TV in one corner. Rado wonders how anyone can pay attention to the screen when there's such a fabulous view from the windows out here on Seltjarnarnes.

Rado stands motionless in the doorway. Bjarki Freyr doesn't notice his presence. There's a sourdough tutorial on the TV. A pleasant-looking twenty-something is kneading dough on a steel worktop, urging viewers to give this most ancient of baking methods a try, and not to give up even if at first they don't succeed.

Finally, Bjarki Freyr gives up and uses the remote control to switch off the television. Rado assumes he had been watching the Police Commissioner's press conference, announcing that Morgan has been found. As he watched it in the car on his phone outside Runólfur's house, it hadn't escaped his notice that Bjarki Freyr hadn't been present. So he guessed – correctly – that he had to be at home. The strange thing is that Bjarki Freyr doesn't seem surprised to see him. He comes across as completely relaxed as he puts aside the remote control and turns to face him.

'What do you want?' he asks placidly, almost in a tone of resignation.

'Sorry to ask you straight out, like an idiot, but what did you actually do? I mean ... I've worked most of this out.'

'I thought she was dead,' Bjarki Freyr says after a long silence.

'Who? Who do you mean?'

'Well, Morgan. I suppose you and Elliði have questioned Huginn,' Bjarki Freyr says with a hint of irritation. 'Otherwise, you wouldn't be here.'

'You helped him?' Rado asks.

'Yes.'

'Why?'

'My wife. She gambled everything on this. If Huginn had been found out to have abducted and murdered a teenage girl, the whole thing would have collapsed. We'd have lost everything. Nobody would have wanted an apartment in the tower. I wasn't thinking clearly ... I ... everything happened so fast,' Bjarki Freyr says.

'Huginn contacted you?'

'He called me. I know him through my wife. She was always dragging me with her to see something in that fucking tower. He said the girl had taken an overdose. He needed help ... If he hadn't run into Dóra at the site and pretended to be some kind of foreman then all this ... she would never have ...'

'So how come Morgan is alive?'

'He said he'd given her something at Thingvellir. When he went to fetch her. She was going to go with him, to start with. Then she changed her mind. So he gave her something to calm her down. He said she stopped breathing on the way into the city.'

'He wanted you to help him get rid of the body?' Rado asks.

'No. He said he'd deal with that himself. The problem was ... Dóra. I had helped him out with the foreign employment contractors. That was when there was trouble with construction at the tower. Artur is behind one of these. Through my dealings with him, it dawned on me that he was the one behind Jurek's gang. It was obvious that the foreign work crews were terrified of him. So I sought his help.'

'You warned him? So he could hide the drugs away somewhere? In exchange for murdering Dóra?'

'That was never the ... I never thought it would go so far ... we never spoke about ...'

'And Huginn? He fooled you as well?' Rado says. 'Sold you a story that Morgan had overdosed? Are you genuinely that stupid?'

'I won't be continuing in my position as chief superintendent. I resigned today,' Bjarki Freyr says, and flushes.

'Resigned? You think that's ...?'

'Rado. You have nothing on me. So I may as well tell you. I know your brother was given a contract on Dóra. Your wife's brother sent him after her. No doubt to provide himself with a hold over me. But you must surely be able to see how all this looks? Who do you think is going to take any notice of what you say? Or Dóra? She's mentally unstable and hasn't been fit for duty for years.'

'And you made sure the medication disappeared from the cell when my father-in-law died. Teddi told me. I have a witness.'

'Did he say that, Rado? Really? Did he see it? You're sure?' Bjarki Freyr tilts his head to one side. 'Don't be like that, Rado.'

'You could speak up!' Rado snaps. 'You could ...'

'Rado, this is over. My involvement in this matter ends with this,' Bjarki Freyr says. 'Now I will ask you to leave.'

Rado stands as if frozen for a moment before he stirs and glances around the living room. Framed Icelandic nature hangs on the walls. The chief superintendent and his wife are people with taste. Some of the artworks remind Rado of those he saw at Hotel Holt. There are also newer works. In these, nature isn't quite so colourful. These pictures are emptier. The depth of field is tightened in the quest for meaning and clarity.

One shows a bare wasteland with a few tussocks in the foreground. It's as if the artist has tried to erase everything about the landscape but the fog. But aside from the vintage of these images, Rado recognises the subject. It's coded into them. Iceland. Old and new. Rado looks at Bjarki Freyr's stony face and understands that the two of them aren't necessarily meeting in this Seltjarnarnes living room as representatives of the old and the new. Bjarki Freyr doesn't see Rado in that context. Not as a representative of the new Iceland that's challenging the old Iceland. As far as he's concerned, Rado's just one of those hordes who mop floors and wipe arses.

'This is far from over,' Rado says at last. He turns, leaves the house and gets into the jeep.

The weather is beautiful. There's not a cloud in the sky. A gaggle of youngsters rushes past the parked jeep, laughing. They're full of hope and life. His phone buzzes. Elliði's calling. Rado hesitates and then picks up.

'She's awake,' Elliði says hoarsely. Rado hangs up, and a sob rises in his throat. He glances at the house he's just left and for a moment feels a glimpse of something at an upstairs window. That's probably nothing. He's starting to catch glimpses of the Groke in the most unlikely places.

45

Hector stands at a tall table in the smoking area at the Leifsstöð international air terminal. The wind moans outside. It's spring, and summer will be here any minute. As much as it ever arrives on this benighted rock. Things have been better. The last few months, since the Sons of the Gods stole that speed shipment from Artur, have passed in a flash. Jerking like a movie with just a few frames. Too much stuff, far too fast, way too much money. Too much of everything.

It's as well he wasn't at the club house when the raid took place. Nobody knows who the attackers were. All they know is who sent them. The Sons of the Gods no longer exist. One by one they showed up at A&E departments or health clinics across the city to have their injuries dealt with. He doesn't know what happened to Nóri. Or if there's a chance of saving any of his fingers. The tales don't all add up. Some people reckon that they could all be grafted back on. Hector feels it's possible. There was a guy who had new hands grafted on. He's seen a picture of him at the beach with his wife, putting sun cream on her back with his brand-new hands. But whether Nóri's fingers will ever have the strength to squeeze the throat of someone who owes him money is another matter entirely.

Nóri had given Hector around half a kilo of speed to sell himself. Hector sold the whole lot in one go. He got some kids to change the money into Euros. Now he's on the way to Málaga. He's going to where his aged mother lives in Fuengirola. The thinking is to hole up in her guest bedroom until he can find himself a little flat. Everything's so much cheaper down there in the south. Iceland's so expensive.

But first he needs to get fit. He's pretty sure he wasn't stopped at customs because he looks like a cancer patient, thin as a rail and with black shadows under his eyes, like a negative image of himself. But it's not just that. He reeks of hopelessness, desperation and pain. All the same, this is yet another fresh start. The hundredth, at least. It's going to get harder and harder to patch himself up. It's more comfortable to do it where the sun shines. Despite being worn out, he has a few ideas. Marbella's not that far from Fuengirola. He knows a few people there. He has contacts, and once he's regained his health it might be worth showing his face. No harm in that.

There's one thing that bothers him. Maybe it's because of the way he's wired. It's the photos he took from the ventilation shaft at the meat packing plant. These are the ones he's not shown to anyone. He told Nóri that the camera malfunctioned, but that the gear was there.

Two hundred kilos of speed. Packed into a steel table. But there are also pictures of two men with a white van. One has a fire-red birthmark on his forehead. The other had weirdly broad hips, like a woman. They were carrying a girl between them, the one there had been an appeal for. She looked dead or unconscious as they stuffed her in the back. Hector has photos of the whole thing. He's looked at them a million times. And a million times he's meant to send them to a cop he knows. He arrested Hector ages ago, but he's still a decent guy. He could find him on Facebook. He could easily send him the pictures. His phone has internet and he has plenty of battery. Hector shakes his head at the memory. Back then when he met this cop, he was in a bad way, totally off the rails. Trashed a house he was supposed to be looking after. The cop calmed him down and sang a Michael Jackson song for him.

'*You are not Alone*'

* * *